MANHATTAN SERENADE

A NOVEL

JOSEPH STEVEN

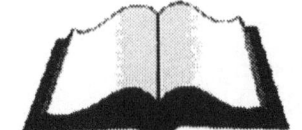

CCB Publishing
British Columbia, Canada

Manhattan Serenade: A Novel

Library and Archives Canada Cataloguing in Publication

Steven, Joseph, 1955-
Manhattan Serenade: A Novel / written by Joseph Steven – 1st ed.
ISBN 978-0-9784388-6-9 (bound)
I. Title.
PS3619.T48M36 2007   813'.6   C2007-906976-2

Publisher: CCB Publishing
British Columbia, Canada
www.ccbpublishing.com

For Marisa and to the memory of our parents.

Other novels by Joseph Steven

The Spanish Enigma

Dancer in the Dark
(Re-released as 'The Vitruvian Sequence')

Reviews

The Spanish Enigma

'Good things come in small packages' might be the description for *The Spanish Enigma*. The balance of the characters is interesting… The story is believable and extremely fast-paced leaving the reader breathless.
- **ReviewingtheEvidence.com**

A fast-paced thriller, *The Spanish Enigma* never gives the impression that it is a debut novel… it succeeds in grabbing the attention of the reader from the first line, and keeps him riveted to his seat till the last line is read.
- **Bookwire.com**

Dancer in the Dark
(Re-released as *The Vitruvian Sequence*)

Thrilling… if you're new to Joseph Steven you will quickly become a fan after reading *Dancer in the Dark*. Fine writing… a great story… engaging characters and realistic dialogue.
- **The Guardian**

Intriguing characters, more twists than a corkscrew and an ending that caught me completely off guard… Joseph Steven tells his tale in a clean, no-nonsense manner. *Dancer in the Dark* held my interest from start to finish, and I felt it was well worth reading.
- **Charles Cordova, national media critic.**

Steven is a gifted writer who keeps his readers riveted and guessing to the end. Even then the conclusion is a shocker.
- **OnceUponaMystery.com**

MANHATTAN SERENADE

CHAPTER 1

NYPD Lieutenant James Francis Moran pushed open the door of Dr. Benjamin Cook's waiting area on the fifth floor of Sloan-Kettering Memorial Hospital. He had come to pick up his wife, Sandra. Six months earlier, she had been diagnosed with Adult Acute Lymphoblastic Leukemia and had spent the previous night at the hospital undergoing extensive testing.

Moran glanced at the clock on the wall behind the reception counter: 11:30 a.m. He was an hour early for his appointment with Dr. Cook. The doctor had telephoned the night before and asked to speak with Moran alone. The doctor's ominous vagueness weighed heavily on his mind. Moran took off his topcoat as he neared the dour, stiff-looking receptionist with her hair in a beehive and gave his name.

"You're early," the woman said in a flat tone while she continued to watch her computer screen.

Moran winked, "Thought we could spend more time together." The remark was greeted with a grunt. The lieutenant shrugged his wide shoulders lightly and started to walk toward the waiting area. "You know where to find me."

When he reached the waiting area, Moran slumped his trim six-foot-three-inch frame into one of the waiting room's vinyl upholstered chairs and steeled himself for the meeting that lay ahead.

Lacing his fingers and crossing his legs, the cop let his brown eyes float around the room. On an end table next to him was a haphazard pile of reading material: *Style; Women; Elle; National Enquirer* and others.

Bored, Moran turned his attention to the other people in the waiting room. He began his favorite mental exercise, one he engaged in when riding the subway, or a bus. Or like now, waiting for Dr. Cook. As if, for any reason, he might someday have to describe the people in the waiting room at a trial. It was also a way of keeping his powers of observation keen. He enjoyed guessing what they did for a living, why they were there, and even if they were happily married. It was James Francis Moran's version of *'What's My Line'*; his way of keeping those little gray cells alert, as his favorite fiction detective, Hercule Poirot, always said.

He started by concentrating on the rotund man seated to his left dismissively flipping through a magazine: Asian, eyeglasses, about fifty, right-handed, five-five, and two hundred pounds. The stranger's pleasant expression told Moran the man was happily married or newly divorced. *Probably here because of a weight problem or diabetes.*

Moran turned his attention to the woman in front of him: Latina, less than a hundred pounds, a slight tic in her right eye, about forty, five-two, and a wedding band on her left hand; probably here to cure her anorexia or wants to get pregnant and can't. When Moran finished assessing her, he turned to his right and focused on the stout middle-aged woman with the sad black eyes who nervously fingered the rosary in her hands. He was about to begin his evaluation when the receptionist called out.

"The doctor will see you now, lieutenant."

When Moran entered Dr. Cook's office, the doctor rose from behind his desk. "Good morning." He held out a meaty hand. A gold ring with a large sapphire in the center flashed from his pinky finger.

"Doctor," Moran said and took the man's hand.

"Sit down, please, lieutenant." Cook cast a critical, cold eye at Moran's rumpled off-the-rack-navy-blue suit. Moran caught the look and shrugged inwardly. He liked buying his suits at The Men's Wearhouse, where he didn't have to put up with prissy, overly sweet salespeople, and where he saved a bundle.

The doctor pulled at his closed suit jacket, whose buttons strained, and cleared his throat. Moran flicked his eyes at the doctor's generous mid-section.

Noticing, Cook said, "Too much pie a la mode," and patted his stomach.

Moran lowered himself into one of the two Chippendale armchairs that faced Cook's desk and squirmed into the hard seat.

"By your tone when you called, I gather the news is not good. What's wrong?" Moran asked.

Cook remained silent, letting the question hang in the air—the question that's always asked. Finally, the doctor cleared his throat and sat down behind his desk. He opened the file that lay before him and ceremoniously placed a pair of Benjamin Franklin eyeglasses on the bridge of his wide nose, cleared his throat and began to thumb through the thick stack of pages in the file.

While Cook skimmed through the file, Moran stared at the doctor and thought of how he didn't particularly like the man, although he recognized Dr. Cook's competence in his field. Moran was put off by Cook's arrogant attitude, his overuse of jewelry—like that five-figure, oversized gold and diamond Rolex on his left wrist, and the way he painstakingly combed strands of dyed black hair from his left side over his bald pate. *Right, Cook, that really fools everyone.*

Moran pushed aside those thoughts and downshifted mental gears, realizing he didn't want the doctor to be a cheerleader with rah-rah messages and bubbling over with enthusiasm. What Sandra needed was Cook to be like a good ballplayer, capable of hitting cancer right out of the ballpark—a home run over the center field wall.

When Cook finished reviewing the file, he grunted, and the answer to Moran's question came straight, a doughnut with no glaze.

"A.L.L. can be a very stubborn adversary. It's now been six months since we began administering chemotherapy with central nervous system preventive therapy. I was hoping by now to have significantly reduced the leukemic cell population." Cook poured a glass of water from the pitcher on a tray next to the telephone. "Unfortunately, the CNS hasn't produced the results I expected. What was diagnosed originally as L3 morphology has unfortunately become what is known as PH1 morphology." He paused and rotated the oversized ring on his left pinky while he looked at Moran whose face became a question mark. "Which is?"

Cook slowly removed his eyeglasses and held them daintily between his pudgy fingers. "It only occurs in one to two percent of patients with A.L.L., and hers is the worst type." He leaned forward and placed his forefingers together. After another clearing of the throat, he continued. "I'm afraid that without a bone marrow transplant the outlook is bleak." Cook's tone, with its hint of superiority, chafed Moran's nerves. The detective also found Cook's habit of clearing his throat increasingly irritating, like a rat scratching on glass.

The doctor wiped his eyeglasses with the back of his broad violet striped yellow tie—a silk banner of bad taste. "It's unfortunate that your markers didn't—"

"Markers?" Moran asked with a puzzled look.

"Human Leukocyte Antigens."

"Ah, yes… you explained that. If I remember, you said because of her advanced condition all six antigens had to match. And mine only matched four. But she has a half-brother, Alfred Abravanel, in upstate New York. Could he be a donor?"

"If the leukocytes," Cook said, and stopped. He gazed at Moran's questioning face and then continued. "Those are the white blood cells used to test for the antigens. If the six antigens match, I see no problem." Cook returned the eyeglasses to his nose. "If not… well, the donor list is backed up three years, and she doesn't have that long."

"Can't we move her up the list? After all you said she'd die without a transplant?"

The doctor adjusted the knot of his tie. "I'm afraid that would require the approval of the hospital board. Preferences are only granted in extreme cases."

Moran's face tightened and he uncrossed his legs. "Excuse me, Dr. Cook, but doesn't dying qualify as an extreme case?"

Cook leaned back in his chair. "I can certainly petition the board on your behalf if you wish, detective, but—"

"Yes, I *do* wish it; in fact, I insist."

Cook stood and snapped the file shut. "Very well, I'll see what I can do. In the meantime, I suggest you contact your wife's brother and have him schedule an appointment so we can conduct the necessary compatibility tests." He smiled, "I am, however, encouraged by the fact that during the past three months the milder chemotherapy I put on her on has given her body's immune system an opportunity to strengthen."

Moran stood, flattened a wrinkle in his tie with the palm of his hand, and riveted his eyes on the doctor. "Thanks," he deadpanned.

"I'm sorry, but please realize that this is all very embarrassing for me. I was confident we'd have better news."

Embarrassing, Moran thought in anger. What kind of a frigging word is that? Spilling soup on your tie is embarrassing; noticing someone see you pick your nose is embarrassing; leaving the house with your fly unzipped, that's major league embarrassing. *Is this guy for real?*

The door swung open and Sandra stepped into the office. She looked up at her husband's flustered face.

"Anything wrong?" she asked.

Moran cast Cook a sideways glance. "Everything's okay. Dr. Cook was kind enough to invite me to wait here for you."

A few minutes later Moran and Sandra stepped out onto the sidewalk. It was a bright brisk early November day with only two

11

or three clouds trailing across a taut blue sky. The city was rushing toward Thanksgiving, Christmas, and the New Year, and the two had made plans the day before to have an early lunch at the Waldorf's Bull & Bear Steakhouse, do some window-shopping, and stop at Gristedes for groceries on their way home, which was a three-story brownstone on West 10th Street.

The street-toughened detective gazed at his wife, and memories of the past began to flicker like a sepia Hollywood flashback in Moran's mind: He had bought the brownstone with the hope that he and his first wife, Sally, would raise a family. That dream vanished when she left him to redefine herself in California. During the next four years, Moran lived alone in the large dark house in monk-like loneliness surrounded only by bitter memories of his failed marriage.

Three years ago, it had all come to a climax when his right knee was shattered by an assailant's bullet. At forty-six years of age, his career seemed over. However, fortune smiled on a depressed Moran when he was given a new knee along with a new job as head of the Cold Cases Task Force, now the Cold Case & Apprehension Squad.

One day when Moran went to the gym as part of his physical rehabilitation to build up his right leg with its new space-age titanium knee replacement, he met Sandra Mazzetti, seven years his junior and a professor of Criminal Psychology at CCNY, the College of the City of New York. With a five-year old sickly boy, she was a single parent whose estranged husband had been killed in a motorcycle accident years before—another one of the walking wounded.

The remembrances stopped with the same suddenness as they had appeared, and Moran swallowed hard. He looked at Sandra and his gaze met hers.

Sandra gave her husband a curious look. "Where were you just now, James?"

Moran smiled. "Nowhere… right here." He caressed her cheek

with the back of his hand. He was back in the present and feeling a sense of relief.

When they reached the corner, Moran hailed a cab. They got in and after a few blocks, Sandra ordered the driver to stop. She wanted to walk she explained, to feel the sun on her skin, the breeze on her face--to feel alive. "I'm fed up with being poked and prodded at by doctors and nurses."

Moran readily agreed, smiling as he recalled his father's words: *"Stay away from hospitals, son; too many sick people."*

Sandra slipped her hand into the crook of Moran's arm, and when he glanced at her, he saw her tired eyes. She peeked at him over her raised coat collar. He was a full foot taller, and when she caught his gaze, she winked playfully and blew him a kiss.

When they crossed Lexington Avenue, Sandra held her five-foot-three-inch body erect and alert against the chilly autumn breeze that blew across the thoroughfare. Moran watched as she turned her head left and right, as if seeing the city for the first time—or was it for the last time? The cold, disquieting, unwanted thought seeped into Moran's mind.

Sandra slid her hand into his while he led her across the street. The thick black hair she had lost during the heavy dosages of chemotherapy was starting to grow back, and she reminded Moran of Tinkerbell—his Tinkerbell. Although Sandra made an effort to look cheery, he knew she was spent. The cancer and the chemo had taken their toll.

Moran squeezed her hand and smiled reassuringly at her when she looked up at him. Their eyes said it all—words were inadequate. A little over a year ago, along with a recipe for chicken with rice from her Sephardic Jewish roots, she had brought joy to the marriage. It saddened him to see her once twinkling, warm brown eyes dimmed by an inner sadness.

"I was thinking about returning to CCNY or maybe writing another book," Sandra said quietly. "I spoke to the chairman of the department, and he said I could have my position back teaching night classes three times a week."

Moran put his arm around her shoulders and drew her close. "I know you're anxious to get back to what you do best, but I'm not comfortable with night school in that neighborhood. Writing a book sounds good, though."

Sandra gazed up at her husband. "You wouldn't be the hero," she said, and he could hear the smile in her voice.

Moran laughed. "Who cares, I sleep with the writer." He squeezed her shoulders.

When they reached the corner of Park Avenue, the traffic light changed to red. Moran wrinkled his face and stretched his right leg. The knee was letting him know it needed to rest.

"You're hurting, let's get a cab," Sandra said.

Moran straightened and gave a dismissive wave. "Not on your life."

While they waited to cross, Moran's cell phone chimed. "Yeah, Frank, what is it?"

"Oh, no!" he said after a long moment. "I'll be there just as soon as I drop Sandra off." He hung up then turned to his wife. "We've got a floater in the East River. Commissioner Newbury's there now."

CHAPTER 2

The sky, like Moran's mood, had turned gray and opaque, with thin slanted rays of afternoon sunlight clawing and scratching their way through the blue-gray stratus clouds that had replaced the bright sunshine. It was typical November weather in the Big Apple: the day would start out bright and cheery and then turn overcast, windy and cold in the afternoon.

Moran's taxi screeched to a stop at the crime scene tape stretched out across an old wooden pier. The detective climbed out and stiffened when he smelled the pungent tang of brine, oil, kelp, and rotted fish that wafted up from the East River.

With his face screwed on tight, Moran slipped under the tape, inched his way between two parked blue-and-white squad cars and stepped onto the pier. The dilapidated wooden planks of the pier creaked under Moran's weight, making the detective feel uneasy. It was one of those abandoned piers the city never got around to demolishing.

Another thing that made Moran uneasy was the fact that Horace Newbury was at the end of the pier waiting for him.

Since Newbury had been named Police Commissioner a year earlier, he was known to be a hardnosed, by-the-book cop who had migrated from Nashville in his late teens and whose main objective was making brownie points with the City Council. Behind his folksy, seemingly easy-going nature lay a tough, uncompromising, career-driven individual.

Moran frowned and hunched his shoulders. He pulled the collar of his topcoat close around his neck to ward off the damp breeze blowing off the river. He hated this time of the year; it reminded him that winter was not far off.

A few feet ahead, the lieutenant spotted three uniforms loitering around a black vehicle with the word CORONER on the rear door. The Commissioner's black limo was parked next to it.

"He's over there," said a bored-looking uniformed cop, and pointed to the middle of the pier. Moran recognized him as the limo's driver. When Moran followed the thumb, he spotted Newbury's tall, athletic figure talking to Detective Sergeant Frank Hernandez, Moran's partner for the last four years. The Commissioner's *they owe me and don't pay me* expression told Moran that bad news awaited.

"Surprised to see you here, sir," Moran said, putting on a happy face when he reached the pair. "Don't tell me you found Hoffa?" He gazed over Newbury's shoulder and recognized Assistant Chief Medical Examiner Milos Chang's trademark salt-and-pepper ponytail. The AME was chatting with two men who wore plastic protective gear as they stood over a body covered by a white sheet.

A stone-faced Newbury gave Moran his steeliest stare. "I cain't find the humor in that," the Commissioner said with a folksy Tennessee twang, where a nasalized vowel was placed before the letter *'n'* so that *'can't'* came out *'cain't.'*

"I'm here to make sure that y'all fully grasp the situation," Newbury continued.

Moran flinched. It was surreal to have the city's top cop sound like the Sheriff of Mayberry. Hernandez shifted his weight from one leg to the other and rolled his eyes.

"We're all ears," Moran said.

Commissioner Newbury flipped a strand of faded brown hair from his eyebrows and eyed Moran's left wrist. "Where's the rubber band?"

Moran glanced at his wrist. "Finally kicked the habit."

"Glad to hear that. Nasty habit, tobacco," Newbury said. He drew a White Owl panatela from an inside pocket, stuck it in his mouth and applied his lighter's flame to the end of it. "The floater's Paul Myer." He then pointed to an old man with a long gray beard, a wool plaid shirt and denim pants. The man was flanked by two cops who were standing next to a blue-and-white squad car. "That's the guy who found him. Thought he'd caught Moby Dick. You want to interview him?"

Moran glanced at the man and noted the fishing pole leaning against the squad car.

"He know anything?"

Newbury puffed out a cumulous cloud of blue smoke. "He only found the body."

Moran shrugged. "Maybe later."

The commissioner let out another plume of smoke and inched in closer to Moran. "Myer was released six months ago. He served just one year of a life sentence in Attica for the murder of Lacy Wooden."

"I read in the *Post* that DNA evidence cleared him," Hernandez chimed in.

Newbury nodded. "Right."

"I don't see how this affects us. We're a cold cases unit," Moran added.

Newbury pursed his lips and unbuttoned his topcoat. "The detectives at the scene of the murder found Myer's bloodstained fingerprints on the wall near Lacy's body, his prints on the handle of the knife—"

"Hold on. I seem to recall that Lacy was shot," Moran said.

"She was, but the bastard disfigured her—cut up her face—and then shot her," Newbury said. "Bill Foyle, the DA at the time, was sure he had an open-and-shut case, what with the prints and witnesses that came forth. They said Lacy Wooden and Myer had a tumultuous relationship. All that, plus Paul Myer's history of violence. He'd been arrested twice for assault on two woman who later recanted. So no one bothered to take a DNA sample from Myer and try to match it to the semen found in Lacy's vagina. All of which now makes the DA's office look like a bunch of dang fools."

Moran fixed his eyes on Newbury. "I still don't see the connection with us."

"As of now, Lacy Wooden's murder is a cold case with top priority. Put everything else on hold. Because of Myer's ties to the victim, I want you to investigate both cases as one."

"Why weren't we asked to look into Lacy Wooden's murder when Myer was released?" Moran said.

Newbury tossed what remained of the cigar into the river. "Because despite my pleas to do so, DA Schilling maintained there was nothing new that warranted re-opening the case. But now that's changed with Myer's murder. I spoke with Shilling and he's very much on board. As Police Commissioner, I'm ordering you to do so, forthwith."

Moran narrowed his eyebrows and peered at Newbury. "But why top priority?" he asked. "This wouldn't have anything to do with the fact that Shilling might make a run for the governorship next year, would it?"

Newbury, who stood at Moran's height, poked the cop in the chest with a forefinger. "Spare me your political insight," Newbury said. He lowered his voice. "I'm going to level with you. Lacy Wooden, was my wife's niece, her sister's only child and—"

"I didn't know that," Moran said while Hernandez stared at the Commish with a dumbfounded look in his blue eyes.

"To tell the truth, we weren't exactly close. I'd just been made commander of Manhattan South when Lacy moved down here from Rochester in search of a Broadway dance career. That was about two years ago. My wife, Margaret, didn't approve of her topless dancing to help pay for her dance classes at Carnegie Hall and, well, just say there were other matters that we didn't see eye-to-eye on." He raised his glance and looked at Moran with saddened eyes. "I'm asking as a personal favor. Give this top priority."

Hernandez took his hands out of the pockets of his three-piece blue suit and stepped forward. "But, what about the cases we—"

"We'll do what can, sir," Moran quickly interjected and exchanged glances with his sergeant.

Newbury's face muscles relaxed and he smiled—a small, tight smile. "With your clearance rate I have all the confidence in the world in you." The commissioner checked his watch. "Gotta go, I'm late for a meeting with the mayor," he added and started back to his limo.

"Hi, Moran. How's your wife coming along?" A familiar voice boomed from behind. Moran whirled around and gazed into Milos Chang's round, tan, ageless face. Assistant Chief Medical Examiner for as long as anyone in the department could remember, Milos Chang's actual age was a source of endless speculation— some swore he had been around since Manhattan was bought by Peter Minuit.

"Coping," Moran said. "Got anything you want to share with me?"

"Nope."

Moran gestured toward the corpse. "I meant about the body."

"Oh, yeah. The photo boys finished a little while ago. Let me show you what we got." Chang started to lead the two cops to the end of the pier. When they reached Myer's body, one of Chang's assistants lifted the sheet. Paul Myer was wearing an open-collar checkered shirt over gray pants. He lay face up on the wooden planks. Moran slipped on a pair of latex gloves and knelt next to the bloated body.

The lieutenant crouched next to the corpse and gingerly turned the dead man's head. As he brushed long wisps of auburn hair from the face, he winced—what had once been a ruggedly handsome square face with a firm jaw was severely chewed, Myer's left eye was missing and strands of algae hung from the empty socket with the left cheekbone exposed. His other eye, a light shade of blue, stared out in lifeless wonder.

The lieutenant's gaze slowly drifted over the body and then stopped. He examined the deep gash on Myer's left temple. "He was bludgeoned on the side of the head," he said. "I'd say it was something with a sharp edge that caused that amount of damage." The detective noticed the gold Rolex on the left wrist. "Seems he was doing pretty well after leaving Attica."

Chang crouched next to Moran, flipped back his ponytail and passed the flat of his hand over his glistening bald head. "Not much left of him, though."

"At least the fish and crabs ate well," Hernandez, quipped from behind them.

Moran nodded. "A regular smorgasbord," he said.

Chang adjusted his rimless glasses and jammed his hands inside his black parka's pockets. "Two shots to the base of the skull," he said, and nodded to the two holes behind the right ear. "You can see from the powder burns that he was shot at close range."

Moran leaned in and peered at the wounds. "Looks like the gun was right up against the skin."

"Any sign of a struggle?" Hernandez said.

Chang gazed up and gave the sergeant an impatient stare. "Sometimes I wonder about you, Frank. We're lucky the fish left *anything* for me to examine," Chang shifted his eyes back to Moran and asked the lieutenant to help him turn the body. "Take a look at this," Chang continued, and pointed to several faded red stains on the back of Myer's shirt.

"Blood?" Moran asked.

Chang nodded. "I'd bet my ponytail on it."

Moran gazed at the AME, smiled tightly and nodded.

"It tells me," Chang said, "that the body was placed in the water several hours after the murder, thus allowing the blood to permeate the fabric. Otherwise, the water would've washed it all away. In my opinion, this is not Myer's blood. There was a struggle and the victim inflicted damage on his assailant who bled

20

onto the back of Myer's shirt."

Moran peered at the faded stains. "Or the killer turned the body over and stained the shirt with the victim's blood."

Chang nodded. "If the bloodstain wasn't so washed out I could probably be more certain from the size of the blood drops and their angle, but under the circumstances you could be right."

"From the wounds I'd say small caliber… possibly a .22, a 9mm or .38 were the weapons of choice." Moran said and stood up.

"Two shooters?" Hernandez muttered.

Moran shrugged. "Maybe." He then turned to Chang. "How long has he been in the water?"

"Hard to tell with the currents in this part of the river, but from the deteriorated condition of the body and the bloating, I'd say three to five days. I'll know for sure after the autopsy."

When Hernandez chuckled, Chang turned and glared at the sergeant.

"Something on your mind?"

Hernandez shook his head. "Haven't said a word, Milos."

Chang grunted. His penchant for performing an autopsy on every corpse, including the decapitated ones, was a running argument between him and Hernandez. The sergeant stepped forward, reached into his topcoat's pocket, and drew out a plastic evidence bag containing a black lizard-skin wallet. "This was on him. Over five hundred dollars in it."

Moran eyed the wallet and nodded. "That and his Rolex rules out robbery as a motive," he said, and turned to AME. "Okay, Milos, he's all yours."

While Myer's body was being loaded onto a waiting gurney, Moran walked to the other side of the pier and gazed out at the turbulent dark green water. The squawking of seagulls flying alongside a garbage-laden barge being towed upriver drew Moran's attention.

"Garbage collectors… that's what we are, Frank; nothing but

garbage collectors," he murmured. His eyes followed the barge.

Hernandez joined him and looked at the passing barge. "It's times like these that make me want to quit the department, switch to day classes, and get my law degree faster."

Moran looked at his partner with feigned surprise. "What, and give up the chance to serve and protect? C'mon, let's move it. You heard the Commish—top priority."

CHAPTER 3

The color slide of a nude ash-blonde young woman filled the screen. She lay face up in a pool of blood on top of a linoleum floor. The gash across her neck was so deep that her head hung at a ninety-degree angle from her torso and although she was naked, her breasts were not visible due to the amount of blood that covered them. Multiple deep slashes had mutilated her face, and two bullet holes disfigured the center of her chest. Her blue eyes stared out at nothing and her mouth was agape in an expression of surprise that said dying had not been on her agenda that day.

"Lacy Wooden, age 24, single, professional dancer, found dead in her apartment on East 72nd Street, with 'Rhapsody in Blue' in her CD player programmed to the 'Repeat' mode" Moran said from the back of the dark room at 1 Police Plaza. "The coroner's report placed the time of death between noon and two in the afternoon, about four hours before the body was supposedly discovered by Paul Myer. Moreover, according to the file, Paul Myer and she were a hot-and-cold item. Statements from neighbors and friends corroborate that they would fight like cats and dogs and then a week later be lovey-dovey again. There are also statements that Lacy occasionally showed up to dance classes with a mouse under an eye, compliments of Myer."

When Moran pressed the remote, the close-up slide of Lacy Wooden's neck and chest wounds were met with a collective gasp. Hernandez was seated in a tattered black swivel chair at a long foldable table. Third grade detective Robert Darcey, a thin, lanky man in his early thirties with boyish features and sandy hair sat next to him, and second grade detective Alice Simms sat across from the two cops, drumming with her fingernails the open file that lay in front of her.

Moran went on. "The gashes were so deep that they almost severed her head. Whoever killed her had a lot of pent up anger. Shot her twice and then butchered her."

Another click and the photo of a large bloodstained ten-inch kitchen knife came on. "This had Paul Myer's fingerprints all over it and—" Moran began and then clicked on another slide. This time an enlarged bloodstained fingerprint on a wall appeared. "This was identified as being Paul Myer's fingerprint." Moran walked to the wall light switch.

"What about the gun?" Hernandez asked.

"Never found," Moran said, and flicked on the lights. The overhead fluorescents flickered for an instant and then glowed.

"The report says she was sexually assaulted," Simms said. She was a slender, green-eyed woman in her mid-thirties with mocha-colored Creole features and short curly mouse-brown hair.

Moran strode toward the whirring projector and turned it off. "Semen was found inside her, and that's where things get ugly for DA Shilling." Moran marched to the front of the table, leaned in, placed his fists on the table, and repeated what Commissioner Newbury had told him about the lack of DNA testing.

"Yeah, but Myer was convicted of first-degree murder and got life without parole, anyway," Darcey piped in.

"Didn't you read your copy of the file?" Hernandez said.

Darcey put on his best little-boy smile and said, "Sorry, I had a heavy date and—"

Hernandez stared at him, shook his head and shot Darcey an impatient look. "Myer was exonerated by the Court of Appeals thanks to a sharp-thinking young Legal Aid lawyer who had a DNA test run on the semen and proved it wasn't Myer's."

"But—" Darcey started to say.

Moran interrupted. "Myer told the detectives that on the afternoon Lacy was killed, he was going to her apartment to patch up a row they'd had. When he got off the elevator at the third floor, a person in a black motorcycle skintight latex outfit wearing a helmet with the visor down brushed by him and headed for the emergency stairwell."

"Says here," Simms said, pointing to the file, "that Myer told police there was something familiar about that individual, but he couldn't remember what it was." She pulled at her hip-long white cardigan sweater.

"He said he handled the knife out of panic and possibly touched the wall on his way to the phone," Hernandez said.

Darcey shrugged and rubbed his eyes with his fingertips. "I think we should check out the victim's apartment and Myer's place."

Moran swung out a swivel chair from the table and lowered himself into it. "Thanks for volunteering; you can take Simms with you."

"Me?" Simms said with broadened eyes.

"Darcey sometimes needs guidance," Moran said. "With regard to Lacy Wooden's apartment, that's a no-can-do. It was rented out right after Myer's conviction. However, there are five boxes full of her belongings that Frank and I will go through."

The phone in the middle of the table rang. When Moran answered, he crinkled his brow, pointed at the receiver and mouthed: S-h-i-l-l-ing.

"Yes, I just finished briefing my people and—" he began, and then listened to the raised voice of Manhattan District Attorney Howard Shilling. Moran pulled the receiver away from his ear and everyone in the room heard the DA's shrill voice.

"I know you're the mayor's fair-haired boy, because you saved him and his wife from Hubert Singer," Shilling shouted, "but I also know that Singer, one of this city's most sadistic serial killers, vanished from under your very nose. This time—"

Moran raised the middle finger of his left hand to the phone, gave the DA the Bronx cheer, and hung up. "God bless his pointy little head."

CHAPTER 4

"**M**oran... Moran!" Shilling yelled into the phone and slammed the receiver onto the cradle when he realized that Moran's voice had been replaced by a dial tone. Through gritted teeth he muttered, "Sonuvabitch."

The door to the DA's office at Hogan Plaza swung open and a thin, middle-aged woman with short graying hair entered the office.

"You said to bring Mr. Morrison in as soon as he arrived," the woman said.

A handsome six-foot silver-haired man with a square jaw that accentuated his patrician features stepped out from behind her. Alan Morrison. His tailored charcoal gray suit had probably cost the lives of thousands of silkworms. Alongside him was a slightly shorter, rougher-looking man with flaxen hair in the Burlington Coat Factory's version of the same suit.

Shilling jumped to his feet and gestured to the two module chairs in the center of the room that faced a black leather sofa.

"Good to see you, Alan," Shilling told the silver-haired man, and then added, "please, sit down, gentlemen," and turned to his secretary. "Janice, could you get us some coffee?"

"None for me, thanks," Morrison said, and lowered himself into one of the chairs. "This is Pete Farrow, our head of security." He pointed to his companion.

Shilling gazed at Farrow's unsmiling, heavy face. It was evident that the man took his position at Morrison Savings and Trust seriously. When Janice left, the DA moved to the sofa where he sat, crossed his legs, and faced Morrison and the head of security.

"How's Helen?" Shilling said.

Morrison leaned back and laced his fingers across his chest. "Visiting our daughter and grandkids in Sarasota. Then she's off to London for her annual holiday assault on Harrods."

"Now, Alan, what could be so important that would bring you all the way from your office on Wall Street?" the DA asked.

Morrison darted his hazel eyes at Farrow and then back to Shilling. "This is a bit awkward, but the bank needs your help. As you know, before Paul Myer was convicted he was the bank's chief investment analyst. At the time, we were shocked by what had happened. He was very good at his job and had an excellent reputation with us. When he was released I felt sorry for the guy and offered him his old job back." He stopped and gazed at Farrow. "You take it from here, Pete."

Farrow straightened his tie and leaned forward. "Two weeks before Myer disappeared, we discovered that over the course of three months he had electronically transferred some ten million dollars from various clients' accounts."

"Ten million in three months!" Shilling said. "Why wasn't it picked up earlier by the bank?"

Farrow rubbed his nose with his forefinger. "It's not that easy. Paul Myer was head of that department, with authorization from clients to invest monies in stocks, bonds, and mutual funds as appropriate. So those periodic transfers were not unusual."

"Hard to believe that you gave an ex-con discretionary power over millions," Shilling said.

Morrison shrugged. "I take full responsibility for re-hiring him, but I always felt that he'd been given a raw deal. Then after his unexplained disappearance, a client of his complained that she hadn't received confirmation of her latest investment purchases. That's when we decided to look into the matter."

"The monies," Farrow said, "went into a bank account in the

Banco de Mejico in Mexico City under the name of Miramar Holdings. When we contacted the bank, they informed us that Miramar, a Mexican company, had closed out the account after having purchased Repsol Oil bearer bonds. Repsol is a multinational Spanish oil company, with refineries in different South American countries."

"I thought bearer bonds were no longer issued." Shilling said.

Morrison shook his head. "That's not quite true. Nevada and Wyoming still allow them. And in Latin America they're quite common."

Shilling gave a half-apologetic shrug. "I don't see how my office can help. Why not contact the FBI?"

Morrison and Farrow exchanged glances. "One of the accounts Myer took money out from a Fannie Mae escrow account," Farrow said. "We'd like to get the bonds back and clear this mess up ourselves."

"Discreetly," Morrison threw in. "When I saw Commissioner Newbury at the Gotham Charity Ball two nights ago, he mentioned that a Lieutenant James Francis Moran was handling the investigation into Paul Myer's death."

At the sound of Moran's name, Shilling bristled, bunched his lips and shifted his weight on the sofa. "So?"

"We would appreciate if Lieutenant Moran would share with us, through your office, any information he might come across during his investigation. Anything that might point us to where these bearer bonds are so the bank can retrieve them as quickly and quietly as possible," Farrow said.

Shilling rose from the sofa and rubbed the back of his neck. "You don't know Moran. I'd be surprised if that big lug ever shared anything with anybody. I've never met a more arrogant individual... thinks the rules weren't meant for him," he said in an agitated voice. He then returned to the sofa and riveted his eyes on Morrison. "And there's another problem."

"I don't understand," Morrison said.

Shilling shot Farrow a look and then darted his eyes toward Morrison. "Alan, can you and I have a moment?"

Morrison gazed at Farrow and nodded, signaling him to leave. A moment later, Shilling rose from the sofa and sat in Farrow's vacant armchair.

"If I do this for you, what's in for me?" Shilling said in a solemn tone.

Morrison wiped his mouth with the palm of one hand and gazed intently at the DA. "How about a large contribution to your political war chest?"

Shilling met the banker's eyes. "How big?"

"Let's say large enough to get you the party's nomination."

A smile crept across Shilling's face as he extended his hand. "Always a pleasure doing business with you, Alan."

CHAPTER 5

Alice Simms and Robert Darcey parked their Crown Vic on Lexington Avenue around the corner from Gramercy Park and East 21st Street but near the building where Paul Myer had lived. The two detectives decided not to attract attention in this otherwise tony neighborhood where the privileged few who lived in the brownstones surrounding the park had their own keys to the private park. In an area where Beemers, Jags, and Bentleys were commonplace, a dull gray Ford would stand out like a Swede in China.

"This area depresses me," Simms said as they walked along the park's wrought-iron fence. "Reminds me of the dump I live in over on Broadway and 95th Street. Not even a pet to keep me company. Landlord doesn't like them. Only cockroaches and fleas are allowed."

"Sounds like you could use a husband or a new place."

Simms snorted. "The latter definitely. As for the husband thing... done that."

"There's an ex?" Darcey said, startled.

"Kevin Palmer, double ex. Ex-husband, ex-Army. Came back from Somalia with what the doctors described as post-traumatic stress syndrome, but it quickly developed into plain old run-of-the-mill alcoholism with physical abuse thrown in for good measure." She turned and looked away. "Kicked his ass out two years ago."

"At least you don't have to worry about what your brother's going to do next."

"Oh, yeah. How is Eddie doing?" Simms said as they crossed

the street toward the apartment building.

"Spends his whole day in the recliner, chain smoking and watching QVC," Darcey said. "His room is full of unopened boxes, stuff he's bought on TV. Says voices make him buy it."

"He really should be in an institution where professionals can take care of him. Schizophrenia is not easy to handle."

"Can't. Promised mom before she died that I'd take care of him. He's my older brother and the only family I have," Darcey said as they neared the green marquee that jutted out over the doorway of Myer's luxury apartment building.

"What I can't figure out is how Myer rated living here," Simms said. "When he got out of Attica he was living in a hole-in-the-wall tenement in the Village. Then two months ago he upgraded to this."

Minutes later, the two cops stood in Paul Myer's living room with a tile floor large enough and a ceiling high enough for a basketball game.

* * *

In Moran's living room, he and Hernandez sat cross-legged on the abstract design carpet amid five open cardboard boxes, sifting through notebooks, jewelry boxes and other knickknacks that had once been Lacy Wooden's personal effects.

Moran's face was screwed on tight, his mood dark as he sifted through one of the boxes. "This is going to take forever. I hope Simms and Darcey get here soon," he growled.

Hernandez peered at his boss. "Besides that, what else is bothering you?"

Moran narrowed his eyebrows and shifted his gaze to Hernandez. "As if we didn't have enough to do. Shilling wants us to look into Paul Myer's embezzling ten million dollars from Morrison Savings & Trust."

Hernandez creased his brow. "Why is that name familiar?"

"It's one of the banks that Hubert Singer did business with."

"Now I recall. Singer closed out all his accounts a week before he…" Hernandez's voice trailed off.

"Go on, you can say it. Escaped, vanished, disappeared—take your choice. And he did it on my watch," Moran's voice was bitter.

Sandra entered the room with a tray of sandwiches and two tall glasses of iced tea. "I thought you could use this." She moved toward the coffee table.

"Sure looks a lot cheerier in here now," Hernandez said. Gone was the dark, stodgy classical furniture that had once sat on top of a dark carpet. Also gone were the heavy mahogany bookshelves that had covered all four walls. They had been replaced by maple bookcases and track lighting. Black and white tile gave the living room an art-deco air, with recessed lighting in the ceiling and modern off-white Swedish functional furniture.

"Did you re-do the rest of the place?" Hernandez asked.

Sandra set the tray down on the coffee table across from the unlit fireplace, shook her head and glanced briefly at Moran.

"No, James only let me change this room. Told me the living room was mine to do with as I pleased, but the other two floors were not to be touched. So, upstairs we're in a world of dark wood and rococo furniture." She gave Moran a bored smile. "Like the Dark Ages."

Moran reached over, grabbed a ham, mayo-and-cheese sandwich and took a large bite. Through a mouthful of food and with his thumb dabbing a spot of mayonnaise on his lip, he mumbled, "I only keep her around because she makes great sandwiches."

Sandra rolled her eyes, "Men!" she exclaimed. "As Zsa Zsa Gabor said, the only time a woman can change a man is when he's a baby."

Hernandez chuckled and hoisted himself up from the carpet. He pointed to a silver frame on the mantle over the marble fireplace. The photograph of a brown-eyed teenage boy with sandy hair and a melancholy smile was in the center.

"It's hard to believe the doctors in London couldn't get all the tumor. How old would he have been now?" Hernandez asked.

Moran and his wife exchanged sad glances. "Fifteen in two weeks," Sandra whispered.

"Sorry. Didn't mean to bring up bad memories," Hernandez said.

"That's okay. We all thought the operation in London was going to work," Sandra said.

Moran got to his feet and moved toward his wife. "There was nothing anyone could do."

Sandra gave a forced smile. "I, eh, better get upstairs and finish vacuuming," she said and hurried out of the room.

After Sandra left, Hernandez sat back down on the carpet and started to flick through Lacy Wooden's diary, a leather bound book with a brass lock. "Hey, check this," he said, and showed the page to Moran.

"*April 6th - S is beginning to become a problem, so I'd better take matters into my own hands,*" Moran read aloud and then shot his partner a quizzical look. "Who the hell is 'S'?"

"More importantly, what did she mean by '*taking matters into my own hands*'?" Hernandez said and flipped through several pages and stopped. "Listen to this," he said and read aloud:

"'*May 15 – M called this morning and canceled our date. Lately he's becoming impossibly jealous. I have to talk to C about keeping his promise—he's so forgetful at times.*" Hernandez turned the page. "*May 16 – Saw H last night and he seemed so depressed. I wish he'd leave his wife once and for all. He's not happy. That's the tall and the short of it for now.*'" He then turned another page. "There's an entry here regarding an '*R*' person and some weekend they spent together," Hernandez said.

"Let me see that," Moran said and grabbed the diary. "*S, M, C, H, R.* What is this, the Alphabet Song book?"

"Maybe she had trouble spelling. I remember in grade school—" Hernandez began.

"Drop it, Frank. One thing's pretty clear, the 'M' could be Myer." Moran handed the book to the sergeant and swallowed a gulp of iced tea, then reached over and picked up a Bowery Bank savings book. He opened the passbook and whistled. "According to this, on the day Lacy died, she had fifty-thousand, two-hundred forty-nine dollars and fifty-five cents saved up."

Hernandez seemed unimpressed. "Wouldn't surprise me. Topless dancers make a lot of money, plus tips and other activities."

"Except," Moran said, and waved the passbook, "four months before she was murdered the account was opened with two cash deposits of five thousand dollars on the same day at two different branches. Bag it."

Moran continued to sift through the contents and pawed out a neatly folded white T-shirt with the purple Arabic cupola logo of the Trump Taj Mahal Hotel and Casino on the front. He stretched it.

"Seems Lacy liked to gamble," Hernandez said.

Moran set the T-shirt aside. "Ho-ho-ho, what's this?" Moran brought out a 5x7 snapshot of a smiling Lacy wearing the T-Shirt posing on a veranda. An expansive beach in the background. The lieutenant turned the picture over. The date scribbled in pencil was two weeks before Lacy's death, and the word 'Jersey' next to the date was underlined in heavy pencil.

Moran handed the picture to Hernandez. "I'd guess the Jersey Shore."

"That's pretty ritzy for a struggling dancer," Hernandez said, and cast the snapshot on top of the T-shirt. He examined more of the strewn contents and lifted up a receipt and peered at it. "According to this, Lacy paid a visit to the Haifa Diamond Exchange on East 72nd Street a week before she was murdered and—" he handed it to Moran—"she exchanged a two thousand dollar ladies Movado for a diamond tennis bracelet."

Moran read the receipt and set it down. "That address is only a couple blocks up from where she lived. I'll—"

The front door buzzer sounded and Hernandez glanced at his watch. "Must be Simms and Darcey."

When Sandra led the two detectives into the living room, Darcey stepped toward Moran and held out an evidence bag that contained a spiral notepad.

"We found it in the dresser drawer," Darcey said.

"The guy obviously believed in the simple life. Two cans of tuna in the fridge alongside a bottle of Stoli, a beat-up sofa in the living room facing a 50-inch plasma television screen, and nothing else. In the bedroom only a bed and the dresser."

As Moran took the bag, Darcey said, "I think you'll find the notations on the second page very interesting."

When Hernandez offered Moran a pair of latex gloves, the lieutenant gazed at his partner appraisingly. "I can't believe you always carry these things with you."

Hernandez smiled. "You're welcome."

Moran slipped on the gloves and Simms said, "Check out the second page."

"Very n-i-c-e," Moran said when he read the page. "July 2, five thousand dollars—good start. August 4, two thousand; September 2, three thou, October 4, six thou; and November 2, two thousand five hundred."

Moran flipped through the rest of the pad. Blank pages. He handed it to his sergeant.

"We found a copy of the lease to the apartment," Simms said. "The rent's three and half grand a month and the deposit was seven thou in cash. Myer moved in on July first, before which he was living at..." She paused and flipped through her leather notepad. "181 West 6th Street."

"I know that area," Hernandez said. "Full of flophouses with hot-and-cold running mice."

Moran asked if there was any cash in the apartment, but Simms and Darcey shook their heads. "Nothing," Darcey said. "But Myer did own a closet full of Armani, Hugo Boss, and Calvin Klein suits."

"Looks like besides banking, Myer was good at extortion," Hernandez threw in. "From the regularity of these payments, I'd say somebody was being squeezed hard."

Simms nodded. "One more thing," she said. "The doorman said that while Myer lived there he had a visitor in black motorcycle gear and a helmet with the visor down. Came once a month."

"Doorman know who the guy was?" Hernandez said.

Darcey shook his head. "Myer always instructed the doorman the morning of the visit that he was expecting a person fitting that description and to just let him through."

"Does 'Evel Knievel' have a description—tall, short, thin, fat?" Moran asked.

Simms said, "Only that he was slender and about five-ten or five-eleven."

"What about the bike?" Hernandez asked.

"Doorman never saw it. Figured it was parked around the corner," Simms said.

Moran and Hernandez exchanged glances. "I want Myer's apartment sealed off," Moran told Simms. "And have a couple of uniforms make sure no one without authorization goes in or out." He turned to Hernandez. "Have Forensics go over it. Maybe our motorcyclist friend left some prints."

CHAPTER 6

The slender woman with flashing dark eyes wore black Capri pants and a sleeveless silver top. It played well against her olive skin. She squirmed forward on the sofa, aimed the remote at the television set, and turned it off. Frank Hernandez seated next to her glowered. "Hey, what're you doing, the 'Double Jeopardy' part of the show was about to start."

Pilar Hernandez pulled back the silky black hair that flowed over her shoulders. "Don't be mad," she said. "I'm sorry I sprung the news on you during dinner, but I only found out this afternoon."

Hernandez kept stoically silent, his gaze glued to the blank screen.

"I understand the idea of having another kid is scary," Pilar went on. "Frankie, Jr. is just a year old, and I know we're trying to save money for a house, but you gotta understand—" She stopped, folded her arms under her breasts and looked away.

Hernandez put his hands on her shoulders and gently turned her around. "Honey, all I'm asking is for time to adjust to the idea," he said. He caressed her face and kissed her forehead. "You know how much I love you... but... well, I thought we decided to wait until I got my degree, passed the bar, and started making enough money to support another kid," Hernandez said.

"Do you know the number of years you're talking about? I'm almost thirty and I don't want to be an old lady with teenage kids."

Hernandez bolted to his feet. "If you wanna know the truth, I'm worried about repeating my father's mistakes. He and my mother had me when they were more or less our ages, and when the pressure of working two jobs to make ends meet was too much for the bastard, he abandoned us and went back to Puerto Rico. I don't want that kind of pressure on us. I still have a year to go in law school, and I'm worried about the expenses that another kid is going to bring."

Pilar rose and faced Hernandez. "Why won't you let me keep my job at the Criminal Courts Building? I'm making good money and the doctor said I was only two-and-a-half months pregnant. When the baby comes I'll take maternity leave and then return to work."

Hernandez shook his head vigorously. "No way am I risking something happening to you while you're pregnant."

"For crying out loud, Frank. That's so old-fashioned. I feel fine. I'm only a court interpreter. It isn't as if I lift heavy objects."

The sergeant rubbed his face with the palms of his hands and gazed at Pilar. "Okay, fine. But when the baby comes, you stay home. If you go back to work after, it'll mean your mother will move in with us to take care of Frankie and the baby. We'll lose our privacy. Don't you see that?"

Pilar stepped back and placed her hands on her hips. Her eyes flashed resentment. "You're tellin' me you don't like my mother?" she said. *"Oye amigo, mi madre es buena gente!"* She took two steps toward Hernandez. The sergeant stepped back and extended the palms of his hands in front of him. It was a bad omen whenever Pilar started to argue in Spanish.

"English, please," he said. "I know your mother is a good person, I have nothing against Antonia. She's great with Frankie, but remember the old proverb: *Juntos pero no revueltos*—close but not together. Too much intimacy always brings problems," he said. He then put his arms around his wife. "Besides, you always complain that she puts too much garlic in her roast pork."

Pilar giggled and stepped back. "You're right about that," she said.

Hernandez's face relaxed—the storm had passed.

Pilar looked at her husband with a solemn expression. "One thing. Forget what your father did, he's been dead for a long time. I know you. No way are you going to fall down on the job. Besides, I could work part-time, eh?" she cooed.

Hernandez smiled faintly. "We'll see." He checked his watch. "Oh-oh, have to run or I'll be late for class."

"Don't worry about Jeopardy, Tivo's taping it," Pilar said.

Striking a mock dictatorial pose, Hernandez grinned and raised his forefinger. "Good, no beatings tonight." He placed the open palm of his right hand against her stomach. "Take care of Frankie's brother."

"Could be a girl, you know."

"Wouldn't dare," Hernandez said, but when he saw Pilar's frown he added briskly, "Just kidding."

Moments later Frank Hernandez walked out of the building. He came into the focus of a 250mm telephoto lens that was aimed at him from the half-opened tinted window of a late model black Mustang. It was parked in the shadows across the street.

Click, click, click, click... The shutter snapped several times as Hernandez walked to the corner and turned toward the rear parking area. When he disappeared, the lens was replaced by a hand that flicked a lit cigarette butt out the window. The Mustang's engine then roared and sped into the night.

CHAPTER 7

The light green dank cement passageway that wound through the basement of the city's morgue led to Milos Chang's autopsy room. It always made Moran's skin crawl. The cop knew he was nearing the '*meat shop*,' as it was known colloquially, by the smell of formaldehyde permeating the air.

"Hi, Milos," Moran said when he walked through the glazed door and closed it behind him.

Chang turned from the sink where he was washing his hands. "Be right with you. In the meantime, he's over there," the AME said. He jerked his thumb at the naked body of Paul Myer. It laid on top a stainless steel table with holes in its surface to drain the blood and body fluids of its occupants.

Moran gazed at Chang's stained surgical gown. "Maybe you'd like to change," he said pointing to the spots.

Chang looked down and then shifted his eyes to Moran. "Nobody here seems to mind."

Moran looked past Chang to the row of refrigerated compartments. They were aligned in alphabetical order and took up the length of the wall. He shook his head— *Morgue humor*—he thought and walked away.

When he reached Myer's body, he gazed down and immediately brought his hand to his mouth and nose. "You forgot to finish sewing him up."

"Look at the greenish discoloration of his abdomen, neck, and shoulders," the AME called out from across the room. "Confirms what I thought. Myer was in the water for about three days."

41

Moran peered at the partially decomposed body, winced and nodded. Then Chang appeared with a large x-ray in his latex-gloved hands. "Wanted you to see this," he said, and moved to a nearby glass-viewing panel. He slipped the x-ray into the clips and turned on the panel's backlight.

When Moran inched forward, he squinted at several small images of a brain. "That's Myer?"

Chang nodded and pointed to a dark spot the size of a quarter in the left frontal part of one of the images. "That's blood," Chang said and moved to the image next to it. "And it was caused by something blunt. See the fracture near the frontal lobe?"

Moran leaned forward and nodded.

"That's what killed Paul Myer," Chang said matter-of-factly. He turned off the backlight.

"What?"

"Step over here," Chang continued and drew the lieutenant to Myer's body.

When they got to the table, Moran wrinkled his nose, pursed his lips and willed himself to stare at the exposed left side of Myer's skull just behind the ear.

Chang pawed under the table and brought up a small basin with two bullets in it.

"Here are the bullets I removed from the skull," Chang said.

Moran gazed inside the basin's contents. "Wait a minute. One's a .22 and the other's a .38. You sure about this?"

"Of course I'm sure, I did the autopsy myself. But like I said, the bullets were not the cause of death."

Moran gave the AME a sharp look. "This better be good, Milos."

"Look closely at the wounds behind the ear."

Moran peered at the bullet holes.

"Notice anything odd?"

Moran leaned in farther, nodded and frowned. "Powder burns. The barrel was up against the skin."

Chang noticed the lieutenant's frown. "What's wrong?"

Moran stepped back and cast the wounds a questioning look. "Ah... nothing... nothing."

"You see something I missed?"

Moran shook his head. "Everything's fine, go on."

"C'mon, tell me what else you noticed?" Chang pressed.

"No bloodstains around the wounds," Moran said.

Chang smirked. "That's because dead people don't bleed. Look at the contusions. They're in the same place as the skull fracture. The fatal blow caused heavy hemorrhaging and accounts for the dark area in his brain. I'd say he was shot thirty to sixty minutes after he was dead."

"That kind of blow would cause some of the victim's blood to splatter on the killer," Moran said. "But why shoot a dead man?"

Chang shrugged. "That's your department. I only cut and sew. But I will say this. Because he was in the water for that length of time, and with the pollution and river currents, it'll be nearly impossible to get any fingerprints or traces of the perpetrator."

Moran walked away tapping his lower lip with his fingertips. "If you're right, it means we're dealing with a pretty strong individual. Someone able to wield something heavy enough to kill a person with one blow."

"Not necessarily. It doesn't take much to kill someone if he's struck in the right spot on the temple."

Moran turned and fixed his eyes on Chang. "Okay, so the perp shot him to throw us off." He winced, then bent over and massaged his right knee.

"Knee again, uh?" Chang asked.

"Word of advice," Moran said. "Don't get shot in the knee," Moran said

"You should see a doctor," Chang said.

Moran gave the AME a pained smile. "You mean Mr. Goodwrench. Naw, it's fine. Must be the dampness in here. What about the blood and skin tissue under Myer's fingernails and the blood on his shirt?"

"The blood found under the fingernails was type AB. It's found in only five percent of the population. The same blood type was on the back of his shirt. Myer's blood type was type O, the most common. I sent the skin under Myer's nails and a bloodstained fragment from the back of his shirt to Forensics. But don't hold out much hope. The skin sample may be too microscopic to obtain results, and the bloodstain was too diluted and possibly contaminated after days in the water."

Moran straightened and stepped forward. "When you did the autopsy on Lacy Wooden, were there any vaginal signs of forcible penetration? I'd like to know if she was raped or had consensual sex before she died."

"I didn't perform the autopsy; I was on vacation at the National Poets' Conference in Hawaii. First time I've left since my wife passed away."

"When you gonna let me read some of your poetry?"

"If it ever gets published, I'll give you an autographed copy."

Moran nodded. "For now, send me a copy of Wooden's autopsy report." His face was dark, like a hurricane about to make landfall. There was more to Lacy Wooden's death than the Commish ever imagined.

* * *

In another basement in another part of the city, a pallid red light illuminated a dark room. A pair of hand rubber-gloved hands held a set of tongs. They dabbed at an 8x10 inch sheet of photographic paper that floated in a tray of developer. Slowly, the image of Frank Hernandez seated behind the wheel of his car began to emerge.

A moment later, a dark figure silhouetted by the red light moved to a row of clothespins that held six drying photographs strung across the room. The figure gingerly added the seventh picture.

When the stranger stepped back, his gaze floated across the pictures. He had placed them in the order in which they had been taken--from the moment Frank Hernandez had left his building until he climbed into his Camry. A smug smile peeked across the photographer's face.

CHAPTER 8

Moran entered the elevator and pressed the tenth floor button to the NYPD's Forensics' Laboratory. While he rode up, he reached into his pocket and brought out the evidence bag that Chang had given him earlier. Moran gazed at the two bullets. *Two different calibers, two different guns. But why?* The two-gunmen theory didn't make sense, especially when the shots were not what killed Myer. The case had taken a new twist.

Minutes later, Moran stepped into the lab and walked past its four long rows of technicians hunched over microscopes and other state-of-the-art equipment. Moran craned his head and spotted an emaciated-looking man in a white lab coat at the last station. The man was peering at a computer screen whose glow lit his bony features. The lieutenant recognized him as Manny Langdon, Chief of Forensics, a man in his mid-fifties. His thick, horn-rimmed glasses and spiky red hair made him seem like a heron standing in a marsh waiting for its prey to surface.

When Moran reached the chief, he noticed a network of branching vessels on the screen.

"Didn't expect to find you here," Moran said. "Where's Maureen?"

"Called in sick. Some kind of bug," Langdon replied in a high-pitched, squeaky voice. He didn't take his eyes off the screen.

Moran pointed to it. "What is that?"

"Blood vessels."

"You said on the phone there was something I should see," Moran said.

Langdon raised his head and turned to Moran. "I did?"

Moran emitted a thin smile. Langdon was famous for accuracy and meticulousness, but short-term memory was not his strong suit. Then he said, "Ah, yes. Stay here, let me get the file." He strode to his cubicle a few feet away. "Here," he said when he returned, and lay a thick file on the countertop. He opened it, thumbed through a stack of reports, drew one out, and handed it to Moran who examined the two-page report.

When he read the last paragraph, Moran raised his eyes and shot Langdon a surprised look.

"You got all this despite the condition of the body?"

Langdon's face brightened with pride. "That's why we have all these toys." He gestured to the elaborate equipment in the room. "Water can destroy a lot of things, but not everything. Oh, and there's something else, come inside," Langdon said.

He walked back to his office with Moran behind him. When they entered the Lilliputian space with its large steel desk littered with stacks of haphazardly strewn papers and reports, the chief motioned Moran to take a seat in front of the desk. Langdon lowered himself into his swivel chair, reached into a drawer, and brought out a small envelope.

"Here's what we found imbedded in a minute crack between the heel and sole of Myer's right shoe," the chief said. His fingertips drew out two thin fibers about an eighth of an inch long—one red and the other black—and held them up. "They're rug threads and the dye comes from a plant not found in the States. It's mainly used in expensive Afghanistan and Iranian hand-crafted rugs. To get those threads imbedded, Myer had to dig his heels into the rug with tremendous force."

"Which indicates there was a struggle," Moran said. He leaned forward to scrutinize the fibers. He picked them up with his fingertips and held them close to his eyes.

Langdon said, "Microscope analysis exhibited signs of wear and tear on them, so we know the rug was old."

"It's a start," Moran said as he set the threads back down on the desk.

"Don't get too excited, lieutenant. The same threads with the same dye are also used in the cheaper versions made in China," Langdon said. "I have one at home with these same colors."

Moran slowly lifted himself out of the chair and bit his lower lip. "What about the particles of blood and skin tissue found under Myer's fingernails that Chang sent over?"

Langdon slowly shook his head. "Not good. The sample is very tiny and in a deteriorated state," the Forensics chief said. He leaned back in his chair, pulled a pack of Camels from the top pocket of his lab coat, shook out a cigarette, and lit it. Moran's eyes went to the glowing ember and he moistened his lips. The words that he'd said to Newbury on the pier, *Finally kicked the habit,*' rang in his mind and he realized that he should have added, *'Maybe.'*

CHAPTER 9

"The Combined Ballistic Identification System in Albany couldn't come up with a match on the bullets," Hernandez said. He was in Moran's living room, talking to him, Darcey and Simms. "I also ran them through Integrated Ballistic Identification System and got nothing there either," Hernandez said. He inserted his chopsticks into an open container of Hunan Spicy Pork. This container rested on the coffee table next to three others. He drew out a large piece of meat, dropped it into his mouth, and tossed the chopsticks inside the container.

Moran frowned. "That only tells us the gun wasn't bought in-state, and the results from IBIS just mean the gun can't be linked to any previous crimes." He gave the sergeant an appraising look and shifted his weight in his chair. "All of which does squat for us."

Hernandez dug into his pocket and pulled out a Blackberry. "I checked with the Taj in Atlantic City and their records show that Lacy stayed overnight a couple of weeks before she was killed," he read from the handheld's screen.

"That puts Lacy there on the date we found on the back of the snapshot," Moran added.

Hernandez went on. "Hotel records indicate that someone else paid the bill—in cash."

Moran narrowed his eyebrows. "What about a credit card as a guarantee for incidental expenses?"

Hernandez shook his head. "Also cash. Paid by a Patricia Wooden. Claimed she and Lacy were sisters."

"Didn't know they accepted cash as a guarantee," Simms offered.

"Normally they don't," Hernandez said, "but the employee that handled the registration was new and made a mistake."

Moran snorted. "According to the Commish, Lacy was an only child. I think she was staying with whoever owns the house where the picture was taken, and they both spent a night out at the casino."

"How's everyone doing?" Sandra called out from the kitchen. "You guys need anything, just holler."

Darcey, who was seated on the sofa next to Hernandez, opened the large file in front of him. He drew out a newspaper clipping and a one-way Aero Mexico ticket. "Forensics didn't find any prints other than Myer's at his place. Seems the guy was a loner." Darcey handed Moran the clipping and the ticket. "They did find these in a folded envelope at the back of a shelf in Myer's closet. Somehow, Simms and I missed it. The ticket was for two weeks ago. Destination: Acapulco."

Moran gazed at the clipping. "*New York Times* society page from eight months ago," he said, and fixed his eyes on the group of men and women in the center of the picture. They were posed with wide smiles while clusters of other couples loitered in the background. Moran read the caption: "Among the attendees at last night's Muscular Dystrophy benefit performance of 'Cats' at Radio City Music Hall were Mrs. Nora Shilling; State Senator George J. Halpern and his wife, Samantha; New York City Criminal Court Judge Edwin Corbin and spouse and..." Moran paused and studied the face of the handsome man with graying temples and a Pepsodent smile. "Greg Saunders, star of the popular soap opera 'Bachelor Dad', " Moran read on and looked up at the group. "Seen him on 'Dancing With Celebrities.' "

"Plays James Fox on 'Bachelor Dad' My next door neighbor watches the show every day. Saunders's very popular with the ladies," Alice Simms chimed in from her chair on the other side of the coffee table.

Moran nodded. "Why would Myer stash away a six-month-old society page clipping?"

"Maybe he was blackmailing someone in that picture," Simms said.

Darcey shook his head. "I can't buy that. You're talking about the DA's wife, a respected judge who's been on the bench for over fifteen years, a four-term state senator, and Greg Saunders, who's on every woman's dream list," Darcey said. "A little farfetched, don't you think, lieutenant?"

Moran sat with his chin resting on his steepled fingers, staring down at an invisible spot on the carpet.

"Sir?" Darcey repeated when Moran didn't respond.

Moran jerked his head up, tossed the clipping onto the coffee table and pointed at Darcey. "I want you and Simms to show this photograph to everyone who knew Lacy Wooden. If you want to find out why someone died, it helps to know how he lived and whom he loved. Check the hospitals and ask if around the date Myer's was killed, they treated anyone for cuts or knife wounds."

Hernandez asked. "What do you want me to do?"

"I've got a special job for you." Moran held up the plane ticket. "Myer was obviously planning to permanently leave the country. Something or someone was waiting for him in Mexico. Whoever has those bearer bonds may have wanted to get rid of our boy, Myer, to prevent him from talking or claiming his share."

"If you're thinking of sending me down there, my Spanish isn't that good. I... I don't know if—" Hernandez began.

"Don't worry, you'll be fine," Moran reassured his sergeant. "Where you're going I'm sure they speak English."

The phone rang and Sandra's voice could be heard from the kitchen. "Mmm... I see... I guess it was too much to hope for. Thank you for calling." After she hung up, she appeared at the doorway, her face chalk-white.

Moran came up from his chair. "What's happened?"

"That was Dr. Cook--my brother wasn't a good match for the transplant."

CHAPTER 10

'The Little Foxes', a topless club tucked away in the heart of Hell's Kitchen, was still closed when Moran stopped his Mercury Marquis in front of the club's door. This was an area of the city that spread itself between 34th Street and 57th Street on one end and 8th Avenue and the Hudson River on the other end. Turn-of-the-20th century Irish immigrants settled in the area that now was the heart of the Theater District. After Moran inserted the 'Official Police Business' sign on the dashboard, he climbed out.

"Hey, good buddy, move it!" a hoarse voice with a southern drawl called out from the alley next to the club. The man gestured to the red *No Parking-Loading Zone* stenciled on the curb.

Moran forced an easygoing smile and flicked his eyes toward the stranger standing a few feet away—a slender, fit man of medium height with a smooth-shaven head and a reddish handlebar moustache. The man appeared to be in his mid-thirties, and his deep-set coal-black eyes covered by thick red eyebrows glowered at Moran. The man's ricotta-cheese complexion reminded Moran of someone who had been born at night and raised in a pool hall. Slim, toned arms dangled out of a sleeveless grease-stained undershirt that hung over a pair of blue jeans.

Clearly someone not to be trifled with.

The lieutenant jerked his thumb at the sign on the dashboard. "Read the sign," Moran said. "The owner in?"

"Who wants to know?" The man grumbled and started lumbering toward Moran.

Another one of the Big Apple's morons, Moran thought as he stepped toward the stranger. He sensed the rusted mechanism of the redneck's brain try to kick in and said. "The Prize Patrol."

Moran noticed the arms tighten and the fists clench. "You some kind of wiseguy?" the stranger said.

"Just answer the question. NYPD here," Moran said.

The stranger stopped and squinted at Moran. "How do I know that's true?"

Moran flipped out his badge. "Smart money says the guy with the badge is the law. Lieutenant Moran."

The man unclenched his fists and jerked his thumb toward the front door. "Door's open. You'll find Rose inside," he muttered. When he started back toward the alley Moran heard the man mumble, "Friggin' cop," and then disappeared.

"Nice meeting you too!" Moran called out, and then moved toward the red-velvet covered door and swung it open. In the dark club chairs were piled on top of the small round tables that covered the bar area. The lieutenant walked farther into the club and eyed an aged thin, black man mopping the mahogany floor next to the stage. Two large crystal balls hung from the ceiling, while on the stage were four brass stripper poles.

"You know where Rose is?" Moran asked.

The man inserted the mop's wet end inside a pail of dirty water and jerked his head up at the cop.

"She's probably in her office," he said, and turned his creased face toward Moran. "Just go through that curtain and make a right."

A moment later, Moran rapped his knuckles on the door with an 'Office-Private' sign.

"C'mon in, Lieutenant Moran," a husky female voice said from inside.

Moran opened the door and stepped in. "Nothing gets by you, does it?" he said.

"Earl Schuyler may not be the brightest bulb on the tree, but he's loyal," the woman said. "I'm Rose Chiu." She took a bite from the Reuben sandwich she clutched in her right hand.

Moran eyed the woman while she chewed: a slender, woman with henna-colored hair in a butch cut. The navy blue silk blouse she had on contrasted nicely with her dark skin, her small features, high cheekbones and almond eyes. Moran noted the Marlboro lines around her mouth and he figured the woman to be somewhere in her late forties. When she lifted her arms, Moran noticed the padded arms of a wheelchair.

Rose raised her head and her black eyes met Moran's curious gaze "My father was from Singapore, mother from Harlem... go figure. This," she said and slapped the wheelchair's arms. "Traffic accident, four years ago." She rolled herself closer to the desk. A pile of glossy headshots of young women and a messy collection of CDs flanked the other half of the Reuben. She gestured to a tattered cloth armchair that faced her desk. "Take a load off. What can I do for you?"

Rose set the sandwich down then grabbed a pack of Marlboro Reds that lay next to a half-empty basket of French fries.

Moran glanced at the armchair's dilapidated fabric with coffee and grease stains and decided that was safer to remain standing. He stepped forward and drew from his inside coat pocket a folded black-and-white headshot of Lacy Wooden—a wisp of a smile, jet-black hair in a French twist and a face that oozed *'just off the bus from Hicksville'* innocence.

When he tossed the picture on top of the desk, it landed next to the Reuben. Rose studied Moran, lit the cigarette, and slowly let out a blue circle of smoke while she maintained her gaze on the cop. The two eyed each other for a long, silent moment.

"You look like you could use one of these," Rose said and held up the cigarette that lay limp between her fingers.

Moran saw the cigarette and his right hand searched his left wrist for the rubber band. *'Damn it'!* he thought as he watched Rose's sardonic grin.

"It doesn't take a genius to peg an ex-smoker," she said and picked up Lacy's picture. She glanced at it before flicking it back on the desk. "Let me save you the trouble and time of asking questions," Rose said and blew out another cloud of smoke. "Lacy was here for only a year before she went and got herself killed. Lacy wasn't the best dancer I've ever had, but she knew how to make the customers happy. As soon as she got up on that stage all eyes went from the other girls to her. The DJ would put on her favorite, 'Rhapsody in Blue' and she'd start bumping, grinding and shimmying... low and slow, I tell ya, she was smokin'. Phew, mercy, that was one white chick who had stone killer sex appeal."

Rose continued and wagged her forefinger at Moran. "The funny thing is that you'd never think that a kid from the sticks would've had that kinda of street-wise know-how, if you get my drift."

Moran nodded. He knew exactly what Rose meant—he had busted enough of them for prostitution. Their stories always began with, *"Please, mister, there was this man when I was very young..."* And the 'johns' in their search for lost youth or escaping unhappy marriages would open up their wallets and unzip their pants.

"She score with any of the customers?" Moran asked.

Rose crushed the cigarette out in a ceramic Cinzano ashtray and chuckled. "Now you know that's against the law. Don't be tryin' to mess with Rose's mind. I have no idea what she did on her own time, but I can tell you the other girls didn't like her. Lacy came off as being too good for them, always flashing her latest piece of jewelry or showing off her newest designer dress, going on and on about someday being on Broadway. Kept mentioning this Broadway producer she'd met. But I tell ya, even though she pulled down good money here, in order to maintain her lifestyle she had to be gettin' extra bread somewhere else."

"You know this producer's name?"

Rose Chiu looked off for a brief moment and then returned her gaze to the cop. "Eh... no, she never mentioned him by name. After a while it got so no one believed her."

Moran didn't recall reading any of this in Lacy Wooden's file or diary.

"Did you tell this to the police after Paul Myer was arrested?"

"I did, but they didn't seem interested. Didn't even bother to take it down. Only wanted to know about Myer."

Moran nodded. "So you think Lacy had a sugar-daddy?"

"Or sugar-momma."

"You're saying she was—" Moran began.

Rose turned the palms of her hands up. "I'm not sayin' anything. But there was this woman, slender, attractive, always in a pants suit and dark glasses. She came in twice a week around closing time, sat alone in one of the booths in the back, ordered a couple of apple martinis and at the end of the night left with Lacy. And, it wasn't her mother."

"Got a name?"

Rose snorted. "I gotta business to run. Long as the customers behave and pay their bill, I mind my own business. See no evil, hear no evil and speak no evil, that's my motto."

Moran stepped in closer and glared at the club owner. "C'mon, Rose, you must know what she looked like."

"Gimme a break, lieutenant. It was almost a year ago. A lot of bodies have come and gone through these doors since then. All I know is that she was attractive, not what you'd call beautiful, but nice looking, with brown hair... I think."

Moran sat on the edge of Rose's desk. "Let's move on. So you think Lacy was AC-DC?"

Rose shrugged lightly. "Who knows? She sure was pretty enough to attract both sexes."

"When was the last time you saw this lady?"

Rose scratched her chin with the tips of her fingers and looked up at Moran. "The night before they found Lacy dead."

"Was Lacy supposed to work the night she was killed?"

"That was her night off."

Moran said. "So tell me about Paul Myer."

Rose gave Moran a disinterested glance. "I already gave a statement to the cops."

"Now you get a chance to tell me."

Rose gave Moran a bored look and reached for another Marlboro. "The answer then and the answer now, is that I only saw him three or four times." She lit the cigarette and puffed out a trail of smoke from one corner of her ruby lips. "He always sat at the end of the bar, nursing one beer for hours. Seemed uncomfortable in the place."

Moran gazed at her and smiled inwardly. She may have been running a sleazy strip club but he admired her gutsy, take-no-prisoners attitude. Rose wheeled herself around the desk, grabbed the Marlboro pack, plucked one out and again offered it to Moran. When he shook his head, she stuck the cigarette inside his topcoat's side pocket.

"In case things get tough," she said and winked.

Moran moved toward the door. "I think that's all for now. I may be back."

"I'm counting on it," Rose purred.

As Moran walked to his car his mind replayed Rose's words: '... *always flashing her latest piece of jewelry...*' Something was wrong with that. Except for a few pieces of cheap bling-blings, there had been no jewelry among Lacy Wooden's personal effects.

Where the hell was the jewelry?

The Haifa Diamond Exchange receipt suddenly flashed in his mind.

A preoccupied Moran walked to his car, and when he jammed his hands into his coat's pockets to get the car key, he felt Rose's cigarette. He took it out, studied it for a moment, then crushed it and tossed it into the gutter. It felt like stepping away from the precipice.

The cell phone vibrated against Moran's waist. He brought it out and looked at the screen—Sandra.

CHAPTER 11

"Autologous stem cell transplant?" Moran said. Sandra, seated next to him, gave the doctor a quizzical look. Dr. Kruger's, youthful face, complete with rosy cheeks, bright blue eyes and a tuft of limp blond hair that fell persistently over his right eyebrow, belied his forty-five years. Despite this, Kruger was a highly respected specialist in the field of advanced leukemia. He rested his forearms on top of his desk and laced his fingers.

"Autologous means that the donor and recipient of the transplant is the same person," Dr. Kruger said with a mild Midwest accent. "Stem cells are immature blood cells that are removed from the blood or bone marrow of the patient. My specialty is peripheral blood stem cell harvesting, which is why rather than wait for a bone marrow donor, Dr. Cook referred you to me. It's also less invasive." He gazed at Sandra. "I've added Prednisone, Cyclophosphamide and Cytoxan to your high-dose chemotherapy treatment. Then at the appropriate time—"

Sandra looked up quickly. "*Appropriate time,* what exactly… I mean—" She stopped when she heard the catch in her own voice.

"We need to destroy as much of the cancer in the bone marrow as possible before we can begin to harvest. I've increased the chemo dosage as much as your body can tolerate in order to shorten the treatment period to three to six months… maybe shorter."

Sandra cupped her husband's hand and squeezed hard. It meant returning to the bouts of nausea and loss of her newly regrown hair along, with the loss of appetite that made her sick just to look at food.

"What's involved in this harvesting?" Moran asked.

Kruger cast Moran a tolerant smile—the kind teachers give impertinent students.

"Stem cells are collected through a small catheter inserted into the patient's vein. The number of circulating stem cells is increased in patients whose bone marrow is recovering from chemotherapy. Then by injecting Cytokines, or blood cell growth factors, we stimulate the production of immature and mature bone marrow stem cells as much as one hundredfold."

Moran grimaced. "Have you had much success?"

Dr. Kruger gave another smile. "This procedure has been successful in forty percent of the cases it's been used."

"What happened to the—" Moran stopped when he realized what the answer had to be.

Sandra let go of her husband's hand and stretched forward in her chair. "What exactly are my chances?"

The doctor cleared his throat. "In order to have any shot at success we need to infuse over five million cells per kilogram of your weight over a period of nine to ten days."

Sandra's eyes widened.

"Since we don't know what the minimum amount is, I like to go for the gusto." The doctor spoke with the enthusiasm of a cheerleader. "As my son says, the whole enchilada!"

When he saw no one else shared his zeal, Dr. Kruger continued. "The great advantage of this procedure is that you will experience a faster recovery of your bone marrow compared to having undergone a traditional transplant."

Sandra frowned. "What if you can't collect enough stem cells?"

"Then we try again until we have enough of them. In the meantime, we freeze the ones we've collected. I'm not giving up, Mrs. Moran—and neither are you."

It may have been the middle of November when Moran and Sandra walked out of Sloan-Kettering Memorial Hospital, but it felt like spring. The city was under a canvas of a cloudless blue sky and the temperature felt in the seventies; it matched their renewed hope and optimism.

Maybe Kruger was capable of hitting one over the centerfield wall.

CHAPTER 12

The brass nameplate on the tooled mahogany desk identified the woman seated behind it as, "Linda Garcia, Manager." She looked exactly like who she was supposed to be, the manager of the largest branch of the Banco de Mejico. She was attractive, mid-thirties, flawless white skin, strong chin, a small, straight nose, high cheekbones, and bright steady dark brown eyes. Her chestnut hair was closely cropped, and she was decked out in a tailored navy blue pantsuit that covered a fuchsia silk blouse.

Linda Garcia rose and greeted Hernandez. "Please sit down," she said in a perfect English —the accent neutral. She gestured to the large stuffed chair in front of her orderly desk. Like the desk, the rest of the office was impeccably neat, decorated with colorful lithographs of Mexican landscapes.

Hernandez sat and watched while Garcia poured herself with liquid grace into a soft leather chair.

"I went over the Miramar account and made copies for you," she said and pushed some Xeroxed documents to the edge of the desk.

Hernandez grasped the set of five pages of deposits, withdrawals, interest, and other miscellany. He pulled out the last page and studied it. "This only confirms what we already know, that ten million dollars was transferred from various accounts at Morrison Savings & Trust during the same period that Paul Myer worked there." Hernandez looked down at the name and signature that appeared on the notarized authorization form in his hand. "Who's Maria Luisa Torres?"

The bank manager shook her head. "No idea," she said tersely.

"What about the address and phone number that appear here?"

There was another shake of the head. "When we tried to reach her at that address the mail was returned 'addressee unknown,' and when we called, the phone had been disconnected," the bank manager deadpanned.

Hernandez gazed pensively at Garcia. "Didn't that strike you odd?"

"Not really. People disappear all the time in Mexico City."

Hernandez lowered his gaze to one of the pages. "I see that she purchased ten million dollars of Repsol Oil bearer bonds in one transaction only four months after the account was opened and then closed it. Suspicious don't you think?"

Garcia leaned back in her chair. Holding a Montblanc ballpoint pen between the first two fingers of her right hand, she slowly tapped it against the leather blotter. "Unlike American banks, it is not the policy of this bank—or of our government—to interfere in the private dealings of our citizens," she said in rapid-fire staccato. "Are you familiar with the word *privacy*, sergeant?"

Hernandez smiled. "Maybe if you spelled it slowly. Do you know the broker who handled the transaction?"

Garcia checked her watch and heaved an impatient sigh. "The bank offers brokerage services for its clients," she said and let the pen drop from her hand. She sprang up from her chair and extended her hand to Hernandez.

The sergeant gazed up at her. "Does this mean our chat is over?"

"I have another appointment."

Hernandez slowly pushed himself out of the chair and stood. "I'm disappointed. Thought that two Latinos could help each other."

Garcia leaned into the desk. "Please, spare me. You're as much of a Latino as I'm Irish. You may have a Hispanic name but you're *gringo* through and through. I've told you all I know of the matter. There's nothing else I can add."

Hernandez swallowed hard, rolled up the documents in his

hand and squeezed them. He then blew out a breath and stepped back. *Hell, next thing she'll scratch my eyes out,* he thought.

"Thanks for your time," Hernandez called over his shoulder as he walked to the door.

"You won't find her," Garcia said.

When Hernandez reached the door, he turned around and faced the bank manager. "How do you know?"

Linda Garcia gave Hernandez an icy stare. "Have a good day, sergeant."

Chapter 13

Moran listened patiently while Hernandez told him about his meeting with Linda Garcia. When Hernandez finished, Moran drew back his arms, placed his hands behind his head, and intertwined his fingers. "And then they say it doesn't snow in Mexico City," Moran said.

Hernandez twisted his mouth. "Played me for a chump," the sergeant said and slapped the surface of the office's conference table with the palm of his hand.

"Relax." Moran said. "Happens to the best of us."

"There were three women named Maria Luisa Torres in the Mexico City area phone listing, but the police told me that one had died two months ago, the other has been in prison for the last two years on a drug trafficking charge, and the last one was a patient at a local nuthouse."

"I've had your Dragon Lady from the bank checked out and something's not right," Moran said.

The door to the office opened and a middle-aged stout man in a white lab coat marched in. The laminated photo ID that hung from his coat's breast pocket said he was Roy Fielding, Chief of the NYPD Ballistics Unit.

As Fielding walked toward Moran and Hernandez, the thick tuft of mussed brown hair that capped his head bounced as if on springs, giving him the appearance of some sort of mad scientist. His right hand clutched two typed pages while his left hand gripped a half-eaten onion bagel.

"I completed the ballistics tests," he said when he reached the table. "Sorry it took so long." He took a large bite from the bagel, wiped his mouth with the hem of his lab coat and set the report down on the table. "It's the same weapon that killed Lacy Wooden."

"Thought so," Moran said. "The wounds were similar."

"There's more, my children." Fielding began with a professorial air. "The .22 has a left-hand rate of twist 1 in 10, and the .38 right-hand rate of twist of 1 in 12. You'll find that one bullet came from a barrel with six grooves while the other came from a barrel with eight grooves."

For a long moment, the words hung over the room like a thick fog. Moran and Hernandez looked at each other.

"Are you saying that two guns were used?" Hernandez said.

"That's where I have a problem," Fielding said. He picked up the report and flipped to the last page. He pointed to a paragraph that was highlighted in yellow. "Read it."

Moran grasped the report and when he finished, he dropped it on the table and rose from his chair. "Both casings were struck on the same side and with the same firing pin indentation," Moran said.

"Exactly," Fielding said. "You and I know that no two pins strike the primer at the same angle and with the same indentation. All of which throws the two-gun theory out the window."

Moran slid the report to Hernandez and turned to the ballistics chief. "What's your take?"

Fielding massaged his chin. "Never seen anything like it."

"What about a derringer?" Hernandez asked.

"If it is, it's got to be one hell of a custom job," Fielding answered.

Hernandez scratched his head. "Then it's got to be two killers and the firing pin markings are just a fluke. Which could mean the killer used two guns to make it look like two shooters."

"And both guns left the identical firing pin markings?" Roy Fielding said. "I can't buy that."

"I agree," Moran said. "Two separate shooters can't produce a pattern that tight. It's impossible for two separate weapons to produce the same angle of entry."

Hernandez furrowed his brow and his gaze drifted back and forth between Moran and Fielding. "Maybe you're right."

Moran began to pace. "Let's play it out. Myer and his assailant have a violent argument. They struggle, and in the heat of the fight, the killer strikes Myer on the side of the head with a heavy object, and then shoots him twice," the lieutenant stopped and faced Fielding and Hernandez. "If it was a planned hit the killer would've just shot the guy and been done with it," Moran said.

CHAPTER 14

Alice Simms floated in through the glass doors of the Haifa Diamond Exchange. The store's large windows contained pricey objects that ranged from gaudy Rolexes to oversized diamond rings. But it wasn't in the city's Diamond District, home to wholesalers and retailers of ninety percent of all the diamonds that entered the United States. In fact, the jewelry store was flanked by a Falafel eatery on one side and crates of tropical produce from, 'La Isla,' a bodega, on the other. The several glass counters with expensive jewelry on display were busy with salesclerks attending clients. From nearby a man with thick eyeglasses wearing a long black beard and ringlets that ran down the sides of his thin, pallid face moved toward Simms.

"Can I help you?" he said. The man's long black coat sagged over his lanky frame and he tipped the wide brimmed black fedora that rested on his head.

Simms showed him her badge and ID. "I need to talk to someone about this," she said and drew out Lacy's Movado exchange receipt.

After examining it, the clerk gazed at her appraisingly. "This is over a year old," he said and grinned at her. "Go to the back and see Max Roth, one of the owners. Maybe he can help."

When Simms knocked on the glazed door of Max Roth's office, a small ruddy-faced man with a long white beard and blue glistening eyes opened the door and doffed his black fedora. He was attired like the clerk.

"I was told you could help me," Simms said when she stepped inside and identified herself. She handed Max the receipt. "I'd like to know more about this. Police investigation."

Max Roth shrugged and gestured to a chair next to his roller-top desk. "Please, make yourself comfortable." He gazed at the receipt as he lowered himself into his roller chair which creaked under his weight. "Is there something wrong?"

"That's what I'm here to find out," Simms said. She sat and placed her business card on Roth's desk.

Max eyed the detective, setting aside an open ledger that lay atop a pile of bills bound by a rubber band next to a computer. "Excuse the mess, I still have to plug these into our database." Roth tapped the pile with the pads of his fingers. He returned his attention to the receipt. "Aha! I remember this," the jeweler finally said.

Simms arched her eyebrows. "Oh?"

"The original purchase, a lady's diamond Movado watch, was bought by this gentleman client of ours who always paid in cash and—"

"What was his name?"

Roth massaged his forehead. "I, eh… don't know." He gazed at Simms with soft, moist eyes. He gave a smile—a patient smile. "Young lady, when a man his age buys so many expensive baubles so often, you know they're not for his wife. So you do the obvious thing and don't ask questions."

"How old was this man?" Simms said.

"Oh, maybe late forties, early fifties. I'm not very good at guessing ages," Roth said.

"When was the last time he was in?"

The old jeweler chortled and raised his hands. "Oy, my memory is not as good as it used to be. But he was a regular for about a year. I haven't seen him for over eight months. Always purchased the finest and in cash." Roth emphasized the last word *cash*. Then he turned to the computer keyboard and clicked a few keys. His eyes, beneath his dark closely-knit eyebrows darted across the flickering screen. A spreadsheet appeared and Roth sat back in his chair. "Here it is," he said with pride.

Simms pushed her chair closer to the desk and looked at the screen. Next to a date was an entry for the purchase of the Movado for two thousand dollars in cash. When she shifted her eyes to the next line, she saw that Lacy had exchanged the watch for a diamond tennis bracelet the next day. The detective reached inside her purse and drew out a folded copy of the *New York Times* picture. She placed it on the desk in front of Roth.

"Do you see your client in this photo?" Simms asked.

While Roth slowly examined the picture, Simms watched him, for any sign of recognition in the old man's face. Suddenly, she noticed Max's eyes flare for an instant and his right cheek twitch.

"Which one is it, Mr. Roth?"

The old man tipped the fedora back and passed the palm of one hand over his creased brow. "I'm sorry, but it's none of these people."

Simms maintained her gaze on Max Roth. "Funny, I would've sworn you recognized someone," she pressed. "Can you at least tell me what he looked like?"

Roth squirmed in his chair and moistened his lips. "He was tall… very distinguished looking." He paused for a moment and then continued. "Oh my, I'm afraid that's all I remember. That's what happens when one gets old," He smiled tightly.

Simms rose from her chair. "It's only been eight months since you saw him, and before that you said he was a steady customer for a year. Your memory can't be that bad," she pressed.

"My dear, I've seen so many people by the end of a day, customers, buyers, colleagues… as you've noticed we're very busy. It's impossible to remember everyone's face with any detail. Besides, I wasn't the only one who tended to him."

"Who else?"

"I'm sorry, young lady, but I don't remember."

Simms leaned in and gave the jeweler her best NYPD intimidating stare.

"I think you should know we're investigating the murder of the woman who made the exchange. You may have read about the

70

case. A Lacy Wooden found brutally murdered?"

Roth's eyes widened. "Oy vey! So, that's who she was."

"She was murdered the day after she exchanged the watch," Simms said.

The old man swallowed hard and rolled his chair to face the detective. "But I thought the murderer had been caught."

"A man was, but he was recently exonerated, so the case is still open," Simms said. "I still find it strange that you didn't think it peculiar having someone pay such large amounts of cash."

Max chuckled. "Not at all. Many of our customers pay in cash. Frankly, I prefer it, less paperwork... just like the old days," he said. "I'm afraid that's all I can tell you. I'm sorry."

Simms's eyes swept through the small cubicle. "I'm curious as to why you're not in the Diamond District. I mean, this isn't exactly a high-brow neighborhood."

Roth grinned broadly. "Precisely. Less competition and lower rent."

The detective nodded and stood. "Thank you for your time, sir. I'd like a detailed list of all the purchases this client made. My e-mail address is on the card."

When Simms left the Haifa Diamond Exchange, she knew that sweet Max Roth had played her for a patsy. Despite his attempts at seeming to be a doting old man with a short memory, the momentary flash in his eyes and the facial twitch told another story.

* * *

In another part of Manhattan, the green recording light of an answering machine in a dark, empty room glowed while it recorded the message that came through the machine's speaker. "It's Max. The police were here today and showed me a newspaper picture with you in it. Don't worry, I was like a dead person and said nothing. Just thought you should know."

When the machine stopped recording, the door opened and a

wedge of light carved its way into the room. A silhouetted figure stepped into the light, crossed the room and pressed the 'Replay' button. When the figure finished listening to the message, the 'Erase' button was pressed.

CHAPTER 15

"**A**lice," Hernandez said, "do you realize that if you're right it could be anyone in that photograph— Shilling, Judge Corbin, or even Greg Saunders. They all more or less match the age of this mysterious cash customer."

Simms sat upright in her chair and faced the sergeant. "I'm tellin' you Max Roth's face lit up when he saw the photo." While Simms detailed her encounter with Max Roth, a thoughtful, silent Moran sat in a swivel chair at his desk gazing out of the office's meshed window at the Municipal Building. He was weighing her every word and visualizing her meeting with the old jeweler.

At the time when Commissioner Newbury decided to increase Moran's staff, the lieutenant immediately thought of Alice Simms over at Missing Persons. He knew her analytic mind was being wasted looking for persons who had gone missing without having committed any crime—usually people who didn't really want to be found. Simms had an almost photographic memory for details and an engrossing narrative style—all beef, no filler.

When Simms finished, Moran spun around and with his lower lip caught between his teeth hoisted himself off the chair. He walked toward the two cops, his usual bounce replaced by a noticeable limp. The knee again.

"I agree with Alice," Moran said. "Max Roth was lying." He pointed to the boxes that contained Lacy Wooden's personal effects; they were stacked against the far wall. "I want to go through them again. Now that we've a clearer idea of what we're looking for, there might be something among her things connecting her to somebody in that photo that we missed the first time."

"Why don't we just question all of them?" Simms said.

Moran waved his hands dismissively. "Much as I'd like to there's no way we can lean on this crowd like they were run-of-the-mill thugs. We need compelling evidence before we brace them. Let's go through Lacy's stuff again and then we can weigh our options."

The purr of the fax machine caused everyone to focus on the document that started to come through. Moran stepped toward the machine and pulled out the paper. It was a black-and-white photograph of a pretty, swarthy, shapely, smiling woman. Her straight jet-black hair was gathered in a tight bun. The lieutenant read the paragraph under the picture and walked back to the table. He set the fax down in front of Hernandez and jabbed his index finger on top of the picture.

"That's the real Linda Garcia—age fifty and vice-president of Banco de Mejico's main branch for the past five years," Moran announced.

Hernandez's jaw dropped as he gazed at the picture. "How... how did you get on to this?" he stammered.

"The day after you returned," Moran said, "Miss Garcia phoned, apologizing for having not kept her appointment with you. She had gotten a call that her car had been hit by another vehicle in the bank's parking structure across the street. Turned out it wasn't true. She dismissed it as a prank. As you can see, she doesn't match the description of the woman you met."

Hernandez gave Moran a quizzical look.

"When I spoke with Linda Garcia to set up your meeting, she was very cooperative and pleasant on the phone, and she sounded like an older woman. Much different from the Linda Garcia you met. So I had the bank's Human Resources department fax me a picture of Linda Garcia on the pretext that we needed to clarify a possible identification snafu."

"Then who the hell was the woman I met?" Hernandez said.

Moran shrugged. "Had to be someone who knew Garcia and

the bank's procedures in order to give you a copy of the bond transaction. Someone in the bank."

"Which would explain her curtness; she wanted me out of there before the real Linda Garcia returned."

"Exactly."

Simms asked. "But why give Frank anything at all?"

"Giving him nothing would've seemed suspicious," Moran said.

Hernandez gazed at the picture again, made a face, and bolted out of his chair. "I could use a friggin' drink," he said. "This case is becoming weirder with each turn. What's next, running into *Chupacabra?*"

"What the hell's that?" Simms said.

"The Latin-American version of Big Foot," Hernandez answered. "Depending on whose version you hear, it's supposed to be a five to seven foot half-alien, half-dinosaur creature that sucks the blood out of goats and other animals."

"Nice," Moran muttered.

"But who the hell tipped off whoever in Mexico? We were the only ones who knew I was I going," Hernandez said.

CHAPTER 16

Frank Hernandez was in a foul mood when he walked under the arches of the NYU Law School building and skipped down the steps to the sidewalk. It had not been the best day in his life—the meeting that morning with Moran and all its implications had taken the wind out of his sails. The fact that someone had tipped off the Dragon Lady in Mexico kept eating away at him. To make matters worse, the Evidence class had been a disaster.

Professor Fagan wasn't pleased when Hernandez tried to bluff his way while trying to explain the hearsay evidence rule and let the sergeant know it: '*Mr. Hernandez, the holiday season is not upon us yet, so please spare us the window dressing,*' Fagan had said when he interrupted the detective's flight into fantasy.

The sergeant raised his eyes and gazed across the street to Washington Square and the stone arch that marked the beginning of Fifth Avenue. He pressed his attaché case against his chest as he hunched his shoulders and leaned against the cold wind coming off the Hudson River. Minutes later, when he climbed into his three-year-old Camry and pulled away from the curb, he caught a glimpse of a late model black Mustang that fell in behind him. When Hernandez made a U-turn and then a left onto Canal Street, he noticed the Mustang close behind. The glare of the headlights made it impossible to see the front license plate.

When Hernandez neared the West Side Highway, a Lexus SUV with a young couple in it pulled in directly behind him. Hernandez looked into his rearview mirror and noticed the driver arguing with his female passenger. She was gesticulating violently with her hands. When Hernandez drove up the on-ramp, he looked at his dashboard clock: 10:45 p.m. He darted his eyes to the rearview mirror—the Mustang was gone.

A relieved Hernandez sped past the 23rd Street exit. The Lexus veered to the right and a red minivan took its place. Two exits later, the van turned off at the 42nd Street exit, and to the detective's surprise, the mystery car was following twenty feet behind. The sergeant accelerated and the speedometer reached 70 mph. Hernandez's gaze flitted uneasily back-and-forth from the rearview mirror and to the side view—the Mustang was there. It wasn't making any aggressive maneuvers, only keeping up with Hernandez.

The sergeant's stomach tightened and he felt shortness of breath as anxiety began to swell up. *Who is this moron?* Ever since he and Pilar had almost been rammed off the road by a Hummer two years earlier, Frank Hernandez was more than a little touchy about being tailed.

He reached under his coat and fingered the Glock in the holster strapped to his waist. At the 72nd Street exit sign, he gunned the car into the right lane. A silver BMW 750i sped up in his rear lane, and when the sergeant looked into the rearview mirror, he saw that behind the Beamer was a U-Haul truck. The sergeant let out a breath—the Mustang had disappeared.

When Hernandez drove down the 96th Street exit, he looked into his mirrors there was no sign of the mystery car. The Camry slipped into its outdoor parking space in the back of Hernandez's apartment building at the corner of 100th Street and Columbus Avenue. He grabbed his attaché case and climbed out. The sergeant looked up. Black clouds covered the sky, and the temperature had gotten colder. Now and then, lightning flashed, bright bolts shot across the sky and a few second later, earsplitting thunder shook the earth as heavy raindrops began to fall.

Hernandez quickened his pace and regretted not having heeded Pilar's suggestion that he taken an umbrella. When he trotted across the dimly lit parking lot, he heard the purring of an idling engine and the muted thumping of windshield wipers. The cop looked in the direction of the sounds and stopped in his tracks. The shadow of a car made his eyes broaden. It was the black Mustang.

Anxiety had given way to anger. Hernandez lowered the attaché case and set it down. He opened his coat, brought out the Glock and chambered a round. He started toward the car, his eyes-- two embers of coal--and his jaw set square. Suddenly, the car's motor revved. When it tore past, Hernandez banged the car's rear right fender with the butt of his weapon.

"What the hell do you want?" Hernandez yelled as rain streamed down his face. Seconds later the car turned right and vanished into the storm. Everything had happened so quickly that he didn't see the license plate. He asked himself, "*Who the hell was that?*" and when *Chupacabra* popped into his mind the sergeant shook his head and chuckled.

CHAPTER 17

When Darcey stepped off the elevator of Carnegie Hall's fifth floor, the sound of tap dancing to a piano's syncopated music blended in with a soprano doing scales and struggling to reach a high C. From another rehearsal room across the corridor, a tenor was doing his best to ruin Turandot's *Nessun Dorma*. The detective neared a closed door at the end of the hallway. On the wall next to the door, a sign was inserted into a glass frame: **Rand's Advanced Master Classes.**

Darcey entered the room. He stopped and gazed at ten young female tap dancers in leotards with top hats and canes dancing in line to Irving Berlin's 'Blue Skies.' The number was being banged out on an upright piano in a corner by an elderly man squinting at a sheet of music.

A tall, svelte, long-legged woman with her back to Darcey called out, snapping her fingers, "One, two, three and step right... one, two, three and step left." She appeared to be in her mid-thirties; her lithe figure made the baggy brown knit sweater over black leotards look chic.

The cop watched the dancers strut their stuff on the room's hardwood floor while a wall-length mirror reflected their images. Not only were they all about the same age, late teens or early twenties, but they all seemed to be two to three inches taller than his five-foot-eleven-inch frame. As Darcey's eyes took in the room, he noticed three framed theater posters on one of the walls—one was from the Schubert Theater '*Damn Yankees*'; the second one, '*42nd Street*' was from the Music Box Theater; and the third was from the Albee Theater '*Can-Can.*'

Jessie Rand headlined all three shows. When the dance instructor moved to the front of the chorus line, she looked up and met Darcey's stare.

"Okay, girls, take five and then we'll take it from the top again," she said in a soft English accent that reminded the detective of Julie Andrews. The detective watched her closely as she floated across the floor toward him with gazelle-like grace. When the instructor reached him, he stepped forward and flipped out his ID.

"You are?" Darcey said.

In a warm, velvety voice, she said, "Jessie Rand." Her pleasant smile revealed two perfect rows of capped teeth that would have made any dentist proud.

Darcey pointed over his shoulder to the posters. "You still dance?"

A glimmer of annoyance flashed in Rand's sapphire-blue eyes. "I prefer teaching. Now how can I be of assistance, officer?"

"We found your name among Lacy Wooden's things, and I'd like to ask you some questions."

Rand gave Darcey a quizzical gaze—those sapphire eyes again. "But she's been dead for almost a year." She brushed a wisp of hair from her brow.

Darcey took her in. She was beautiful and elegant, her strong features softened by her ebony-black lustrous hair; the woman moved with natural grace. Under her leotards, Darcey imagined she was firm yet soft, tight and yielding. When the detective realized he was staring, he shifted his gaze to the side. He told her about Paul Myer's release and subsequent murder. "I'd like to verify a few things with you," he said when he finished.

Rand gave him a warm smile and drew him to the piano.

"What can you tell me about Lacy Wooden?" Darcey said.

Rand pressed her hair back with the palms of both hands, her focus, razor-sharp. "Lacy was a good student with a lot of promise. But, she was too distracted with other things to really fulfill her potential," Rand said and shifted her weight from one to leg to the other. "Pity, because if she had applied herself she could've had a brilliant career."

"What do you mean by distracted?"

"The girl was too bloody interested in men. Always someone new coming to collect her after she finished here... mostly older men. I didn't care for that at all, and I let her know several times."

Darcey then showed her the *Times* society page photograph. "Was anyone in this picture among those callers?"

Rand grasped the clipping and peered at it. Darcey scrutinized the dance instructor while she scrutinized the photo. Suddenly, Rand's peaches-and-cream complexion flushed and the muscles around her mouth tightened. "I'm afraid not." She returned the picture to Darcey.

"You sure?" Darcey said.

Rand's warm smile returned. "Quite."

"Is it Mrs. or Miss Rand?" Darcey asked as he pocketed the clipping. *Never seen eyes that blue in my life,* he mused.

"Miss."

"Oh," Darcey said with a hopeful glint in his eyes. "I... eh... was thinking that maybe... ahem... when I'm off duty, I could—"

Rand smiled and drew closer to Darcey. Her bedroom eyes bore through the cop like a laser while his hopes rose and his knees weakened.

"That's sweet," she said. She lowered her voice and whispered in Darcey's ear, "Except, that I play for the other team."

CHAPTER 18

"I find this case bizarre at best," a jacketless Shilling said as he turned away from the window and walked back to his desk. The starched, form-fitting white shirt revealed a trim torso that belied his fifty-two years of age. "Six months after he's cleared of Lacy Wooden's murder, Paul Myer is killed by someone who shoots him twice for good measure after he's dead." He paced with his hands in his pockets. "Which leaves your niece's murder still unresolved." He pointed at Newbury.

Shilling reached his glass-top chrome desk, plopped into his chair, and maintained a steady gaze on Newbury and Moran both of whom were seated in front of him. When no one spoke, Shilling added, "Not only that, but Myer is also suspected of bank fraud, which brings me to this Maria Luisa Torres. No one knows anything about her. Plus the waste of time and money on Sergeant Hernandez's trip to Mexico to meet with an impostor." Shilling threw up his hands. "Am I the only one getting the feeling this is all being filmed in black-and-white with only Mary Astor and Sydney Greenstreet missing?"

"I'm not Sam Spade," Moran began, "but—" He reached down, grasped the manila envelope that rested against his right leg and opened it. "—I want you to see this."

Moran stood and stepped toward Shilling's desk. "I printed this from the Banco de Mejico's website." He set down a color printout on the desk next to a small framed photograph of a younger Howard Shilling in U.S.M.C. combat fatigues alongside four other Marines crouched in front of a tank. In the left-hand corner was inscribed in ink—'*The Desert Rats, Feb.2, '91.*'

"I showed this printout to Commissioner Newbury before we came in," Moran said. "The woman who appears in the inset next to her biography is Rosario Mendez, head of the bank's brokerage services."

Shilling leaned over, slid the print closer and examined the black-and-white image of an attractive mid-thirties woman, with short brown wavy hair, a Mona Lisa smile and bright dark eyes.

"Who is she?" the DA said.

"She's the one who met with Sergeant Hernandez."

Shilling pressed the palms of his hands against his face. "Oh, boy."

"According to her biography, Rosario Mendez is thirty-seven, got her MBA from Columbia University ten years ago and has been with the bank for the past five."

Newbury stood and joined the lieutenant. "Moran told me that when he ran the picture through the database it brought up Miss Mendez's mugshot after she was arrested for DWI while at Columbia. She was slapped with a fine plus ten days for disorderly conduct."

"Actually it was more like DWPO," Moran added quickly.

Shilling cast the lieutenant a questioning look. "What's that?"

"Driving While Passed Out."

The DA threw a somber gaze at Moran. "Let's stick to the facts. Why disorderly conduct?" Shilling said.

"At the time of her arrest, she assaulted the officer claiming he was abusive to her because she was Hispanic," Moran said. "Proved to be BS, but it would explain her dislike of cops."

"So where and who is Maria Luisa Torres?" Shilling asked.

Moran and Newbury exchanged glances. "She may not exist," Moran said.

"Great!" Shilling exclaimed. "Just what Morrison will want to hear." He looked at Moran's tight face. "I can tell from your look there's more. Bring it on."

Moran reported on his meeting with Rose Chiu, Simms's meeting with Max Roth, and Darcey's encounter with Jessie Rand.

However, he omitted the showing the *Times* photograph that included Shilling. "We're waiting for the complete list of the jewelry bought for Lacy from the Haifa Diamond Exchange. It might give us a lead as to the identity of Lacy's generous benefactor," Moran said.

Newbury stiffened at the word *benefactor,* pawed into his inner coat's pocket, and brought a leather cigar holder. He placed a panatela in his mouth and chewed on it. The building was a smoke-free area.

"Lacy's post-mortem indicated she had consensual sex shortly before she was killed," Moran said. "Which could mean she knew her killer."

Newbury pulled the cigar from his mouth and clucked. "Always told my wife I thought Lacy was bad news," he said, and clenched his teeth.

Shilling said. "What about the payments to Myer?"

Moran said, "We're still working on that. Without leads, it's going to be tough."

Shilling's phone jangled.

After he answered, the DA said. "It's Detective Simms asking for you, Moran." He held the receiver in his outstretched hand.

"Alice, what's up?" Moran said. While he listened, his face hardened and his fingers drummed the glass-top. A moment later he said, "Thanks for calling," and hung up. When he looked up, he saw Shilling and Newbury staring at him, their faces question marks.

"Max Roth died an hour ago at St. Clare's from an apparent heart attack," Moran said.

* * *

Three floors down, in Part V of the Criminal Courts Building, Pilar Hernandez sat in the jury box with her chin resting on the palm of her hand while her other hand toyed with the pearl necklace that rested over her blouse. Next to her sat two other court interpreters with the same bored expression. The minutes passed like hours while a variety-pack of Manhattan's less desirable citizens paraded before Judge Edwin Corbin during the arraignment and bail setting process. Unlike the Farsi interpreter, a dark-haired woman with flashing black eyes and a scarf loosely wrapped around her head and the short, middle-aged Armenian interpreter who had been busy all morning, Pilar hadn't been called on at all. It was a startling reminder of how the city's demographics had changed in recent years.

Judge Corbin, a blonde bushy-haired man, glanced up at the clock over the courtroom's entryway when the last defendant was led away.

"It's almost one, and the clerk tells me we've cleared this morning's calendar, so let's break for lunch and be back at two," he said.

Moments later Pilar Hernandez walked out of the building onto Centre Street and headed to the long line of pushcart vendors hawking their fare of hot-dogs, hamburgers, falafel, knishes and other food to the crowd of cops, lawyers and defendants. When she neared one of the carts, a tall, attractive, white-haired man with a smooth olive-skinned face and almond-shaped brown eyes materialized at her side.

He tapped Pilar's shoulder. "Excuse me," he said, with a soft Spanish accent.

Pilar whirled around and faced the stranger. "Sorry, friend, but I haven't got any change to spare," she snapped and started to turn her attention to the cart's menu.

"No, no," the stranger said in a wheedling voice. "I'm not asking for a handout, Mrs. Hernandez. I need to talk with you." He walked around to face her.

Pilar softened her attitude when she noted the man's neat cream-colored suit and well-groomed appearance. "Look, I'm hungry and I'd like to get something to eat. Go inside, to the Interpreters' Room on the second floor and make an appointment."

The stranger moved closer to her and leaned in. "I'm..." he

started to whisper in her ear just as two hook-and-ladder fire engines roared by in front of them. The deafening blare of the sirens made it difficult for Pilar to hear the man so she cocked her head while he continued to whisper.

"What!" Pilar said, as the fire engines rounded the corner.

"Let me buy lunch and we can talk over there," the stranger said and pointed to Foley Square diagonally across from them.

CHAPTER 19

When Simms and Moran arrived at St. Clare's overflowing emergency room, a deep familiar voice called out. "If it isn't Lieutenant James Francis Moran."

Simms and Moran turned, and Moran wrinkled his forehead when he saw Manny Friedman, a sturdy, ruddy-complexioned man in his fifties with long, reddish hair in an open soiled trench coat. "Detective Sergeant Manny Friedman, what are you doing here?" Moran said.

Friedman pulled the coat's lapel open and pointed to the star-shaped badge that hung from his jacket's breast pocket. "*Lieutenant* Manny Friedman now, outta Brooklyn and here at Midtown North's 19th Precinct."

"That's the 19th's loss," Moran said.

Friedman frowned. "Not a very nice thing to say, especially since you and I are now equals."

"Not even in your dreams, Manny," Moran snapped. "Now if you'll excuse us." He started to walk away.

"Hold on," Friedman pressed. "This is my beat and I'm in charge."

"Of what?" Simms chimed in.

Friedman stared briefly at Simms and then sneered at Moran. "I see you're taking Affirmative Action to heart, Moran. What happened to the Newyorican?"

"Sergeant Hernandez is on another assignment; however, he knew you'd ask about him and sends his best," Moran shot back.

Simms folded her arms across her chest and bristled. Moran

touched her arm. "Don't mind Friedman, he's an Equal Opportunity Bigot, hates everybody." He turned to Friedman. "Meet Detective Alice Simms."

Friedman gave Simms a dismissive glance. "We found your card in Mr. Roth's wallet. The man suffered an apparent heart attack at his office and we treat all suspicious deaths as homicides until proven otherwise. The key word being *apparent.*"

"You think he was murdered?" Moran said.

Friedman shrugged. "Dunno, I'm waiting for the doc to come and tell me. I did, however, notice that all the drawers in his desk were open which could indicate burglary. Why are you here?"

"The deceased was a witness in an open homicide that we're investigating and that makes what happened to him our business," Moran said.

Friedman's face flushed and the tips of his ears reddened. "You pulled this crap on me once before at the Dream Pizza Parlor killings in Brooklyn. This time, I'm not—"

"You got a beef, take it up with Newbury and Shilling," Moran interrupted. His eyes bored through Friedman. "Pick up your ball and bat and go home, Manny."

"I know you're tight with the Commish and Hizzoner," Friedman hissed and peered at Moran's nose. "You know, I'd swear that brown spot at the end is a little darker than the last time I saw it."

Moran gave a wry smile. "I can always wipe it off, but that blockhead on your shoulders is permanent."

Friedman stepped forward. "One of these days, Moran—"

Moran's jaw clenched. "One of these days what?"

Simms moved in. "Not here, people are watching." She gestured to the sea of brown and Asian faces that crowded the Emergency Room, their dark eyes staring at them.

The two large doors at the end of the emergency room whooshed open, and a small dark-haired female doctor in surgical greens entered the room. She strode toward the cops. Her laminated ID read: *Nancy Suarez, Trauma Surgeon.* In her hand was a clipboard with several pages attached.

"Lieutenant Friedman, I—" Suarez began.

"I'm the officer now in charge," Moran interjected and turned to Friedman. "Thanks, Manny, but I'll take if from here."

The surgeon turned to Moran. "I'm the attending physician and I'd like to talk to you about what we found." She led Simms and Moran to the rear of the ER where Max Roth lay covered on a bed. Suarez closed the curtain around the space and faced the two detectives.

"When the EMTs arrived at his store after a 911 call from a salesclerk," Suarez said, "Mr. Roth was found in his office suffering from ventricular arrhythmia and gasping for breath." She looked at her clipboard briefly. "The EMT notes have him down as *CTD.*"

"What's that?" Simms asked.

"It's hospital lingo for Circling The Drain—in other words, he was near death."

Moran said. "Go on."

Dr. Suarez went on. "Mr. Roth said he was a diabetic with heart trouble. Two pill bottles were on his desk. One contained Type I diabetic pills; the other was opened and contained nitrolingual a form of nitroglycerin. Mr. Roth passed away just moments later."

The doctor gazed at her clipboard and lifted up a page. "From the blood tests we ran on the deceased, the cause of death was nitroglycerin poisoning. He overdosed. The diabetic pills dosage called for three pills per dose, while the nitrolingual dose is one."

"Two pills could've made a difference?" Simms asked.

"Normally it would cause a mild heart attack but nothing fatal. However, Mr. Roth's heart disease was degenerative, and when you factor in his age, it doesn't take much to cause death."

"You suspect foul play, doctor," Moran said.

Suarez shrugged. "Hard to tell. My guess is that he mistook one medication for the other."

* * *

Later that afternoon when Moran and Alice Simms entered Max Roth's office in the store, the lieutenant noticed the open drawers and disordered state of the desktop: folders, stacked bills bound by rubber bands and other papers. He turned to Simms. "What do you think?"

Simms shook her head. "His desk was just as messy when I interviewed him. As for the drawers, he could've been looking for his medicine. No one has come forward saying anything's missing."

Moran nodded. "I guess we can accept that for now."

Simms sat down in front of Roth's computer and opened up the *My Documents* folder. "Let me try to access that client list he was supposed to send me." She peered at the screen and scrolled down a list of subfolders in the file. She stopped, at a folder labeled *Accounts Receivables,* and opened it. Simms clicked a few more keys while she watched the screen.

Moran looked admiringly over her shoulders as Simms' fingers did their magic dance on the keyboard. Moran's own typing method was something that resembled Lionel Hampton playing the vibraphone.

Suddenly, a spreadsheet appeared on the screen. "Bingo!" Simms exclaimed, and she began scrolling down. Simms pointed to an entry. "It corresponds to Lacy Wooden's Movado watch purchase and the date is the day before she came in and exchanged it for the ten-carat diamond tennis bracelet." She leaned forward and gazed at the entry for a moment. "Look." She pointed to the word *Yehoshua.*

"What does that mean?" Moran asked.

Simms shrugged. "Sounds like Hebrew." She entered the name in the *Search* window and it brought up seven entries: a diamond necklace, an 18k gold bracelet, an emerald broach, a platinum pin, a 14k gold compact, and the Movado watch and a three-carat diamond ring. The purchases were made within a year prior to

Lacy Wooden's death for a total of more than twenty-thousand dollars—in cash.

"Lacy struck the mother lode with this *Yehoshua*," Moran said. "After you print it out, I'm confiscating the computer as evidence. It might contain more info about this person." He turned to the digital phone next to the computer and pressed the '*Calls Received*' button. He scrolled down the screen's ten stored phone calls and the callers' names.

"All suppliers," Moran said. He pressed the *Redial* button. "Let's see the last number he called." The lieutenant said and hit the *Speaker* key as the number rang several times. "*Thank you for calling the Brooklyn Chabad House. Sorry, we're not in. Please leave a...*" the answering machine's taped voice said and Moran hung up.

"That was Max Roth's voice," Simms said.

"And that place sounds familiar," Moran murmured.

CHAPTER 20

"**Y**ehoshua, is Hebrew for Joshua," Sandra said while she kneaded puff pastry dough and Moran spread a generous amount of paté de fois gras over the browned filet mignon that lay on the cutting board in the kitchen. It was Thanksgiving and he had promised to make Sandra her favorite dish, Beef Wellington, in the hopes of improving her appetite. Moran set down the spatula he was using, wiped his hands on his apron, and gazed at his wife.

"You sure?"

Sandra twisted her mouth. "No, I just made it up," she said. "You forget I come from a long line of rabbis and speak some Hebrew."

Moran smiled. "Sorry," he said, and moved toward the door. "I'll be right back," he added as he raced out of the kitchen. When Moran returned, he had the *New York Times* clipping in his hand. "I think I know who it is," he said. He laid the cutout on the counter and pointed to the couple standing next to Shilling.

Sandra looked at the group photograph and the couple under which Moran's finger lay. "State Senator George J. Halpern and wife," she read aloud and glanced at the strikingly handsome man with patrician features, light brown hair with brushstrokes of gray. The tall, svelte blond woman next to the senator with a smiling face had more jewelry on her than King Tut.

"George *Joshua* Halpern," Moran stated. "To be exact."

"What!"

"Simms said that when Roth saw this there was an instant of recognition in his eyes. I'll bet my pension it was Halpern he recognized."

* * *

The following Monday morning, Moran used most of the two-and-half-hour Amtrak train ride along the Hudson River to reflect on the long holiday weekend. It had been quiet and restful; he and Sandra spending afternoons lazing in the warm sun at the lake in Central Park and visiting the Empire State Building like two tourists on vacation. As the scenery along the Hudson blurred past, he gazed out the window and smiled inwardly. How mysterious and exotic Sandra had looked with the beige turban that covered her head—like Lana Turner in *The Postman Always Rings Twice*. The conductor's announcement that he had reached his destination, the sleepy town of Rensselaer, across the river, from Albany snapped Moran back to the present.

When Moran stepped out of the cab and looked up at the 1899 granite and brick State Capitol Building, he checked his watch. 1:10 p.m. His appointment with State Senator Halpern was for 1:00 p.m., but as usual Amtrak had left Grand Central late. Moran shrugged and made his way up the stone steps.

Halpern's secretary, leggy and statuesque, close to six-feet tall with shining shoulder length blonde hair, strong cheekbones and large blue eyes, greeted Moran with all the warmth of the Hubbard Glacier. She glanced up at the clock behind her and gave the cop her 'bad-dog-no- biscuit' look. Moran eyed her. She wasn't beautiful, but sexy... a very sexy woman.

"Sorry, I'm late, Senator," Moran said when the blonde led him into Halpern's spacious office.

Halpern, speaking on the phone, waved at the lieutenant. "Look, Samantha, for the umpteenth time, I'm sorry, but I can't leave Albany just now, so you can entertain Sabrina's dance class friends with a dinner party this weekend—" Halpern stared at the receiver—the line apparently dead. "Impossible woman," he muttered and dropped the receiver back onto its cradle. The senator turned to his secretary.

"That'll be all, Cynthia," he said to the iceberg. She left the office, and Moran felt the room's temperature rise from glacial to normal. Halpern came around his oversized desk and strode to meet Moran with a full-dental-plate grin.

He was taller than Moran expected, and his tanned face set off his piercing violet-gray eyes. Halpern's athletic build was covered by a double-breasted Armani. The senator's perfectly coifed hair with streaks of gray told Moran the man was not only a health nut but also a vain tight-ass. The *'stick a coal up his rear and in a week you've got a diamond'* variety.

"Now you know why I've been trying desperately to get the bullet-train bill passed," Halpern said. Motioning to the soft leather sofa that sat against the wall opposite his desk, he added. "Let's sit there."

Moran quickly took in the room—there was an oak bookcase filled with hardcovers on one wall, and a thick Persian carpet extended itself across the floor. A cherry wood coffee table in the middle was flanked by two Louis XIV style chairs. In the background, soft classical music played through the office's hidden sound system. It all matched Halpern's puffed up image.

Moran recalled his father's favorite phrase, *"Some people are, some people think they are, and some people ain't."* Halpern definitely belonged in the second category.

"You were fortunate to find me home when you called on Friday," Halpern said. "Samantha changed her mind and decided to spend the Thanksgiving holiday in the city. Now, what exactly did you mean by *'it's vital that I speak with you'?*"

Moran reached into his coat's pocket and brought out Max Roth's client list. "Are you familiar with these items?"

When Moran handed the list to Halpern, the senator quickly reviewed it as Moran watched.

The senator cleared his throat when he finished. "Yes," Halpern said and returned the list to Moran. "Lacy was a very attractive and persuasive young woman whom I met at a fundraiser for the performing arts. We had an affair for about a year."

Moran's eyebrows arched.

"Don't look so surprised," Halpern said. "Samantha and I have an understanding--I let her indulge her appetite for luxury cars, jewelry, and expensive jaunts to Europe, and she lets me live my life. Part of that agreement is to never publicly embarrass each other. It's worked rather well for the past ten years."

"Did you and Max Roth know each from any other place?" Moran asked.

"Yes, he was head of the Brooklyn Chabad House, my favorite charity. I do my best to help young people."

"Where were you on the day Lacy Wooden was murdered?" Moran said.

"That's easy. Here, attending the Council on Economic Growth dinner at the Clarion Hotel," Halpern said and let out air. "I'll never forget that day and the ghastly news of Lacy's demise."

"Can anyone confirm this?"

Halpern smiled—a condescending smile. "I was the keynote speaker, which means that two hundred guests saw and heard me."

Smooth operator.

Moran said, "One last thing. How well did you know Paul Myer?"

"I didn't," Halpern answered instantly with a firm voice and steady eyes.

Moran peered closely at the senator. "What if I told you there are witnesses who will swear they saw you and Myer together several times?"

Halpern blinked briskly and moistened his lips. "I'd say they were very much mistaken."

CHAPTER 21

"One of these days, police placard or not, you're gonna get a ticket," Pilar said as she pointed to the Official Police Business card on the dashboard. She climbed out of the car and stepped around a fire hydrant.

"Never happen. Now what's this mysterious evening all about?" Hernandez said over the roof of their car as he locked his door.

"Don't be so impatient. All in good time," Pilar said from the curb. "The *Time*'s food critic mentioned the Trattoria Vitello as the latest rage in town."

"I also heard it requires taking out a small mortgage on a house we haven't got," Hernandez said. He came around and took his wife's arm. He liked how she looked—a Burberry shawl around her shoulders that covered a black turtleneck sweater over a pair of dark-gray wide silk pants—'chic' was the word that came to the sergeant's mind.

When they were mid-way across Thompson Street in the heart of Greenwich Village, Hernandez noticed the throng of couples loitering outside the restaurant. "Let's leave. I'm not waiting hours for a plate of pasta," Hernandez said.

Pilar tugged at his jacket. "We've got reservations. The owner and I went to high school together. A guy named Miguel."

"Miguel?"

"His partner's the Italian cook, Claudio Renzi."

"The TV cook you're always taping?"

"The one and only. He owns several restaurants around the country and this is his latest," Pilar said as they reached the sidewalk. The sergeant stopped abruptly and gazed at the rear of the car that pulled up in front of the restaurant's valet service—it was a black late model Mustang.

"Wait up," Hernandez said to Pilar and started to walk briskly toward the vehicle.

"Frank, we're gonna miss our reservations," Pilar pressed and tugged at her husband's arm.

A frustrated Hernandez stopped. "I know that car," he said.

"You know how many black Mustangs there are in Manhattan? C'mon let's get inside," Pilar said. Hernandez turned around.

When they entered the crowded entrance, they snaked their way through the swarm of lingering patrons to the Maitre D's lectern. There Miguel, a slim well-dressed mid-thirties man with long, sleek black-hair greeted them with a warm smile and immediately escorted them to a secluded table in a corner.

"I set this table aside just for you," Miguel said over his shoulder as he guided the couple through the main dining area to an intimate table set in an alcove. After being seated, Hernandez gave his wife a polite, uneasy smile and proceeded to peer into the faces of the multitude of diners that filled the place. The sergeant craned his head and shifted his gaze to the customers at the bar as if searching for someone as Pilar eagerly looked over the menu's five pages.

An annoyed Pilar lowered the menu and eyed her husband. "Will you please forget that car?"

"I've got the feeling that we're being watched."

"Of course, we're being watched." She pointed to the pert, young waitress in a dress shirt, bowtie, and ankle length apron who had materialized at the table. "She's waiting to take our order."

A moment later, Miguel appeared and set down two strawberry martinis in front of Pilar and Hernandez. "Compliments of the house," he said and returned to the front door.

"I'll take these," Hernandez said, and pulled Pilar's drink toward his own. "You can have your choice of water or iced tea."

Pilar made a face and creased her brow and eyed her martini

with a forlorn look. "Not even born yet and he's already changing my life."

"He?"

Pilar reached into her purse, drew out a black-and-white blurry picture and set it down on the table.

"Surprise, Frank. Meet your new son," she said.

Hernandez picked up the picture and studied the blurry sonogram of the fetus—his son.

"So this is the reason for tonight. I hope when he's born he's better looking than this."

"I'm glad to see you're getting used to the idea."

"Slowly... very slowly."

An hour later after Hernandez and Pilar pushed away their half-eaten Tiramisu, Pilar rose from her chair. "I'll be right back."

Hernandez gave Pilar a curious look. "Where're you going?"

"The Ladies' room," Pilar mouthed, and gently made her way to a small rear corridor.

Hernandez leaned back, reached into his pocket, and drew out the sonogram. He was scrutinizing it when an "Ahem" from above interrupted him. The sergeant looked up and met the dark eyes of an elderly man in a cream-colored suit gazing down at him.

"Yes, what's the—" Hernandez said and stopped. The stranger seemed oddly familiar.

The sergeant's eyes quickly traced the smooth olive-toned face and the groomed white hair. A series of images sped through Hernandez's mind. Slowly, like a ship emerging from a fog bank, an uneasy sense of recognition became a certainty. The face had a name.

The stranger gave Hernandez a weak smile. "It's me, Victor. Your father." He nodded toward the sonogram. "How do you like my new grandson?"

CHAPTER 22

Later that evening, at the end of a row of red vinyl-covered booths in Joe's Coffee Shop a short walk from his apartment building, a tight-lipped Frank Hernandez's fingers tapped the side of his mug of coffee. Across from him sat his father. The two had hardly said a word since they sat down five minutes before. The atmosphere was charged with tension.

Finally Victor spoke. "I approached Pilar at the courthouse, and after much persuasion, convinced her to help me get in touch with you." He fixed his gaze on Hernandez's moving fingers. "I felt it was time you knew the truth."

Hernandez shifted his gaze and looked out the glass window that ran the length of the wall. "I know Pilar meant well... forget it," he said. "So that was your black Mustang at Vitello's and the other night in the parking lot?"

Victor nodded. "A rental."

"But why not just come up and talk to me?"

Victor shrugged. "I got cold feet. How do you approach your own son, a son you haven't seen for nearly thirty years? A person doesn't get over family. Look, Chico—"

Hernandez closed his eyes with a pained expression. He raised his hand and gave his father a cold, steady look. "Don't... please... no one's called me Chico since I was five."

From the counter near the door, a man with a heavy Russian accent said, "I'm closing up." He sounded like a cement mixer.

Hernandez looked around and noticed they were alone—the two couples that had been there earlier were gone. "We won't be long," the sergeant called back at the oily mastodon who squatted by the cash register.

"I was the only one who called you Chico," Victor said.

Hernandez drained his cup. "It's kinda late for trips down memory lane." He pushed the mug aside. "Mom said you died years ago."

A wry smile slowly crept across Victor's face while his fingers turned his coffee mug.

"That's almost true. I was in a boating accident off Cancun. Me and a couple of buddies went fishing for tuna when a squall came up and overturned the boat. I woke up on an island off Cancun and wasn't found until a week later. In the meantime the Mexican authorities, thinking I was dead, notified your mother and—"

"Does mom know you're alive?"

Victor shook his head. "No. I figured that as far as she was concerned I was better off dead. Which is why I kept quiet when I heard she had filed for divorce."

"Okay, so you're not dead. So where the hell've you been for the past thirty friggin' years?" Hernandez felt his brow prickle as he gazed intently at his father. He tried to overcome the urge to get up and run out of the place.

"Look... um... I can't blame you for not being overjoyed to see me, but just hear me out," Victor said.

Hernandez leaned back and stretched open his palms on top of the table. "This better be good."

Victor wiped his face with one of his large hands and then placed his fingers on the table. He looked away for an uncomfortable moment before returning his gaze to his son. "I was working for your mother's father, Eddie Flanagan, at his bar and grill up in the Bronx, washing dishes, when I met your mother. Like two love-crazed teenagers, we fell in love and eloped. Until you came along, her old man wanted nothing to do with us." Victor rubbed his hands together and continued. "That's when things started to go wrong... at least for me. Your mom had a hard time giving birth, and for the first couple of years, she was too weak to work. I was scared and overwhelmed by it all. I held down two jobs, came home, slept three hours and went to work again. In those days, I think I drank every bar in the Bronx dry and then some." He heaved a sigh. "I'm sorry, I left, but it was—"

"Gee, let me finish that for you... *too hard to bear*," Hernandez said.

Victor clenched his fists and his face reddened. "I can't change the past. No one's perfect. I was wrong and I've got to live with that for the rest of my life. I tried to come back, but your mother wanted no part of me. For a while I sent money from San Juan but she returned it. Stubborn woman!"

Hernandez smiled. "Well, you're right about that, she can be hard-headed."

Victor gazed at his son. "You've got my coloring, but your mother's eyes. I know you're studying law and that's a good thing. First Hernandez to ever amount to anything. I'm proud of that."

The sergeant wiped his brow with a paper napkin. The *feely-touchy* tone was starting to chafe his nerves. "So, what did you do all these years? It certainly wasn't worrying about me."

Victor studied his son, took a sip of coffee and swallowed hard. "I went to Mexico, where I worked for a while as a security guard in an oil field and managed to put some money together. Eventually I bought a tapas bar, '*Montezuma's Corner*,' with a friend in Mexico City's financial district. Now we own five of them. It's working out pretty good, a lot of steady important clients, and we cater corporate affairs for many of the banks in the area." He rubbed his forefinger and thumb. "Lots of *dinero*."

Hernandez stoically stared while the man took his son through his life in Mexico. Victor said he'd even gotten married once, but after four years it ended in divorce. "I was her fifth husband and it was a case of knowing what to do but wondering how to make it interesting," he quipped. "I'm seeing someone now. She's pretty high up in a bank near one of my restaurants."

"Thinking of remarrying?"

Victor gave his son an appraising look. "Naw... maybe moving in together, but who knows?"

Hernandez found himself starting to feel sorry for the guy. Despite the white hair and being in his early sixties, Victor Hernandez was still a good-looking man. But his eyes seemed tired, the spark the sergeant vaguely recalled as a child was gone. Maybe the time had come to let go of the past and start afresh. After all the man was his father. *How long can you hate someone?*

"Where are you staying?" Hernandez asked.

"At the St. Regis."

"We're not the St. Regis, but you could stay with us if you wanted," Hernandez said. The words came out easier than he expected.

Victor gazed at him. "That'd be nice," he said softly. "But, I can't. It's very nice of you to offer, but I think we both need more time to get to know each other."

"Then how about dinner tomorrow and get to know your grandson?"

Victor nodded and extended his open hand over the table. "You've got a deal... son."

Hernandez flinched at the word, but managed a thin smile and as he took his father's hand.

CHAPTER 23

*I*t's a pitch dark night. The only sound is the howling wind. That and the sting of blowing snow against the stranger's face. To the figure lying face down in the snow-covered ravine, it is like an eternity. There is pressure of something heavy against the legs and searing pain. The eerie sound of an animal howling in the dark adds to the terror. The watch's crystal is broke and the hands have stopped at eleven o'clock—morning or afternoon? The dark surroundings are starting to blur. There is the sensation of freefalling, hurdling and spinning downward inside a black vortex. A sound. The denseness of the trees and the high snow drifts prevent the helicopter from finding what it is searching for. Something has to be done to let the chopper know where to land. Terror replaces desperation and then it happens: the sound of approaching footfalls in the soft snow, a voice yells, "Over here!"

From the Bose Radio/CD player on the nightstand, music suddenly filled the room. The stranger curled up in the bed snapped its eyes open. Dabbing away beads of sweat from the forehead, the stranger sat up. The nightmare was over—until the next time.

The figure turned to the left and saw the empty pillow. "Honey, where are you?"

"In the kitchen, making breakfast," a soft, mellow woman's voice came through the open bedroom door. "Thought we'd take the Harley out today. Go up the Saw Mill River Parkway and have lunch at Dobbs Ferry."

"Great idea, let me jump in the shower."

The stranger slid out of bed and winced. It was the same every morning: the left ankle would be stiff from the scar tissue. After ten skin grafts and hundreds of hours in therapy, that was the best the doctors could do. The figure shuffled to the dresser, slid open a drawer, and brought out a pack of cigarettes. Next to it was a snapshot of Lacy Wooden stretched out on a beach.

"You goin' to be much longer?" the woman in the kitchen yelled out. "You'd better not be smoking."

"No... no... just putting on my robe."

An hour later, a black Harley-Davidson FLTRI roared out of a parking structure. The driver, in black skin-tight biker gear and a black helmet with a small decal of a six petals red rose superimposed over handlebars on the back, maneuvered the eighteen-thousand dollar Hog with dexterity through the busy intersection. The woman at the back wrapped her arms around the driver's waist.

* * *

"Lacy Wooden's killer suffers from malignant narcissism with overtones of antisocial personality disorder—more commonly known as sociopathic behavior," Sandra said from her seat at the head of the conference table. Around the table Moran, Darcey, and Simms sat in silence listening. "The extreme violence exhibited by the multiple stabbings, the deep gashes in the throat area, and then shooting Lacy twice all are indicative of the kind of uncontrollable anger that a person suffering from malignant narcissism would demonstrate."

"You're saying we're dealing with a nutcase?" Simms said.

"No. Narcissism is something from which most of the human race suffers, albeit in small amounts. It's a good thing, self-love and self-admiration are needed to give us the confidence we require to take risks and succeed. Humans need to feel important. Men stand up for their country, a cause or a principle, while women want to feel important to their job, children, husbands or lovers. However, in large doses, malignant narcissists don't take criticism or rejection well. When opposed or slighted, they become angry, sarcastic and even vengeful. The narcissist takes it one step farther. In addition to all of the foregoing there's an element of sadism and enjoyment at watching their prey suffer, which is what Lacy's killer did. He enjoyed killing her."

"You think it's a man?" Moran said.

Sandra shook her head. "Not necessarily. Malignant narcissists come in all sexes, sizes and ethnic groups. When you combine this with overtones of sociopathic behavior then you're throwing into the mix a very dangerous component. They feel no repentance for their actions unless caught, and any remorse they feel isn't for the victims but for themselves. What makes them that much more dangerous is that they're experts at masking their inner feelings and can function in the real world undetected." Sandra leaned back in her chair and shifted her eyes from Moran to Darcey and finally to Simms—she was in full teaching mode. "I wanted to make you aware of what to look for and what you face."

The mobile phone clipped to Darcey's waist rang. The ringing split through room with the suddenness of a tree limb snapping in a snowstorm. His eyes widened when he read the caller's ID on the screen. "Yes," he answered with trepidation. While he listened and massaged his left temple, he nervously switched the phone from one hand to other. "Mrs. Beasley, please wait, I'll be right over."

"What's happened?" Moran asked.

"I have to go," Darcey said. "That was my brother's new caregiver calling from the house. She says she's quitting."

CHAPTER 24

Out-of-breath, Robert Darcey jammed his key into the door's lock and entered his apartment. When he announced himself and no response came from inside, his stomach did a somersault. The detective warily pushed the door closed with the heel of his foot and ventured farther in.

He stopped when he entered the living room and saw the gaunt, middle-aged black woman who sat on the edge of the couch. She wore a pink pillbox hat atop her braided, cornrow hair.

"Mrs. Beasley, I'm glad you're—"

"I wasn't going to wait much longer," the caregiver said in a West Indian accent.

The loud blare of a television program from Eddie's bedroom startled Darcey. "What the hell's that?" he said, and turned toward the sound.

"That's his newest purchase, a 55 inch flat screen TV," Mrs. Beasley said. "It came this morning and ever since it was installed, he won't come out of the room or take his medication." The woman gestured to the prescription bottles of Thorazine and Lithium that lay on the small table next to the couch.

Mrs. Beasley puffed heavily as she gathered her purse and rose to her feet. "When I tried going into the room, he hurled a chair at me and called me a..." Mrs. Beasley said, then stopped. "Well, I don't want to repeat what he said. You should really think about putting him in an institution," she said over her shoulder as she left the apartment.

A stunned Darcey stared at the closed door for a moment and blinked. The dreaded 'Bad day at Black Rock' feeling started to well up inside of him. The detective gathered himself and marched toward his brother's room.

"Eddie, we need to talk," the cop shouted over the television din. When no response came, he called out again, "Please lower the sound we need to talk, now!"

The ominous silence that followed caused rivulets of sweat to slide down Darcey's back. A crisis was the last thing he needed. Ever since he took his brother in, Moran had been very patient and understanding, but the truth was that he was part of a murder investigation which demanded his full attention.

When Darcey reached the bedroom door, he cocked his head and placed an ear to it. The only sound was the blaring of the television. Darcey slowly turned the brass knob and in a low voice said, "Its okay, Mrs. Beasley has left."

The deafening QVC's programming made Darcey wince when he entered the room. His gaze floated over the tall pile of unopened boxes from UPS and FedEx that took up one corner of the room. He pursed his lips and shook his head at the sight. Two full ashtrays rested on the table next to the empty Lazy Boy recliner and Eddie's unmade rumpled bed.

There was no sign of his brother. Darcey's heart rate picked up when he gazed down to the other side of the bed—Eddie's right hand clutching the TV remote lay motionless on the carpet near the foot of the bed. Darcy hurried toward the hand and gaped when he saw his brother's emaciated, pajama clad body lying on its side. His light brown spiked hair was matted with dried blood.

CHAPTER 25

Moran wove his way through the three-deep crowd at the bar of the 'Little Foxes' and made his way toward a solitary table in a corner. There, Rose Chiu sat in her wheelchair sipping a Mai-Tai. The loud music coming from the stage mixed in with the crowd's hoots and hollers.

"Hey, baby, take it off—"

"Come to papa, honey—"

"I got the money if you got the time—"

When Moran passed the bar, he noticed Earl bartending. A starched white formal shirt with a winged collar and a black bow tie had replaced the undershirt. "How's it goin', Earl?"

The bartender didn't respond but kept frowning icily at the lieutenant.

"Happy to see you," Moran added and waved at the man.

"Lieutenant!" Rose called out above the music. "Over here, I'll buy you a drink."

When Moran reached her, he gave her a tight smile.

"I can tell from your street face that this ain't no social call," Rose said and lit a cigarette.

Moran brought the *Times* clipping out of his coat's pocket and placed the photo next to the Mai-Tai. "I have a question," Moran said. "Take a look at this. Anyone in that picture look familiar, or been here?"

"That's two questions," Rose said. She slowly moved her gaze away from Moran and glanced at the clipping. "Nope," she answered and slid the picture aside.

Moran reached down and pushed the picture back toward Rose.

"Take your time, somebody might come to mind."

Rose gave the picture a second glance. "No need, the answer is still the same," she said coldly. "These people are all big shots in the city. I'd remember them if they ever came in."

Moran slowly folded the clipping and slipped it back into his coat's pocket. "What about someone in a motorcycle outfit?"

"Man or woman?"

Moran lowered himself into a chair next to Rose and gazed at the small woman. "Don't know."

Rose raised her drink and took a long sip through the straw. "There were a couple of times a person dressed like you say picked up Lacy when she finished."

"How come you didn't say this when I was here before?"

Rose shrugged and emitted a dismissive puff of smoke. "You didn't ask."

Moran smiled. *This was one tough cookie.* "What can you tell me about this individual?"

Rose took another sip, set the glass down, snapped her fingers at Earl and pointed to her empty glass. "Hey, Sky, two more!"

"You don't call him Earl?" Moran asked.

"Can't stand the name, too country bumpkin. '*Sky*' for Schuyler... Classier." Rose carelessly looked over at the bartender, whose jaw was set hard. "He doesn't like it, but I'm the boss so I call him whatever I want." She crushed out the cigarette.

Moran smiled and gazed at the little umbrella that rested on the edge of her glass. "Never had one. Taste any good?" He motioned to Rose's drink.

"You want one too?" Rose asked.

An amused smile crossed Moran's face and he shook his head slightly. "You were about to say?"

Rose took out a Marlboro from the pack that lay on the table and brought the ashtray closer. After she lit the cigarette, she slowly blew out a column of smoke over Moran's head. "Help yourself," Rose said and pushed the pack toward the cop. Moran eyed the cigarettes for a long moment and then shook his head.

"I don't know what this motorcycle person looked like," Rose began. "Never came in. When Lacy finished, she'd dash out the back door, run to the front of the club and jump on the back of the bike. Never saw a face. I can only tell you, that whoever it was, was slender and seemed very fit."

"Know the bike's make?"

Rose shrugged. "All I know is, it was big and black."

Earl materialized with Rose's drinks and shot Moran an '*I'm gonna get you, sucka*' sneer. The lieutenant winked at him.

"Hope that helps," Rose added when Earl left. "Like I said, Lacy Wooden wasn't my best dancer, and she wasn't a very nice person. But she didn't deserve to be butchered like that."

Moran hoisted himself out of the chair. "Despite how hard you work at being tough, I think that down deep you're a nice person."

Rose snorted and pointed to her chest. "Wrong, lieutenant. No heart of gold beats here." She took a long swallow of her Mai-Tai. "Can't afford it."

CHAPTER 26

"According to the DMV," Hernandez said, "no one in the *Times* photo has a motorcycle registered in their name and none have withdrawn any large sum of money from their bank accounts. Nothing that matches the amounts or dates on Myer's payment list." He was seated across from Moran in a posh booth at Rafferty's. The popular restaurant was near 1 Police Plaza where judges, lawyers, and people from the District Attorney's office congregated at the end of a long day. But it was unusually quiet that afternoon.

A well-dressed bearded man with a black skullcap resting on his oblong-shaped head appeared. "Welcome to Rafferty's Chinese Kosher Restaurant & Bar. I'm Rudy, one of the new owners. Can I get you anything from the bar?"

Moran glanced at the menu's drink section. "I'll have a Mai-Tai."

Hernandez gave Moran an odd look and then looked up at Rudy. "Uh... the same for me."

When Rudy left, Hernandez said. "What's with the Mai-Tai? You're a Chivas Regal man."

Moran shrugged. "Thought I'd give it a try."

The sergeant looked around the empty dining room. It had polished dark wood paneling, and small shaded red lights were mounted on the walls in the center of the booths that lined one wall. From the bar area near the entryway could be heard the murmur of conversations.

"Except for the high prices, it's certainly not the old Rafferty's," Hernandez said. "Chinese Kosher? What's next?"

"That's New York, a work in progress," Moran said.

"I checked on the Internet and found out that there's a national group of bikers who get together a couple of times a year to raise money for battered woman, under-privileged kids, and other charitable organizations. They all own Harley-Davidsons, and their trademark is a red rose on the handlebars of a Harley. They call themselves 'The Harley Rose Club,' and Greg Saunders is very active in the group."

Moran arched his eyebrows. "That means he must own a motorcycle. But you said—"

"The fact that he doesn't have one in his name doesn't mean he can't borrow one or rent it. Or the bike might be under somebody else's name," Hernandez quickly interjected.

Someone clearing his throat interrupted. "Glad I ran into you, Lieutenant Moran. I trust you're off duty," a deep mellow voice said from above. When Moran and Hernandez looked up, they saw the ruddy-complexioned round face of Judge Edwin Corbin, his brow lightly beaded with perspiration.

Moran eyes zeroed in on the tumbler of scotch-on-the-rocks that Corbin's unsteady hand grasped. The cop then directed his gaze to the attractive young blonde who stood a few feet behind, an impatient frown on her face.

"Actually, we're both off duty, judge," Hernandez jumped in.

Moran nodded to the woman. "New assistant?"

Corbin glanced at his companion. "Eh... no... A niece visiting from out of town," the judge said, and inched closer to the table. "Listen, I want to know why you're going around town showing an old newspaper picture of me?"

Moran asked. "How'd you come by that bit of information?"

"Don't get cute with me, lieutenant," Corbin snapped back. "Judge Potter told me all about your antics before he retired. How I got the information is my business. Now answer the question."

Moran rested his hands on the table. "Judge, we're not in your courtroom and I don't have to answer."

"I know you're looking into the Lacy Wooden and Paul Myer

killings," Corbin said flatly. "And I find it offensive that you have the nerve to consider me as a suspect."

"That's not true," Hernandez said. "We're conducting routine questioning, and no one has asked anyone specifically about you. The photo from the *Times* was found safely hidden away in Paul Myer's apartment and we just want to cover all the bases as to why he would hang on to it."

Corbin narrowed his eyebrows and peered down at the sergeant. "You're Frank Hernandez, right?"

"The one and only," Hernandez said and flashed the judge a '*vote-for-me*' grin.

"I like your wife's attitude better," Corbin said, and shifted his eyes to Moran. "If you want to know something, ask me directly, Lieutenant. I don't like being spied on." The judge moved toward the waiting blonde.

"Say hello to Mrs. Corbin for me," Moran called out to the rapidly moving judge. *Another BLT who thinks he's a Hero sandwich.*

"Hope he's not driving," Hernandez piped in.

The two cops exchanged glances. "You thinking what I'm thinking?" Moran asked.

Hernandez nodded. "The honorable judge likes them young," he said.

Moran said. "We've only showed that clipping to three people: Lacy's dance teacher, Rose Chiu, and Max Roth. One of them told Corbin about our inquiry. Have Darcey brace the teacher. Let's you and me have a *good cop- bad cop* talk with Chiu. Maybe it'll open her up."

"We'll probably get the same noise from Halpern and Greg Saunders."

Rudy arrived at the booth and set the Mai-Tai's on the table. "Sorry, for the delay but I didn't want to interrupt," he said and went back to the bar.

Moran stared at the pink rum-based drink and pushed the little umbrella with the pad of his index finger. "Must rain a lot where they invented this drink," Moran said. He then took a sip of the cocktail. "Not bad, but too sweet." He slid the drink aside. "Think I'll stick to my Chivas." The lieutenant picked up the embossed red menu, opened it, and scanned the entrees. "Hmm, no seafood or pork dishes. You're right, the place sure has changed."

Hernandez's face hardened and when he rested his elbows on the table he steepled his fingers. "There's something I want to bounce off you." He laid out his recent meeting with his father. While he spoke, Moran remained quiet, gave a few nods, and grunted a couple of times.

When Hernandez finished, Moran looked down, twirled the Mai-Tai's umbrella, and shifted his gaze to his sergeant. "You did the right thing. We all make mistakes, which is why they put erasers on the end of pencils. Your old man screwed up, and he recognizes that. Time to think of your son and the one coming. They need--better yet—deserve a grandfather. Lose the baggage, Frank. Travel light through life. Have you told your mother?"

Hernandez shook his head. "Still trying figure that one out."

Moran sat back with an intrigued look. "You said your father owns a restaurant in the financial district of Mexico City?"

"Yeah, why?"

"Uh… nothing… Nothing," Moran said, and fixed his eyes on a vague point somewhere over Hernandez's shoulder.

CHAPTER 27

"My, my. Isn't this my lucky day?" Rose Chiu said from behind her desk when she saw Moran and Hernandez walk in. "Nice of you to stop by to wish me a happy birthday," Rose added. She nodded her head at the sergeant, "Who's the hunk?"

"Sergeant Frank Hernandez," Moran said. "You're a fickle woman. Thought I was the only man you cared for."

Rose shrugged. "Like the scorpion said after he stung the turtle who gave him a ride across the pond, *'sorry, but it's my nature.'* " Rose swung her wheelchair and started to come around the cluttered desk.

"I gather this isn't a social call."

"Nope," Moran said.

Hernandez stepped forward and stood in the woman's path. "Why did you tell Judge Corbin that Lieutenant Moran had been here asking if you knew anyone in the Times clipping?"

Rose gazed up at Hernandez, her face stern, her eyes radiating anger. "You're in my way," she said. When the sergeant stepped aside, she wheeled herself to the center of the room and pivoted the chair toward the two cops and glared at Hernandez. "I don't think I like you very much," she said and looked away to Moran. "What's with your friend?"

"Take it easy, Frank," Moran said.

Hernandez shrugged and stepped closer to Rose. "So, what's the answer?"

Rose shook out a cigarette from the pack on her lap, placed it between her lips, and lit it. She puffed out some smoke in

Hernandez's face and chuckled. "I didn't. You think someone like me knows a judge well enough to call him?"

"Don't be a smart-ass," Hernandez said. "I own the copyright."

Rose gave the sergeant an unwavering look. "Now I *know* I don't like you. Unless you've got some kind of warrant, I'd appreciate it if you'd both leave."

Hernandez looked around the office with disdain. "I bet the vice squad would have a ball staking out this place."

Rose backed herself to the desk, crushed out the cigarette in an ashtray as she glowered at the sergeant. "That kinda jive doesn't cut any ice here, sergeant. Save it for some two-bit hustler who doesn't know any better." A wicked smile crept across her face. "Because today is my birthday and I feel good. I'll tell you fellas what I know. Corbin--Judge Corbin came in once in a while with some of his cronies. They'd have a few drinks, smoke cigars, and tip the girls very generously. And they paid in cash. But I never called him or told him about you being here. That's the honest truth."

Hernandez scoffed. "Honest, that's a strange word coming from you."

"Easy, Frank. Can't you see the lady's cooperating?" Moran interjected. He pawed into his pocket and brought out the clipping. "Now that your memory has improved, are any of those cronies in this picture?"

The smile remained on Rose Chiu's face. "Oh, you're good... really good." She took the clipping and glanced at it. "Yeah, there is. This here fine-looking dude with just the right touches of gray to make him interesting," she said, and pointed to Halpern. Then she pointed to the man standing next to the senator. "And this fella," she said, tapping Howard Shilling's picture. "Didn't care for him, too full of himself." Rose handed the picture back to Moran. "The last guy I think is some kinda TV actor. I don't watch much television. Like I said, they'd come in once in a while have a few drinks and leave."

Hernandez stepped in inches away from Rose and peered down at her. "You like pulling our leg don't you?"

"Frank, let it go," Moran said and turned to the woman. "We appreciate your help, Rose. And, happy birthday."

"Thank you. You're a gentleman and a scholar, not like some people in this room." Rose shot Hernandez a dirty look.

When Moran and Hernandez stepped out into the street, the sergeant turned to Moran. "Tough broad."

"Yeah, no grass grows under her wheels."

"If she didn't tell Corbin, who did?" Hernandez asked. They quickened their pace toward their car as heavy raindrops began to fall.

"My money's on Halpern," Moran said. "Corbin and Halpern belong to the Carmine DiSapio Democratic political club, which means that not only do they attend functions together as evidenced by the *Times* picture, but most likely are friends. Let's see what Darcey comes up with."

CHAPTER 28

Robert Darcey pushed through the curtain of heavy rain that pelted the city on his way up from the IRT subway station to the safety of Carnegie Hall's marquee. He didn't mind the rain. The news earlier from the doctors at Roosevelt Hospital had been good. Eddie would be okay from the head wound he had sustained when he'd fallen against the steam radiator in his bedroom. The doctors said that because Eddie hadn't taken his medication for so many hours. nor eaten anything, he had fainted against the radiator. They insisted on keeping him a few days for observation and to stabilize his system.

Darcey's thoughts turned to Jessie Rand's sapphire blue eyes as he trotted up the steps into the concert hall's vestibule. The cop zigzagged between small clusters of young men and women who loitered in the marbled foyer while immersed in animated conversations. Some wore leotards with sweaters wrapped around their shoulders; others were clad in sweatsuits clutching instrument cases. As Darcey darted past them, he picked up snatches of dialogue that ranged from the latest cattle call on Broadway to who had slept with whom to get the lead in a show.

When Darcey reached the row of elevators, one of the doors slid open, and seven people spilled out with Jessie Rand in the lead. She looked smart in her black sweater and tan raincoat as she marched toward the street, a small umbrella in her right hand. *Shabby chic* was the phrase that popped into Darcy's mind.

"What are you doing here?" she said when she and Darcey crossed paths. The cop smiled, his eyes brightened—the velvety voice and British accent had taken their effect.

"Ah… eh… Well, just a couple of questions I wanted to ask," Darcey said, his attention drawn to the blue eyes. The strong scent of lavender and rose petals from the perfume she wore added to her allure.

"Ask them while I walk out; someone's waiting for me," Rand said.

"A date?"

Rand glanced at Darcey and pursed her lips. "What's the question?" the dancer asked. They continued to move through the large vestibule.

"Do you know Judge Edwin Corbin?"

Rand stopped and looked at Darcey. Their eyes locked for an instant. This time the sapphire eyes' warmth was replaced by a cold stare. "You asked me that before, and the answer is still the same. No. I don't know anyone in that bloody newspaper picture and that's the tall and short of it."

"Then how do you know it was Judge Corbin in that photograph?"

She glanced at the nearby main door and then returned her gaze to the cop. "Detective—"

"Robert… That's my first name," Darcey said in a soft, intimate tone.

"Whatever," Rand said with a look of indifference. "I'm not an idiot. One sees the same people quite often in the papers. There's no secret as to their identity. Now, if you'll excuse me?"

"Lacy talked a lot about a Broadway producer. Know who that might be?"

"Sure, Saul Goodwin, I introduced them."

"The same name that's on your posters upstairs," Darcey said. "What exactly was their relationship?"

"I suggest you ask him," Rand said. She turned and hastened toward the door.

When Rand walked out of the concert hall Darcey followed her. As he reached the building's steps, he saw her opening the passenger door of a waiting silver Mercedes S65 AMG. Intrigued,

Darcey ran down to the street, only to see the six-figure car swallowed by the flow of traffic.

* * *

At a quarter to eight that same evening, in another part of town, a shadowy figure in a black motorcycle suit emerged from a narrow alleyway and hugged the wall of the building in an effort to avoid the heavy rain. He turned left and headed to the doorway of the 'The Little Foxes.' The sign on the closed door said: '*Closed – Open 8:00 p.m. to 1:00 a.m.*'

Inside, Rose Chiu sat behind her desk hunched over a stack of 8x10 glossy headshots while earsplitting heavy metal music from the stage penetrated the wall. Rose rubbed her left temple with her fingertips as she studied the picture of a young woman for a moment before adding it to a pile of rejected candidates—too fat, too skinny, too homey-looking, too old, etc. The reasons for rejecting them varied depending on how Rose felt that day. Today her mood was dark and stormy as the weather outside, and the music wasn't helping.

Chiu pressed the intercom button on her phone set. "Sky, if you can hear me get me a Mai-Tai and don't spare the rum. And tell Mike to lower the friggin' volume. You'd think he had to fill Yankee Stadium with that new sound system."

Minutes later, the sound of footsteps made Rose look up and gaze at the door. Her eyes widened when she saw a figure in a motorcycle outfit march through the open door and close it with one heel. Chiu's mouth gaped at the figure. "What the hell are you doing in—"

CHAPTER 29

Rose Chiu was in her wheelchair, her head resting crookedly on the headrest, her blank eyes staring at the popcorn ceiling as if mesmerized by its starkness. Her arms lay folded on her lap and her ruby mouth was partially open, as if about to speak.

"How long has she been dead?" Moran asked Chang, who was examining the corpse. The AME peered at the tissue around the two blood-caked wounds in the middle of her chest. While Chang worked, he hummed an unrecognizable tune. In white coveralls a four-man Crime Scene Unit team was busy collecting evidence in different parts of the room.

"You seem cheery tonight," Moran told Chang. His gaze drifted over the bloodstained desk and the scattered headshots sprinkled with droplets of blood.

Chang turned and looked up. "My poetry book's getting published."

Moran and Hernandez exchange surprised looks. Moran said, "What's the title?"

"Passion and other Vices: The Poetry of Sex."

"What?"

Chang shrugged. "Call it, my dark side." He smiled wryly.

"And, when may we read this opus?" Hernandez asked.

"Soon. But enough about me," Chang said. He gestured to the body. "From the size and shape of the entry wounds I'd say it was the same gun that killed Paul Myer." He pointed to two dark spots. "Rigor mortis hasn't set in yet, so I figure she's been dead about two hours. However, she didn't die immediately. She probably lived for a few minutes after she was shot."

"How do you know that?" Hernandez said.

"See the position of the head, tilted to the side? If she had died immediately the head would be laying on her chest or on top of the desk. She probably survived for a while and then died."

Moran and Hernandez came closer to the body. The two wounds were next to each other. The upper wound was a small hole with a little blood around, and the lower bullet hole was larger, with severe trauma to the skin.

"Look at this," Chang said and gestured to a stack of yellow Post-Its on the table. "She either was writing when the killer walked in or tried to write out a message after she was shot."

Moran peered at the notepad. Two letters were scribbled in black ballpoint and trailed off.

Hernandez leaned in and examined the writing. "Hard to make it out," he said, "but I'd say it's a capital S followed by a lower case 'a'."

Moran nodded and hummed acquiescence. "Rose Chiu wrote this after she was shot. Everything on the desk has bloodstains, except this pad. Why would she take the time to write something unless it was the name of her killer?"

Hernandez moved around the desk and eyed the area under the wheelchair. The sergeant noticed a Bic ballpoint on the carpet. He bent over, and with his handkerchief, picked the pen by its top and laid it down on the desk. Hernandez then held the ballpoint by the top end and drew a line on a slip of blank paper.

"Ink matches," Moran said. He shifted his eyes to the black lizard-skin phonebook that lay atop several slips of paper with scribbled writings on them. "Bag all this. And by the way, where's Earl?"

Hernandez jerked his thumb to the door. "Still outside near the stage. After he called it in, the first uniforms on the scene found him sitting on the edge of the stage crying like a baby."

"Never fails, the bigger they are they harder they fall," Moran said. "We'll talk to him later."

The two cops moved to one of the CSU agents, a bald stout man with a pair of tweezers in his left hand.

"Find anything we can use, Lewis?" the Moran asked.

Lewis shook his head. "Only a fresh partial thumbprint on the edge of the desk. Not very clear, I'm afraid."

"Over here," another agent called from the doorway. "Think I've got something."

Moran and Lewis turned and moved quickly toward the doorway. When they arrived, the young female CSU there was holding a digital camera. She pointed to a partial footprint on the trodden oriental rug that covered the floor of Rose Chiu's office.

"It's still a little damp and it leads into the room," she said. "And, over here," she continued pointing, "is the same print, only this time it's heading out."

Moran crouched and examined the print: the front part of the foot was clear but only traces of wet dirt remained where the heel should have been.

"The toe appears to be pointed. From the dirt, it's my guess that it was made by a flat heavy heel," the agent said. "More like some kind of boot, but not a cowboy boot. I'd say a size twelve," the female agent continued.

"Sounds like our biker is back in business," Hernandez said.

Moran said. "Nice work. Get me several copies of the pictures." He turned to Lewis. "I need your report ASAP."

Now Chang walked up to Moran. "I'm finished here. Anything further requires an autopsy." He shot Hernandez an expectant look. The sergeant shrugged and smiled.

Once Chiu's body had been removed, Hernandez walked to the dead woman's desk while Moran's eyes lazily floated over the desk's top. The clutter made it impossible to tell whether or not anyone had rifled through the stacks of headshots, bills and mail that covered Rose Chiu's desk.

Hernandez picked up one of the photographs and gazed at a pert brunette with bright blue eyes. "Looks like Rose was in the middle of casting new girls when the killer walked in."

"Let's go pay our respects to Earl," Moran said.

The two detectives found Earl seated at a table in a dark corner of the club that looked down on the stage. The palms of Earl's hands covered his face while he lay slumped over on the table. The first three buttons of his purple silk shirt revealed a hairy chest. He raised his head and looked up at the approaching cops—his eyes red and moist, his nose running.

Moran wrinkled his nose when he reached the distraught Earl. "Phew! What the hell are you wearing?"

Hernandez said. "I'd guess Paco Rabanne."

"And lots of it," Moran said.

Earl lifted his face and gazed at the two cops. "Y'all find the bastard that did this, you hear?"

"We will," Moran said. "You can bet on it. But first we need some details."

He asked the anguished Earl the usual questions, where was he, the time, did he hear or see anything, to all of which the bartender gave the expected answers: *"I was downstairs in the basement getting liquor for the bar,"*... *"It was about 7:15,"*... *"No, I didn't hear anything 'cause Mike had the sound system going full blast,"* and *"I'd didn't see anyone."*

Earl shook his head and blew his nose with a cocktail napkin. "The last time I heard from Rose was through the loudspeaker system when I heard her ask for a Mai-Tai."

"Where were you when she said that?" Moran said.

"In the basement."

"Does a first or last name starting with 'SA' mean anything to you?" Hernandez asked.

Earl raised his head with saddened eyes, looked at the sergeant and shook his head.

"If you think of anything, let us know," Moran said and dropped his card on the table. "By the way, where exactly are you from?"

"Florida. Central Florida."

Moran nodded and began to walk away.

"Wait a minute," Earl cried out. When Moran and Hernandez turned, Earl said, "There is something. I saw a black motorcycle drive out of the alley. I remember 'cause it looked like an expensive piece of machinery. Not something you see too often around here."

"Who was driving it?" Hernandez asked.

Earl shrugged. "Beats me. I only saw the guy's back. Although it was dark, I was close enough to see a red rose on the back of the helmet. Then he disappeared."

"What makes you think it was a guy?" Hernandez said.

Earl shrugged. "Just figures."

"You didn't happen to get the license number or the make?" Moran asked weakly.

Earl gave Moran a confused look. "No, why would I do that?"

"Don't worry about it, just a shot in the dark." Moran said.

The two cops continued to make their way toward the front. As Moran and Hernandez stepped out onto the wet street and walked to the car, claps of lightning and thunder crackled in the eastern sky. Moran stretched his right leg and winced as he bent down.

"You okay?" Hernandez asked.

"Never better," Moran said and cracked a pained smile. "I liked Rose," he said and straightened. "Don't meet too many people like her anymore... a straight shooter. She gave as good as she got."

"Yeah, but she got killed. She knew her killer, which sounds like Rose Chiu was holding out on us," Hernandez said.

Moran chuckled. "I meant she was a straight shooter, *most* of the time."

CHAPTER 30

In the Cold Case & Apprehension Squad's office, the only light came from the glow of a computer screen that bathed Alice Simms' face. She was studying Max Roth's *Accounts Receivable* file. The search of the confiscated computer's hard drive for more clues was beginning to take its toll on the detective's eyes—it had been two hours of squinting at black lines filled with numbers and decimal points. Simms heaved a sigh, stretched her arms, and rubbed her eyes with the knuckles of her forefingers. When she returned to the screen and scrolled to the end of the page, the last entry made her sit up and take notice.

18kt Piaget ladies' watch with diamonds, $6,000 Visa Credit Card No. 4818-6909-0789-1643—E.C. Special Instructions: inscription 'FROM E.C. FOR THE GOOD TIMES.'

"E.C.... Edwin Corbin," Simms murmured. The detective reached across the desk, slid over, and grabbed the Rolodex to look up Visa's Fraud & Accounts telephone number. After ten minutes of digitized music, the petulant Visa Operations supervisor came back on the line and confirmed that the account belonged to a Judge Edwin Corbin.

The door opened and Moran stepped into the room. "You look like you've seen a ghost," Moran said after he switched on the lights.

Simms pointed enthusiastically at the screen. "Visa confirms it was Corbin." Moran walked toward the computer and Simms filled him in with what she had learned. "It was bought three months before Lacy's death."

Moran stood over Simms and studied the entry. "Maybe he

bought it for his wife."

"From what you've told us about the judge, I don't think so," Simms said.

Moran shrugged. "If you're right it would explain why Lacy returned Halpern's Movado; compared to this it was bupkes. Check it out."

A perplexed looking Simms stared at the lieutenant. "How?"

"The shortest distance between two points is a straight line. Call Mrs. Corbin. Tell her you're with the Armed Robbery Unit and investigating a stolen jewelry case," Moran said.

Simms cocked her head. "Oh, boy, that doesn't pass the giggle test. Thanks."

Moran flashed a grin. "You're welcome. That's why I make the medium bucks. Trust me, call her."

"I would've preferred to hear you say, '*Alice, take the rest of the day off*,'" Simms muttered.

CHAPTER 31

Alice Simms slowly shook her head and covered her eyes while Darcey recounted, for the second time, his encounter with Jessie Rand at Carnegie Hall and how blue her eyes were. "Will you please stop going on about Jessie Rand?" Simms said. "I don't think I can take it anymore."

Hernandez added. "Don't get carried away with her until she passes the radio test."

"The what?" Darcey said.

"It goes like this. If on the first date after you start the car and turn on the radio she leans over and switches stations without asking you, she's a selfish dame and you don't want any part of her."

Darcey stared at Hernandez with a blank expression for a moment. Finally, he spoke, "That's a line from some movie."

"Whatever. The point's the same."

Darcey lowered his gaze. "She already told me she was gay." He gathered himself and stood. "What matters is that I think she recognized someone in that *Times* cut-out and this Saul Goodwin is worth looking into."

From his vantage point at the head of the conference table, Moran, who had been listening to the banter in silence, cleared his throat. "I agree. I'd like to hear Simms' report."

Simms' purse lay on top of the table. She drew her notepad out and flipped it open. "The phone company records indicate that on the day I interviewed Roth, he made a call to Halpern's residence here in Manhattan five minutes after I left. The call lasted less than a minute, which means that it was either a short conversation or

Max left a message on the answering machine."

"Just as I suspected," Moran said. "It was Halpern who told Corbin what we were doing." He turned to Darcey. "Besides your mesmerizing encounter with Jessie Rand, anything on Greg Saunders yet?"

"He's still down in Bimini until the end of the week filming a TV movie. I found out he's the honorary president of 'The Harley Rose Club,' and they use his name as a draw. He rides with them occasionally. The club's website doesn't have a nationwide list of its members. You sign up online in your state's chapter, which rules out running 'SA' through any national database."

"Then do it state-by-state," Moran said.

Darcey said. "Done that. The problem is privacy laws don't allow them to publish the members' names. Anything from Chiu's phonebook?"

Moran shook his head and pursed his lips. "Aside from the fact that the woman had lousy handwriting, nothing. Only one last name begins with SA and that turned out to be her dentist, and the only first name with that beginning was her sister in San Francisco."

"What if those letters are the start of a sentence rather than a name?" Simms asked.

After another shake of the head. Moran said, "I'm still going with the name theory. I don't think people who are dying take the time to write sentences. "Let's go with the assumption it's a name." The lieutenant turned to Darcey. "Check Motor Vehicles and see if there're any motorcycles registered to last names that start with the letters 'S' and 'A' as well as first names," Moran said.

A soft rap on the glazed panel of the door was followed by the entrance of a young woman in a white lab coat. Her curly shoulder-length brown hair bounced off her shoulders as she walked toward the group of detectives. An envelope dangled from her right hand.

Moran's face brightened. "Maureen Singleton," he called out.

"I hope you're the bearer of good news with regard to that thumbprint."

Singleton gave a grave nod, pulled out a pair of horn-rimmed eyeglasses from her coat's breast pocket, and planted them firmly on the bridge of her nose. "This is my report," Singleton said, still moving toward the conference table. When she reached it, she handed the envelope to Moran who opened it and drew out a one-page typed report.

"Although it was only a partial latent thumbprint when we applied cyanoacrylate and sodium hydroxide to it, we were able to expose it," Singleton said.

"What's cyanoacrylate?" Darcey asked.

Moran looked up from the report and gazed at Darcey. "It's also known as Super Glue, which is 98 percent cyanoacrylate."

"When we plugged the print into the FBI's Integrated Automated Fingerprint Identification System we got no match. Also, there were no other unaccounted for prints in Rose Chiu's office," Singleton said.

When Moran finished, he handed the document to Hernandez.

"Not good," Hernandez said when he was done with the report. He set it down on the table.

CHAPTER 32

"Other than wanting to talk to Greg Saunders about any possible ties to Paul Myer," Howard Shilling said from his desk, "have you given any consideration to his being a suspect in Lacy Wooden's murder?"

Moran creased his forehead. "Why? There's nothing tying him to her."

Shilling pursed his lips and looked up for a moment. "Oh... I think there might be. I had the misfortune to run into him at 'The Little Foxes' a few times." He paused when he noticed Moran's look of surprise. "C'mon. I'm sure you know by now that several of us used to go there once in a while for good-natured fun. Anyway, I recall Saunders and Lacy making eye contact, the kind that tells you something's going on between them. I think it's worth looking into." Shilling gave a short laugh. "It'd serve my wife right, always strutting around like he was God's gift to women," Shilling gazed at the lieutenant.

Moran pursed his lips and bunched his eyebrows. "That's quite a theory—and imagination—you got there."

Shilling frowned and placed the palm of one hand on the desk. "At least look into it," the DA said.

"I can't expend what little manpower I've got to go on a fishing expedition for you," Moran said standing.

The DA eyes glared at Moran. "That's your problem. You always have to go it alone."

"I'm the cop, not you," Moran said.

Shilling strode toward Moran and pointed his finger at the lieutenant. "Look, Moran, let's not have another one of your 'one-man army' shenanigans," the DA said and snorted. "Everyone remembers what happened with Hubert Singer, a seemingly harmless CCNY comparative philosophy professor turned serial killer who got away under your very nose."

Moran's brown eyes became two glowing embers and his jaw tightened. Like a movie clip stuck in fast forward, he recalled the night a year ago when he had Hubert Singer, CCNY's Philosophy professor-turned-serial-killer, trapped at Mayor Garner's residence in Gracie Mansion. And how Singer had faked his own suicide by appearing to shoot himself. When Moran left the room to call for an ambulance, Singer escaped.

"Are you listening?" Shilling said when he saw Moran's blank expression.

Moran blinked and stared at the DA. "Loud and clear."

Shilling's phone clanged announcing the end of round one. "Yes, Janice," Shilling said, "I can't talk to her right now, tell my wife I'll try and call her later," he snapped and hung up. He gazed at Moran, who was still standing on the same spot. The DA flashed a wide grin. "Look, there's no need for us to fight. We may not like each other, but we're all we've got," he said.

Moran smiled tightly. "Fair enough."

"What about the bank matter?"

"I've come up with something—" Moran began to say when his cell phone chimed. The call came from 'The Little Foxes' club.

"You told me to call if I remembered anything," Earl said. "Well, there was this Saul Goodwin, some kinda Broadway big shot, who phoned Lacy a lot at the club, as well as Greg Saunders. I know 'cause I took the calls."

CHAPTER 33

The dark-blue Mercury Marquis slowly weaved its way through the sludge-like traffic on Eighth Avenue. With Thanksgiving over, the city was in full Christmas Holiday mode, which meant infernal traffic jams and ill-tempered drivers.

"Hit the siren," Darcey's brother said from the passenger seat

"Take it easy, Eddie," Darcey said. "I just picked you up from the hospital and you're already getting worked up. Relax."

Eddie nervously scratched his neck and he gazed at his brother for a moment. With catlike quickness, he leaned forward and flipped on the car's siren.

"What the hell!" Darcey shouted and turned it off. "Don't ever do that again. This is not an emergency."

Eddie fidgeted in his seat while he looked at the passing buildings and the faces of other motorists. "We need to stop for cigarettes," he said.

"After I see Saul Goodwin on a police matter."

"No, I need them now! Friggin' hospital didn't let me smoke," Eddie said.

Darcey looked at Eddie. The man's color had come back. He seemed halfway healthy, even though the occasional twitch of his right cheek didn't ease Darcey's discomfort of having to find a new caregiver. The detective dropped his gaze to the brown bag on the floor in front of Eddie. It contained a small fortune in medicines, to which the doctors had added Prozac and other four drugs with unpronounceable names. Twenty minutes later, the vehicle came to a stop across from Lincoln Center in front of a stone building. It was wedged in between two other stone-faced, gray buildings that reached for the sky competing for light and air. The cornerstone identified it as the Walker Building and dated it as 1935.

"Stay here, and don't even think about getting out of the car," Darcey said. He placed his 'Official Police Business' placard on the dashboard. "I'll get the cigarettes when I come out."

Eddie continued to fidget in his seat and rubbed his hands together. "I'll... I'll be fine," he mumbled.

Darcey cast his brother an anxious look and then climbed out of the car. When the detective reached the building's front door, he looked back. He felt a sense of relief when he saw that Eddie was leaning back, his head resting against the seat's headrest.

Darcey stepped out of the elevator on the third floor. As he walked down the empty hallway, his footfalls echoed on the art deco marble flooring. A moment later, the detective stood in front of a closed door with etched lettering on its glazed glass panel: "Saul Goodwin Productions."

A middle-age buxom woman in a tight yellow blouse was slouched on a chair behind a desk intently concentrating on filing her nails. She looked up and gave Darcey a bored smile. She pointed to the door next to her. "Through there."

Inside, the detective found a heavyset older man with terrace-like eyebrows and badly dyed blonde hair. The man's teeth were clamped on a large unlit cigar. He slowly lifted his portly frame from the vinyl-covered chair. "Saul Goodwin. Always be nice to the local constabulary, that's my motto. Let's talk over here," he said. With a meaty hand and a broad smile, he gestured to two stuffed chairs that faced each other in the middle of the room.

Darcey turned his head and quickly took in the room— autographed framed black-and-whites of actors and actresses on the wall. On a nearby mantle, three Obies, two Tonys and other theatrical awards were also displayed. When the two sat down, Goodwin snapped his bright psychedelic suspenders, crossed his legs and slowly turned the cigar. Darcey focused on the baseball bat that seemed to be surgically implanted in the big man's mouth.

"Quit smoking six months ago, but I need something to chew on," Goodwin said. "Stops me from eating too much," he added. He slapped his protruding stomach, which produced a loud thud.

"You've done some important musicals," Darcey said, and motioned to a wall covered with Broadway show posters. The detective riveted his eyes on two of the posters. He had seen them on Jessie Rand's studio wall. "You know Jessie Rand?" the detective said.

Goodwin chuckled loudly. His body curved inward, his shoulders shook and his wide grin became a moisturized smile. "I gave the woman her first break on Broadway. You know her?"

"Not really. We've met."

Goodwin looked at Darcey oddly for an instant and then said, "When Jessie arrived fresh off a small town—San... something or other in Ohio—trying unsuccessfully to be the next Patti Lupone, I told her to stick to dancing and forget the singing; town's full of canaries."

"I thought she was British."

Another resounding chuckle. "No, no. That's part of the new image I created for her. Even gave her the name Jessie Rand."

"What was her name?"

The burly producer arched his eyebrows and massaged his chin. His face crinkled while he thought. "Mmm... I forget. Some German sounding name, *Schleper or Schoo* something or other. Can't remember exactly. Anyhow, I told her to lose it and get a pronounceable name and an English accent," he said. Goodwin lowered his voice and leaned forward. "Ever since Julie Andrews appeared in 'My Fair Lady,' this town loves British broads. Now, how can I help you?"

Darcey's gaze homed in on the man's wide face, a trick he'd learned from Moran—always read a face. He didn't really suspect Saul Goodwin —the man's girth and physique eliminated that— but it was good practice.

"I understand you knew Lacy Wooden," Darcey said.

Goodwin leaned back in his chair and stroked his face. He kept his gaze on Darcey as if deciding whether to answer or not. "She was part of Jessie's dance class, and Jessie thought the girl had some talent. I went to the strip joint where Lacy worked and watched her do her brass pole routine." Goodwin shrugged. "She was fair, not great, but there's always a spot for a good- looking hoofer in the chorus, especially if she's *cooperative*." Goodwin winked. "If you get my meaning."

"Were you and Lacy seeing each other socially?"

Goodwin emitted another laugh. "I like you--you got a sense of humor. I don't know about my wife, but I'm a happily married man. No, Lacy and I were certainly no item. That's for suckers. I'd call her once in a blue moon, we'd meet at a restaurant, have dinner and then go to her place for some harmless fun, but she had her eyes on Greg Saunders." Goodwin's expression turned dour. "A TV actor with limited talent and a big ego."

"I gather you didn't like him."

Saul Goodwin chortled. "Wanted to star in my next production. Imagine the chutzpah, the guy can't hold a tune in a bucket and stands on the stage like a sequoia. You should talk to him if you want to know anything more about Lacy Wooden. I heard they were seeing a lot of each other."

"What about Jessie? You still keep in touch?"

Goodwin nodded. "Matter of fact, she's choreographing my new show, 'Goodwin's Follies.' "

"She still dance?"

Goodwin bunched his eyebrows and moistened his lips. "Let's just say Jessie Rand is past her prime. But she's a helluva choreographer, not to mention an invaluable money raiser."

Darcey arched his eyebrows. "How old is she?"

"Thirty-seven, but some dancers burn out sooner than others. Anyway, as I was saying, she's a helluva money raiser. Even got Sabrina Van Damme from her dance class to invest in the show."

"Senator Halpern's sister-in-law? Heiress to the Van Damme fortune?"

Saul Goodwin tugged at his suspenders and smacked his lips.

"The one and only, queen of the tabloids. Just thinking about all that dough and beauty neatly wrapped in a tight thirty-four-year old body makes me salivate. Anyhow, she and her sister have each put in almost a half a mil, and with their names on the investor's list I can raise the rest." Goodwin snapped his pudgy fingers. "Like that."

Darcey rose to his feet. "I won't take up any more of your time, Mr. Goodwin," he said, and began to walk toward the door.

"Call me Saul. Everyone does," the big man said.

The detective stopped and turned. He faced the producer, who remained wedged in his seat.

"By the way, do you own a silver late model Mercedes?"

Goodwin flashed a grin, and his cheeks became two red apples. "Got it a couple of weeks ago, great car, why?"

"Oh, nothing."

Goodwin finally unplugged the cigar from his mouth and eyed the detective appraisingly. "You should get one."

"Sure. If I don't eat or pay rent for the next ten years, maybe I could afford the down payment," Darcey responded.

Another laugh. "Like I said, you got a sense of humor, I like that. See you around, detective."

When Darcey reached the street, what he saw turned his blood to ice as his stomach did a small rumba. Eddie was not in the car, but two uniformed cops were loitering next to the empty Marquis.

"What's wrong?" Darcey asked when he reached the car and identified himself.

"You must be the brother Edward Darcey mentioned," the ruddy complexioned older uniform said.

Darcey looked around. "What happened? Where is he?"

The two cops exchanged glances. "Your brother was arrested for shoplifting a pack of Lucky Strikes from over there," the cop said, and gestured to a small bodega. "He was taken down to the stationhouse for booking. Someone saw him come out of this car, so we decided to stick around."

CHAPTER 34

"Thanks for helping my brother, lieutenant," Darcey said from his seat. "Eddie's new caregiver seems to be working out pretty well."

Moran flipped his hand at Darcey. "Forget it. Just saved the guys at the stationhouse a lot of paperwork over a five-dollar pack of cigarettes that was still unopened." Moran turned to Hernandez's father, who sat between Darcey and the sergeant.

"Your son tells me that your restaurant caters to Banco de Mejico," Moran said.

Victor grinned. "One of our best customers."

Moran nodded and opened the file that lay in front of him. He drew out Rosario Mendez's picture and Linda Garcia's faxed photograph and pushed them toward Victor. "You know these women?"

Victor gazed at the fax and gaped. "Hey, it's Linda!" he exclaimed. He turned toward his son. "She's the woman I told you about. Is she in trouble?"

A stunned Sergeant Hernandez looked at his father with widened eyes. "No... eh... the Lieutenant will explain."

Victor gave his son a quizzical look. "If something's going on, I want to know about it."

"There's nothing going on with her, but I'll get to that later," Moran said. "What about the other picture?"

Victor gazed at Rosario Mendez's photograph and creased his brow. "She's an executive with the bank and a frequent lunch customer at the restaurant. Very aloof, not very *simpatica*. Always takes a table in the back. Once in a while she will come in with an older guy. They kept to themselves. I once approached the table and heard them talking in English—American English—so I figured he was from the States."

Moran and Hernandez traded curious glances. "Did you get his name?" Hernandez asked.

Victor shook his head. "No. Like I said, she was very distant. Never chatted with anyone."

"Can you describe the man?" Hernandez said.

Victor raised eyes and looked at the ceiling. He slowly massaged his jaw with the tips of his fingers for a moment and then spoke. "Uh, yeah... he was tall, white hair... and well dressed. You could tell he was rich."

Moran opened the file again, brought out the *Times* clipping and slid it across the table. "Do you see him here?"

Victor grasped the picture and studied it. "Nope," he finally said and set down the cutout.

Moran stood, moved around the table toward Victor and leaned against the conference table. "We need a favor from you."

Victor peered at his son and then looked up at Moran. "Sure, fire away."

CHAPTER 35

He was a little over six feet tall, forty years of age, had close-cropped chestnut hair with touches of gray, and aqua blue eyes that held a tinge of sadness in them. The man stood rigid and his right toe anxiously tapped the cement floor. His right hand gripped a small valise. He stared out at the closed black steel door in front of him with dedicated concentration, ignoring the shrill sound of men talking in loud voices and the dull thud of a steel door opening and closing behind him. He took a deep breath and smelled the pine-scented disinfectant that hovered over the area.

"We're going to open the door now," said a deep monotone voice through the loudspeaker. "Make sure you have all your personal belongings with you."

A moment later, the steel door slowly slid open. The ex-con squinted his eyes as they adapted to the bright sunlight. There was a chill in the air, and he didn't have a coat. He pulled up the collar of his jacket, which was now two sizes too large, hugged the suitcase against his chest, and strode out of the East Moline, Illinois minimum-security prison. When he cleared the gate, he drew a deep breath—his first taste of freedom in a year—and heard the gate clang shut from behind.

It had all been a misunderstanding that had gotten out of hand, and before he realized it, his hand had become a fist and had punched his live-in girlfriend in the face several times. Her name was Amy. They had both been drunk and neither could remember what prompted the assault. When the two cops answered a neighbor's call, Amy insisted that she had fallen. The lead cop, a big redneck with an attitude, didn't buy the story and arrested him for aggravated assault.

The trial judge wasn't any tooth fairy either. Taking the advice of his court-appointed lawyer to plead guilty in exchange for sixty-days in the county jail turned out to be the worse day of his life since his ex-wife had kicked him out of the house years earlier. The judge, a craggy, sourpuss named Rufus Hogg, peered down at him and slapped him with a year in state prison. That morning, Judge Hogg handed out year-plus sentences as if they were samples.

The stranger pushed the memories away and entered the nearby Silver Slipper Bar & Grill. It was a dingy, grimy place with ornate Christmas lights draped over the wall-length mirror behind the bar. At two o'clock in the afternoon, the Silver Slipper's only customer was a grizzly, long-haired elderly man in stained denim bib overalls who sat at the end of the bar nursing a flat beer. The old man gave the stranger an uninterested look and returned his stare to his brewski as if trying to find in its depths the reason life had denied him in his fair share.

"What'll it be, friend?" the sturdy red-haired bartender asked.

When the stranger neared the bar, the odor of stale beer assaulted his nostrils and he could sense the barkeep's eyes scrutinizing him as if he were a bug that had just crawled in. He knew he had been pegged for what he was—an ex-con. He looked up and caught his reflection in the mirror—a pale, thin man with streaks of gray hair in a suit too big for his frame—and turned his head away.

"Bourbon... Double," the ex-con said and set his valise down on the stool next to him. He then pawed into his pocket and drew out a pack of cigarettes, took one out and lit it.

"Sorry, pal, no smoking," the bartender said.

He stared at the man with incredulous look. "You gotta be kiddin'!"

The barkeep shrugged. "Since you went inside, the law's changed. No smoking in public places. Accordin' to the City

Council, second-hand smoke is bad for the help," the bartender said with a sneer and held out an ashtray. "But, we make great burgers. Want one?

The stranger's eyes swept the bar and he wrinkled his nose. "Made on a greasy grill by a five-dollar-an-hour immigrant in a hair net… think not."

He gave the bartender a hard look and ground the cigarette out in the ashtray.

When the double bourbon whiskey arrived, the stranger drained the shot glass in one gulp and asked for another. A moment later, the bartender set down the second double and raised an eyebrow.

"You better be able to pay for this," the barkeep said.

The stranger's face tightened, his eyes radiating defiance. He tossed back the shot of bourbon then reached into his pocket. He pulled out a weather-beaten wallet and slapped a twenty-dollar bill down on the counter.

"Satisfied?" the stranger growled.

When the bartender came back with the change, the stranger stuffed the bills into his wallet and snorted when he looked at his expired driver's license picture—twenty pounds heavier, more hair and a fuller face.

The name on the license was Kevin Palmer.

CHAPTER 36

An hour's drive north from Manhattan, the antebellum-style white mansion cast a watchful eye over the town of Pelham. The building sat on a hilltop and had an expansive lawn so green it looked as though it had been spray painted that same day. Through the years, Pelham had grown from a sleepy suburban village into a wealthy bedroom community. Here, up and coming New York City businessmen and people from the entertainment world whiled away their nights and weekends hosting dinner parties or playing tennis at the country club. The sidewalks of Pelham's main thoroughfare were neatly cleared of litter, and quaint little shops lined both sides of the street. The old white church at the end of the street with its forest-green shutters and a steeple like a crone's hat dominated the tranquil scene.

The black Crown Victoria sped through the opened wrought iron gate, and from his driver's seat, Hernandez waved at the overhead surveillance camera. "This is what God would build if he had the money," he said as he drove up the winding driveway that led to the white house at the top of the hill. "Greg Saunders must be making a lot of dough," Hernandez muttered.

Moran stifled a bored yawn. "He's probably another BLT." He gazed out his passenger window at the passing landscape of shrubs and hedges. "Saw the guy once on '*Dancing With Celebrities*' and he didn't impress Sandra or me—too many teeth, all smiles, no substance," Moran said.

When Moran and Hernandez made their way up to the front door, the lieutenant noticed the open four-car garage and the two expensive-looking shining black motorcycles that sat in one of the bays. Moran head-pointed to the garage. "Look like Harleys to me. Thought DMV said there were no motorbikes registered to Saunders."

"Gives us something else to talk about," Hernandez said and pressed the black double-door's brass bell button.

A moment later the door opened and Greg Saunders stood there in a green long sleeve V-neck sweater, white pants and loafers. He held a cell phone to his ear. "I have to go now, darling, my guests are here." Saunders flipped the phone shut, and turned to the cops and grinned.

Moran studied the actor's face. *All the charm of a cobra.*

"Come in, just finished making Margaritas. Got the recipe from this bartender I know in Puerto Vallarta," Saunders spoke as he led the two visitors through the spacious foyer. They walked past a wide, red-carpeted staircase into an imposing room filled with bookshelves and a billiard table in the center. From a CD player on one of the shelves, *'Rhapsody in Blue'* drifted softly through the space. Saunders quickened his pace and walked briskly to a wall-wide window. He turned a switch and the transparent drapes swooshed open, exposing the fairytale lawn.

Moran and Hernandez looked around the room. "You live here by yourself?" Moran asked.

"Just me and my ego," Saunders said and let out a loud laugh. He stopped laughing when he saw the unamused faces of Moran and Hernandez.

"That's a joke... show biz humor," Saunders said.

The two cops smiled—polite, patient smiles.

Hernandez pointed to the two Emmys prominently exhibited in a glass case. "You must be very proud of these."

Saunders' face brightened. " 'Best Male Actor in a Daytime Drama' award. Two years running. I owe a lot to *James Fox*," Saunders said. He looked for a reaction from the two cops. When none came, he added, "That's the name of my character."

"Sorry, we work during the day," Moran said.

Saunders crossed the room and turned off the CD. He moved to the wet bar where a pitcher of Margaritas and three wide-rimmed glasses with straws waited on a tray.

"You a Gershwin fan?" Moran asked.

"Yes, very much so." Saunders said.

Moran recalled that '*Rhapsody in Blue*' was playing in Lacy Wooden's apartment. He made a mental note.

"You'll love these," the actor said while he poured the drinks.

"We noticed the motorcycles in the garage. Both yours?" Moran asked.

"Yeah, rode one down yesterday from Connecticut."

"Connecticut?" Hernandez said.

"I have a house on the Long Island Sound where I do most of my riding. Less traffic." Saunders said as he balanced the tray and walked toward his visitors.

"Why two?"

"I'm hoping to start a collection of Harleys. Only Made in the U.S. of A. bikes for me."

Moran asked if they were registered in Connecticut.

Saunders nodded. "Is there a problem?"

"No," Hernandez said. "But... eh... isn't it risky for someone in your position to ride motorcycles? You'd think the production's insurance company would object."

Saunders shrugged and an impish smile crept across his face. "Life without some risk is boring." He set the tray down on the square glass coffee table, pulled up his sweater's sleeves, and lifted two glasses of Margaritas. "So, what exactly did you want to talk to me about?" He handed Moran and Hernandez their drinks.

Moran's eyes focused on Saunders' exposed right forearm. "Those seem like pretty nasty cuts," he said, and pointed to several five-to-six inch narrow scars.

Saunders glanced at the forearm. "My own fault," he said, and chuckled. "Skidded on sand with the bike. Should've known better than to ride on the beach without protective gear."

"Speaking of which, do you own a helmet with a red rose set on top of handlebars decaled on the back?" Hernandez said.

"Yeah, I'm the spokesman for 'The Harley Rose Club,' " Saunders said.

"Just wondered if your helmet had the club's insignia," Hernandez said. "What color is your bike riding gear?"

"I have a black latex rubber suit and a powder blue one, why?"

Hernandez pursed his lips and shook his head slightly. "Nothing."

Saunders gave the sergeant a puzzled look, then shrugged.

"Does the name Rose Chiu mean anything to you?" Moran said.

Saunders took a sip of his drink and wiped his mouth with the back of his hand. "Sure, she owns a strip club in the city. Used to go there a lot, then I read she got killed. A break-in, right?"

"You could say that," Moran said.

Saunders took another sip and swallowed hard. "Crazy world we live in."

"Did you know a Lacy Wooden?" Hernandez quickly asked.

Saunders smiled—a flash of perfect teeth. "Sure. It's no secret that we were an item for a while. Jessie took me one night to Chiu's place to watch Lacy dance and that's how we met," the actor said.

"Is that Jessie Rand?" Hernandez quickly asked.

"Yeah, after that I used to frequent Chiu's place. You know, go down after taping the show and relax watching Lacy do her thing on stage. I even got her an audition on 'Bachelor Dad' to play my youngest daughter, but the director said she was too old," Saunders said.

Moran asked. "How did you and Miss Rand hook up?"

"Met Jessie at a party this Broadway producer friend of mine, Saul Goodwin, gave at his place a few years back."

Moran nodded—another mental note. "What about Paul Myer?"

Saunders turned, set his glass down on the coffee table, and looked at the cops. "I don't want to seem uncooperative, but I already answered many of those questions to the police when Lacy was murdered. Should I be calling my lawyer?"

A smile crept across Moran's face. "Not unless you're hiding something. Like I said on the phone, Lacy's murder has been re-opened and we're tying up all the loose ends."

"You know how it is, Greg," Hernandez added. "Everyone who knew Lacy has to be accounted for... purely routine."

Saunders gave an uneasy smile. "As far as that sleaze ball Myer is concerned, the world is better off without him." The actor lowered himself into a nearby soft cloth sofa. "I kept telling Lacy to dump the no-goodnik. Always bugging her with his jealous rants. There was a time I would've gladly punched his lights out." Saunders looked down at his hands. "Except I couldn't run the risk of damaging my career." He raised his gaze at Moran and Hernandez, who stared back at him. "I'm not a tough guy, but I play one on TV," he added and grinned—more teeth.

"We know, more show biz humor," Moran said. "You own a handgun?"

Saunders looked at him, narrowed his eyebrows and cocked his head slightly. "Unless the law's changed, isn't that illegal in New York without a permit?" the actor said. "And the answer is no."

"Any weapons in your house in Connecticut?" Moran said.

"I have a .22 caliber pistol, a .38, and a shotgun with permits," Saunders said. "Here, I have a 12 gauge side-by-side double barrel Beretta which I use for occasional skeet shooting. Aside from the bike, it's the only other hobby I have time for."

"That's a lot firepower," Hernandez observed.

"I feel safer with them. The alarm system alone doesn't cut it for me."

"What about the surveillance camera?" Moran said.

Saunders snorted. "That thing's always on the blink. In fact, I had to call this morning to have it fixed again. I live in the country in Connecticut. My nearest neighbor is half a mile away, and there's only one sheriff," Saunders said. "Last year a crazed fan jumped the wall, broke into the house, and refused to leave, saying she was my wife."

"Would you let us do a ballistic test on the .22 and the .38?" Hernandez said.

Saunders bolted off the sofa. "I don't like where this conversation is going, and I think I'd like to call my attorney."

"So I guess the answer is '*no*'," Moran said. His face turned into a mock pout. "And just when I thought we were getting along so well."

Saunders' face began to redden as if slapped repeatedly. "Listen, I don't have to—"

Moran shuffled up to the actor and placed his hand on the man's upper arm—it felt tight and muscular. "Relax, Mr. Saunders. No one's accusing you of anything," Moran darted his eyes toward Hernandez. "Right, Frank?"

With a polite smile, Hernandez said, "Absolutely."

"Could you tell us your whereabouts on the night Rose Chiu was killed?" Moran said.

"Just routine, Greg," Hernandez interjected.

Saunders sat down on the sofa and brushed back a strand of hair that had fallen over his brow. "It was Monday and I was here going over the new script for the week."

"Can anyone verify that?" Moran said.

Saunders turned his palms up. "Afraid not, I was alone."

Hernandez stepped toward the coffee table and set his drink down next to Saunders' glass while Moran moved toward the actor.

"I think we've got all our answers, Mr. Saunders," Moran said. "By the way, my wife and I very much enjoyed seeing you on '*Dancing With Celebrities.*' You were very smooth and light on your feet." He drew out his notepad and a ballpoint. "Would you mind giving her your autograph? Her name is Sandra."

Saunders' face lit up. "Of course, lieutenant," he said. The actor took the notepad and pen and scribbled out '*To Sandra with kisses and hugs—Greg Saunders.*'

Later as Moran and Hernandez drove through the mansion's gate onto the main street Moran turned to the sergeant.

"Did you get it?"

Hernandez reached inside his jacket and brought out a long see-through evidence bag. He pointed to Greg Saunders' Margarita straw. "Right here."

Moran lowered his window and tossed out the autograph.

CHAPTER 37

The large blackboard had the names: Lacy Wooden, Paul Myer and Rose Chiu written and encircled in chalk. Underneath, another line contained the names: George Halpern, Edwin Corbin, Saul Goodwin, Jessie Rand, and Greg Saunders. Next to the black board, Moran stood with a piece of chalk in his hand. Across from him, Hernandez and Darcey sat at the conference table with their arms folded across their chests. At the far end of the table a pale Sandra Moran sat, her fingers slowly turning a pencil. Occasionally she'd look up and give Simms, who was stoically leaning against a wall, a weak smile.

"Corbin, Goodwin, Rand and Saunders," Moran said while he dashed arrows from each name toward the boxes of Lacy and Rose. "They all had a connection to them, which makes them suspects until proven otherwise."

"Except Halpern," Hernandez said. "He has an alibi for the day of Lacy's murder, and there's nothing to tie him to Chiu."

"For now," Moran said. "But he's not off the hook for Paul Myer. Don't forget Halpern had the hots for Lacy and maybe Myer threatened to tell Mrs. Halpern of his affair unless the senator paid up."

"About the wounds on the killer," Simms said. "No emergency room reports treating anyone for cuts or knife wounds on or about the day we guess Myer was killed."

"The wounds were probably superficial and the killer treated himself," Moran said.

"I was finally able to speak with Mrs. Corbin," Simms said. "Turns out the judge hasn't given her any jewelry since their

150

twentieth wedding anniversary five years ago. She made crystal clear she wasn't very happy about that. Called him a *cheap skinflint.*"

"I'm sure we'll hear from the judge about that," Moran said. He quickly drew another arrow from Corbin to Lacy. "Although his connection to the killings is weak, let's keep him in the running for the moment."

"I think Greg Saunders is our man," Hernandez said. "The scars on his forearm; he owns two handguns of the same caliber as the murder weapon; refused to let us run ballistics on them; he and Lacy were a heavy item; he owns two bikes similar to the one the killer was seen riding, and the fact that he disliked Paul Myer makes him a prime suspect."

Moran stepped forward. "I'm not so sure. For starters, there's the matter of motive. Why kill Lacy, Myer and Chiu?" Moran said. "Besides, the two-gun theory isn't confirmed by the postmortem nor by the position of the entry wounds. As for the motorcycles, we have no proof that either one was *the* bike."

Moran went back to the blackboard and stared at the names. "However, I'm sure it's one of these." He underlined the names of the suspects. "But, Darcey's right. We can eliminate Saul Goodwin. He doesn't fit the profile we have of the biker at the murder scenes." Moran said. He shifted his gaze to Sandra, who was making notes on a yellow pad. Her face seemed pallid.

"Are you all right?" Moran asked.

Sandra emitted a distracted smile. "Just a little tired."

Moran said, "From what we've learned, do any of these individuals fit your criteria for Malignant Narcissistic disorder?"

A tired looking Sandra gazed at her husband. "Everyone who's in public life is narcissistic to one degree or another; but is it to the degree of being malignant? I don't know. That's why I'd like to take another look at the file."

"A new theory running around in your head?" Moran said.

Sandra twirled the pencil between her fingers. "Something's bothering me and I don't want to get into it until I've seen the file again." She glanced at her watch. "I wish I could stay, but I'm taking over Dr. Humphrey's Criminal Psychology class tonight." When Sandra got on her feet, she swayed and brought her hand to her forehead.

Moran rushed to her side. "You're in no condition to go anywhere but home, I'll—"

"No, no, I'll be fine," she said, steadying herself. She gathered her purse.

Moran nodded but kept a watchful eye on his wife. "I'll have someone downstairs drive you, and I'll pick you up later with the file."

When Sandra left, a worried Moran turned to Hernandez. "Have you heard from your father?"

The sergeant wrinkled his forehead. "No, and I hope he's okay."

CHAPTER 38

"**H**ow did you get rid of her?" Victor whispered in Spanish to Linda Garcia when they entered Rosario Mendez's darkened, empty office.

"I didn't. And this is going to cost you plenty." Linda Garcia had a flashlight in her hand. "Rosario is in Acapulco for a two-day meeting," she added. She swung the flashlight's beam toward the computer on Mendez's desk. "There it is."

Victor glanced at his watch. "It's five past eight, when is the security guard due?" he whispered.

"Do not worry about Pablo. He is probably curled up in a stairwell having a pizza and some beer," the bank's manager said as they made their way to the computer. "You sit there," Linda said, and pointed to a chair in the center of the room. "And don't make any noise. This might take a while." She stepped toward the desk.

"I suppose smoking is out of the question," Victor said from the chair.

His companion raised her eyes at him. "Do not even think about it."

Hernandez's father shrugged and slouched back in the chair. He kept his eyes on Linda, who was now staring at the computer screen and clicking keys.

"Someone is going to hear that typing," Victor said in a hushed voice.

"Will you shut up!" Linda hissed. Her face looked spooky as the bluish hue from the screen illuminated it.

The minutes seem to pass like hours while a bored Victor

squirmed in his chair, chewed on a fingernail, and crossed and uncrossed his legs repeatedly. The only sound in the dimmed room was his breathing and the castanet sounds coming from the keyboard.

Finally, Linda stopped tapping the keys and looked up. "Nothing here about any Repsol transactions or any Maria Luisa Torres. Think I'll—"

An ominous silence descended over the room at the sound of heavy footsteps from the corridor. Victor bolted out of his chair and crawled behind it while Linda turned the screen off and dropped to the floor. The door slowly opened and a wide beam from a Magnum flashlight arced across the room.

"Anyone in here?" Pablo said in Spanish. The two intruders held their breath and a rivulet of sweat slid down Victor's nose and caused it to itch. He was on all fours and didn't dare move while he fought off the urge to sneeze. It seemed the security guard had been standing in the doorway for an eternity. Victor's hands and knees began to ache. *Cheap friggin' carpet,* Victor mused.

He lowered his head and looked through the space between the chair's legs and felt his heart jump into his throat when Pablo's heavy black shoes started to move farther into the room.

"Where are you?" a husky male voice called out from corridor. "You better come unless you like cold pizza and warm beer."

"Okay, okay, I'm coming!" the security guard called back. He turned and walked out of the office. When the door closed, Victor pinched his nose and sneezed. "I thought you said he was in a stairwell eating."

Linda hoisted herself off the floor and sat back down in her chair. "I'm going to try Rosario's *Contacts* folder," she said, as Victor picked himself up.

"I'll take the file cabinet," Victor said and started toward a large metal cabinet that was against one of the walls.

"Forget it. Rosario is one of those computer freaks who files everything on the hard drive. You should see the number of files she has here," Linda said, and returned to the keyboard.

Again more nail biting, crossing, and uncrossing of legs and a few impatient sighs while Victor listened to Linda's fingers clicking at the keys. The bank manager's eyes skittered and bounced from line to line, like a car on a bumpy road while she scanned the file on the screen.

Minutes later Linda Garcia whispered from across the desk. "Psst, come over here."

Victor came around the desk and peered over her shoulder. "Hmm, a New York City phone number, and an e-mail address, but no name or address, just the letter 'M.'?"

"All the other numbers but this one have the person's names, addresses, e-mail addresses," Linda said.

* * *

"Area code 212," Moran said. "489-7149." He sat at his module desk and looked up at Victor Hernandez whose face beamed with pride. "I'm surprised Linda was able to access Mendez's files."

"As bank manager, Linda has access to all the computer passwords. They're only changed when someone leaves the job," Victor said.

Hernandez turned to his father. "Any problems we should know about?"

A proud Victor smiled. "Everything went like a James Bond movie."

Moran punched in the telephone number and pressed the *Speaker* button. A digitized woman's voice came through: *"You have reached the New York Athletic Club—"*

Moran hung up and looked up at the perplexed faces of Frank Hernandez and his father. "What about the e-mail address?"

"The Internet provider said it wouldn't release any information without a court order," Hernandez said.

Moran slapped the palm of his hand on the desktop and jumped out of his chair. "Damn privacy laws!" he said. "We don't have grounds for a court order. Get a hold of the New York Athletic Club's members' list."

CHAPTER 39

M oran and Hernandez entered and inhaled the smell of gun powder mixed with the sweet-acrid smell of death permeating the kitchen. On a chair in front of them lay the slumped-over nude body of Greg Saunders. The actor had been gagged with duct tape and trussed like a turkey and was left with his head resting on his chest as in prayer or asleep. Large splatters of blood covered the white porcelain-tiled walls and the granite floor. The room looked like a scene from a horror flick.

"Flora King, his cleaning lady, found him this morning," said a lean, tightly packaged man in his early forties with puffed cheeks. The frosting of gray around his temples was partially covered by a hat that had a row of oak leaf embroidery on its visor and sat squarely on his head. He stood rigidly, almost at attention, in a dark blue, neatly pressed police uniform with two captain's gold bars on its epaulets.

Moran contemplated the man. The embossed name tag read Captain Darryl Benedict, Pelham Police Department. The head of Pelham's Finest was trying hard to impress the *big city cop.*

"When Commissioner Newbury heard about it." Benedict said, "He called me and said the victim was a person of interest to you."

Moran murmured *'yes'* while his gaze followed the taut string that was tied to the dead man's right toe. Its other end extended to the trigger of an expensive silver inlaid double barrel side-by-side shotgun. The weapon was on top of the stainless steel refrigerator a few feet away, and both barrels looked down on the victim. Duct tape wrapped around the shotgun's barrels held it in place on top of a block of wood, while more tape secured the gun's elevated stock to another block of wood.

"The gun's registered to the victim," Benedict said.

"Pretty elaborate," Hernandez said when he looked up at the Rube Goldberg contraption.

Moran said, "Someone had to hate Greg Saunders an awful lot to go to all this trouble."

"Not to mention being very strong," Benedict added. "Our coroner believes that Mr. Saunders was rendered unconscious by ether up in the bedroom and then brought down here."

"Let's take a look at that bedroom," Moran said.

Moments later, Moran, Hernandez and Captain Benedict stood in an oversized, sparsely furnished room. The king-size bed, with its elaborate headboard of an eighteenth century English hunting scene, was unmade. Silk sheets hung over one side and rested on the room's thick carpet. A two-door armoire and the plasma Sony TV that covered the wall in front of the bed were the room's only other furnishings.

Benedict led the two detectives to the bed. "If you get close, you can still smell the ether."

Moran leaned in and sniffed the air. "Are those his?" the lieutenant asked. He pointed to a set of pajamas strewn on the floor at the foot of the bed.

"Yep, we found traces of hair that matched the victim," Benedict said. "As you can see, there's no sign of a struggle and nothing appears to be out of place."

Moran's gaze fell on one of the night tables where a black cellular phone lay next to the lamp. He gestured to the phone. "You check this out?"

Benedict pushed his cap back. "Huh-huh, both the received and dialed calls records are empty."

"Unusual," Moran said.

Benedict shrugged. "People do strange things."

Moran stroked his chin. "I'd like this room sealed off," he said, then turned to Hernandez. "Call Maureen and have her team get over here."

When the trio returned to the kitchen, Moran neared the dead man and wrinkled his nose. The smell from the beginnings of decomposing flesh had started to rise from Saunders' body. Moran's gaze once again traced the elaborate setup.

"Our perp was one cool, calculating individual," Moran said. "Knocks the guy out, undresses him, brings him down here, ties him up and then carefully sets up this contraption. Also, he had to be in remarkable shape to carry Saunders from the second floor to here."

"Nice touch. Saunders regains consciousness and as soon as he moves his foot, he activates the shotgun's trigger," Hernandez said.

"There's no sign of forced entry, neither here at the house nor at the gate and the alarm system was turned off," Benedict said.

Hernandez asked, "Was the gate closed when Flora King arrived?"

"Yes, and as usual she used her remote to get in," Benedict said.

Moran brought over a small stepladder that lay against a wall and climbed up to the top of the refrigerator where he studied the shotgun and the complicated mechanism the killer had devised. String was tied to the two triggers, stretched around the stock, and then back to the triggers where it was tied to the string leading from Saunders' toe.

"12 gauge Beretta," Moran said. "Has it been dusted?"

"Yes, and I'll have the lab send you the results," Benedict answered from below.

Moran descended the ladder and creased his face. "Ouch," he moaned and stretched his right knee.

"Something wrong?" Benedict said.

Moran gave a faint smile. "Just nature reminding me of my age. We'll need to test the gun," he said.

Captain Benedict nodded. "No problem. I understand that this is all part of a larger picture."

Moran asked Benedict if his forensics people checked the rest of the house.

Benedict adjusted his hat. "Afraid not. Our Forensics *'people'* consists of just one person. I thought you'd want to have your own NYPD experts go over the place."

"Anyone see anything... neighbors, passersby?" Hernandez asked.

Benedict slowly shook his head. "The house is hard to access, what with the gate and all."

"The lack of forced entry, no signs of a struggle in the bedroom, and a turned-off alarm system point to the fact that Saunders knew his killer," Moran said. "Did the coroner give a time of death?"

"From the partial stage of rigor mortis, he put the time of death at between four and six this morning."

"Where's the coroner?" Hernandez said.

"He had to leave. There was an accident in town, two people killed," Benedict said. "Damned outsiders, always speeding through the place."

"And Flora," Hernandez said. "Where can we find her?"

"One of my men took her home. She was quite shaken up," the captain said.

Moran added. "We'll need her name and address."

"No problem, she lives in town."

"Mind if we look around while we wait for our CSU people?" Moran said.

Benedict shrugged slightly. "It's all yours, lieutenant. My people are finished. I just waited for you. I'll get rid of the press outside the gate. Pelham is a small village and something like this, involving a celebrity, always attracts the media."

Moran said. "I need the body taken to our morgue."

"I'll make the arrangements," Benedict said. After he left, Moran and Hernandez stepped toward the body. Moran carefully lifted Saunders' head. The right side of the face above the eye was an accumulation of mangled bloodstained flesh and brain tissue. Moran leaned in and scrutinized the gaping wound and with his latex-gloved hand he gingerly removed a shotgun pellet. He held it up. "Looks like double-O buckshot," Moran said.

"Certainly not for skeet," the sergeant said.

"See what shotgun cartridges Saunders had while I check around here," Moran said.

Alone, Moran walked around the bloodstains and examined the marbled countertops. Everything seemed clean and in place. He opened the refrigerator. It contained a half-filled bottle of Finlandia vodka on one shelf next to a jar of olives, a carton of eggs, and a partially eaten macaroni and cheese casserole. Moran closed the door and returned to the body. Saunders' hands were tied behind the chair with the same kind of duct tape as the gag across his mouth. The body was trussed with green nylon rope. When Moran touched the rope, it felt oddly sticky and abrasive. His concentration was broken when Hernandez entered.

"I found these in the living room," Hernandez said and held up an evidence bag containing two glass tumblers. "They still have drops of whiskey in them and two Remington double-O shells are missing from a full box in the gun cabinet."

Moran nodded and peered at the glasses. He shifted his look to Hernandez. "You ever seen rope like this?" He gestured to the body.

Hernandez leaned over and with his fingertips felt the rope. "That's climbing rope. My roomie in college was an avid climber. His closet was packed with it. It's coated with a liquid abrasive to prevent slippage."

"Didn't Saunders tell us that motorcycles and skeet were his only hobbies?"

"He never struck me as the mountain-climbing type," Hernandez said.

"But our killer might be," Moran said.

Hernandez scratched the side of his head. "Seems like everyone we question about Lacy Wooden's murder gets bumped off."

"Not everyone, but close enough."

"Think it's the same perp?" the sergeant asked.

Moran gave his partner a steely look. "Could be. The fact that the M.O. is not the same means nothing. Maybe our killer added a little variety to throw us off." Moran's eyes swept the room. "If it is the same perp, then we've got a very clever killer on our hands."

CHAPTER 40

The rustling of papers and the solitary circle of soften light which emanated from a cubicle were the only signs of life in the Crime Scene Unit's lab. The horn-rimmed eyeglasses rested on Maureen Singleton's face at a slight angle—the right leg lay snug over her right ear while the other leg pressed against the middle of her left ear—belied the CSU's assistant lab chief's reputation for exactness and tidiness. With an impatient sweep of her hand, she brushed aside a strand of blonde hair away from her forehead and checked her watch. It was 6:45 p.m., and it had now been twenty-four hours since she and her team had collected the forensic evidence from Greg Saunders' house.

The silence was broken by the scrapping of shoes at the cubicle's entryway. "Sorry, I'm late," Moran said. "I see everyone's gone home."

Singleton turned and rose. "Nobody wants to work late anymore," she said. She gestured to a chair covered by an orderly stack of files. "Just set them down on the floor and make yourself comfortable."

Moran looked around the space. "How do you keep it all so neat?"

Singleton chuckled while her fingers dug into the neatly piled folders that lay on the desk. "Easy, I'm rarely in here. The real work is done out there," she said and pointed to the darkened laboratory. "We found traces of semen on Saunders' bed sheets; I've sent it over for testing."

She continued to search the folders, then pulled out a red one, flipped it open and tossed a narrow evidence bag on the desk.

"Besides this, we uncovered a latent palm print on the wall above the bed's headboard. The oil from the print indicates that it was a few hours old. I forwarded it to the Feds so they can run it through their database for a match, but don't expect much. Latent palm prints are tough."

Moran reached over and grasped the evidence bag. He pointed to the wisp of blonde hair inside the bag. "Whose is it?"

Singleton bunched her lips and pawed out of the file three 5x7 inch color photographs from inside the file. "That strand matches the hair color of the two women in the pictures. And the chromosome constitution of the sample is XX—female."

Moran examined the three photographs: a slender woman in her late thirties with a long angular, symmetrical face divided by an aquiline thin nose and light blue or violet eyes. Someone in a John Singer Sargent portrait. She had an aristocratic air about her, the blonde hair gently rested on her shoulders. The woman was lying on Saunders' bed wearing only a smile. The other picture was of the same woman alongside another woman who bore an uncanny resemblance to her—two peas in a pod. The last photograph was of Saunders and the second woman. They were both in bike gear standing next to two black Harleys with Niagara Falls in the background. The motorcycles appeared to be as the ones in Greg Saunders' garage.

Moran crinkled his face. "These were in Saunders' house?" Moran said.

Singleton nodded. "In the back of the night table drawer."

"The problem is," Moran said, frowning, "is that we don't know how long that hair wisp has been on the bed," Moran said. "The nude woman in those pictures is Samantha Halpern and the other one's her sister, Sabrina. I recognized her from the media coverage of her antics."

"The dates on the back of the pictures range from three months to a year ago," Singleton said. She removed her glasses and laid them on the desk.

Moran's fingers drummed the photographs for a moment as he

murmured, "S... A," in a barely audible tone.

"You say something?" Singleton asked.

The detective passed his tongue against the inside of his cheek. "Nothing, nothing."

Singleton looked at the lieutenant oddly and rested her elbows on the desk. "I think I know what's going through your head, so bear in mind that the shade of blonde in the hair sample we found is a very popular shade. See?" She tugged at a tress of blonde hair that fell over one of her ears. It was the same shade. "Lots of women use it."

"But their pictures weren't found in the victim's nightstand," Moran said. "Anything else?"

Singleton smiled. "Oh, yes." She reached underneath the desk, brought out a small plaster cast, and set it down. "Size twelve grooved rubber-sole pointy-tipped boot. We almost missed it, but one of the guys noticed fragments of dirt imbedded in the rug just outside the bedroom. When we threw the ultraviolet light on it, the print of a boot appeared. However, I can't determine the wearer's weight because he or she was probably weighed down by Saunders."

"Any sign of him being dragged?"

"No signs of dragging on the runner that covered the stair steps. I'm sure the killer carried the body from the bed to the kitchen. There were no signs of blood anywhere except in the kitchen."

"Did you see boot marks anywhere else in the house?"

Singleton frowned and shook her head. "No, but that's not surprising when you consider that Benedict's people trampled the area like a heard of elephants before we got there."

"Could it be a motorcycle boot?" Moran asked.

Singleton shrugged. "Hard to tell, but a size twelve is a fairly common size boot, man or woman."

Moran tapped his chin with the tip of his forefinger and nodded while he listened. When she finished Moran lifted the cast and examined it. "The grooves have sharp edges. Is that something normal for this kind of boot?"

Singleton pushed herself off the chair and walked toward Moran. "It depends on the manufacturer. A boot like that could also serve as a hiking or mountain-climbing boot."

"Which would account for the rope," Moran said.

"Speaking of which, the killer is left-handed."

"How can you be sure?"

"From the manner in which the knots were tied," Singleton said. "When a right-handed person ties a knot the pattern is from left to right. The rope around Saunders was tied right to left."

"Anything on the cell phone?"

Singleton lowered her eyes to the folder's sheet of notations. "The only fingerprints on the phone belonged to the victim."

"I noticed the phone was a camera/phone. Any pictures?"

"I tried accessing that feature's folder but it's locked," Singleton said. "It requires a password." She stood up. "Now, for the second half of the show. Come with me." She put on her glasses.

"You certainly earned your pay with this case," Moran said. "Should've had kids before you got divorced, Maureen. It would've given you more of a life."

Singleton laughed. "I saw '*Rosemary's Baby*' and there was no way I was going to have children with that man."

"Well, whatever else you've got I hope it sheds some more light," Moran said as he followed her out. "This case has more angles than a Picasso painting."

A moment later, the lab assistant perched herself on a stool, snapped off her eyeglasses, and cast them aside as if discarding a bad poker hand. She peered into one of Crime Scene Unit's microscopes. It was attached to a computer. After slowly adjusting the focus knob, she raised her head. "Here it is." She said and hopped off the stool.

Moran lifted himself onto the stool and looked through the microscope's two eyepieces.

"Looks like blood."

"It's a specimen from a small piece of latex similar to that used in medical gloves."

Moran straightened and faced Singleton. "Where did you find it?"

"We found it wedged at the base of the refrigerator," Singleton said. "The tests reveal that its chromosome composition is XY, a male. Greg Saunders was blood type A, this is B. The bloodstain's fresh, no more than thirty-six to twenty-four hours from the time we found it, and from the serrated edges of the latex, my guess is that it's the result of a cut."

"Maybe when they were rigging up the shotgun," Moran said. "Which means that possibly a man and a woman were involved in Saunders' death?"

* * *

At Moran's brownstone, Sandra yawned and stretched her arms above her head. She leaned in and hunched over the Lacy Wooden file her husband had given her. Sandra checked her watch and saw that it was six forty-five in the evening. Three hours had passed since she had begun studying the notes, pictures, the *New York Times* society page clipping, and the other material. She rubbed her forehead with the palm of her hand; it was cold and clammy.

Hoisting herself off her chair and clenching her teeth, she slowly moved to one of the bookshelves in the living room and let her gaze float over the spines of several criminal psychology books, two of which had been penned by her. When she reached a book titled: *"The Destructive Narcissistic Behavior: Clinical and Diagnostic Implications"* by Doctor Horatio Polk, she stopped.

She drew the book out and then brought her hand to her brow. The cold, clammy feeling had progressed to nausea. She reached out and held on to the bookshelf when she felt the room start to spin. Soon she was spiraling down a dark tunnel, and then everything went black.

CHAPTER 41

When Moran arrived in Riverdale, a small elite community just north of Manhattan, he was tired and grumpy. Earlier that morning, Dr. Kruger had informed him that Sandra's loss of consciousness was due to her doubled dosages of Cytoxan and 25 Cyclophosphamide. The doctor had given her a strong sedative that put her into a deep sleep in order to stabilize her. The question as to why Sandra had doubled her meds remained a mystery.

When Moran drove past the two granite pillars that flanked the start of the blacktop driveway, he caught sight of the house. It was hidden from the main road by a tall stone wall, as were the other homes along the elm-shaded Pinedale Drive. He steered his car up the winding driveway past the expansive lawn and parked behind a black BMW 750i with the license plate: 'IM HOT'.

As Moran got out of his car, he looked up at the stately, two-story colonial brick house. It looked as if it had been shipped over brick-by-brick from England. He climbed the broad stone steps that led to the heavy double-oak entrance and rang the bell. The light-skinned man who opened the door appeared to be in his fifties. In striped black pants, a black satin vest, a starched white shirt and a wide silk tie, the man stood rigid and gave Moran an icy glare.

Moran's gaze swept over the tall manservant; the fine blond hair was held in place by a generous amount of gel, the form-fitting valet vest revealing a strong build. The servant's haunting pale blue eyes centered themselves on the detective. The valet smiled tightly. "Can I help you?" The voice was deep, and clipped with the trace of a Hispanic accent.

Moran identified himself and explained that he needed to speak to the owner of the house. The manservant's smile was quickly replaced by a stern look. "You wait here," the valet ordered and left Moran cooling his heels on the mohair welcome mat. A short while later the man reappeared. "Follow me." He led Moran through a wide, darkly furnished foyer, around a corner, and across a formal living room sprinkled with antique furniture, then down a carpeted stairway and into a large room. The place was lit by the stream of light coming through the lace curtains that covered the ceiling-to-floor glass windows.

Moran inhaled the air dense with a floral scent that reminded him of either a French brothel or a funeral home. The lieutenant's eyes swept the room--the walls were yellow, the moldings a celestial blue, and the floor was made of large black and white tiles. Against a wall stood a gun cabinet displaying four shotguns. The decorated twelve-foot goose-down Christmas tree that stood in one of the corners reminded Moran that he hadn't bought Sandra's present.

A throat clearing from the shadows made Moran turn quickly toward the sound.

"You always scare your guests that way?" Moran asked.

A sultry female voice said. "Thank you, Carlos, you can go now." She continued, "First of all, lieutenant, you're not a guest, and secondly, a veteran NYPD detective shouldn't scare so easily. I'm Sabrina Van Damme. Why are you here?"

Moran neared. The Rembrandt lighting that fell on the woman revealed her high cheekbones and strong features. The svelte looking woman was seated in a red loveseat with her long legs daintily crossed, while her hands rested on her lap, one on top of the other. Her blonde hair was in a French twist and her face was alabaster white—like her sister, Samantha.

The detective noticed that Sabrina Van Damme didn't seem as thin as in the images he had seen of her in the media. He estimated her weight at one twenty to one twenty-five pounds, and her height at about five-eleven. The subtle eye shadow brought out the violet of her eyes; her skin was smooth with light dusting of freckles sprinkled in all the right places. A knee length black sleeveless dress. A single strand of pearls around her neck. Moran did some quick math in his head and figured that the price of the dress could've fed a small village in Costa Rica for a year. It was obvious that his hostess shopped in stores where every price tag had a comma.

Sabrina caught Moran's nonplussed gaze. "Sam's my twin. Not identical, but close enough. I was three minutes behind her, but I've made up for that."

"You're taller than in the newspaper pictures," Moran said.

"That's because they were only three by five inches," Sabrina said, smiling.

Moran allowed himself the trace of smile—*Another comedian.*

Sabrina floated up from her chair and started across the room; she moved in sections—alluring and sensuous. When she reached a brass cart on wheels with more liquor on it than any human being had a right to have, she turned and held up two highball glasses.

"You look like you could use a G&T," Sabrina purred.

"No thanks, water will be fine," Moran said. "I noticed that Carlos isn't your typical Latino."

"That's because although his mother's Colombian, his father was Russian. His last name's Ivanovich."

Sabrina mixed herself a Gin &Tonic with more G than T. With her left hand, she dropped several cubes from the silver ice holder into a second tall glass and then added sparkling water.

"So what made you drive all the way up here, detective... eh... what was it again?" Sabrina said as she walked to Moran with the two glasses.

"Moran. Lieutenant Moran. And I'd like—."

"Ah, yes. Sorry," Sabrina said.

As she handed Moran his glass of water, he saw that her

fingers were long and lithe, just like their owner. Her body was tight, her calves muscular—the result of hours at the gym and Jessie Rand's dance classes. Sabrina slithered to the couch, lowered herself, and crossed her legs. With the tips of her left thumb and index finger, she held the plastic stirrer that protruded from the glass. She stirred her drink.

"Now tell me why you're here," Sabrina cooed.

Moran swallowed some water and eyed the woman over the rim of his glass. She didn't seem to be the wild party, orgy kind of woman the media had made her out to be; she was elegant, neatly put together and in full control of herself—*maybe too much*. The detective smiled a neutral smile, and moved toward the couch. "Miss Van Damme, tell me about Greg Saunders."

Sabrina lowered the drink to her lap, her face sad with moist eyes. "I was devastated when I read about it. Who would've done such a horrible thing? He was such a handsome man."

Moran sat down and faced her. "You haven't answered my question, Miss—"

"Call me Sabrina." She gave him the look of a little girl unable to answer the teacher's question.

Moran smiled and nodded. "And the answer is?"

"Greg and I were going to be married."

The words jerked Moran to attention and he spilled drops of water on his trousers. "Married? You're kidding?"

"When a man gets on his knees and asks you to be the mother of his children, most people would interpret that as a proposal of marriage."

A stunned Moran lowered his glass. "How long ago was this?"

"Three months ago when we motorbiked to Niagara Falls. At the time, I attributed his proposal to the romantic setting, but I was wrong. When we got back, he repeated the offer. Naturally, I accepted."

"When were you getting married?"

"We hadn't set a date. Greg had to talk with his agent and

make sure there were no conflicts. I wasn't in any rush."

"I don't remember the media ever mentioning it," Moran said.

Sabrina shrugged lightly. "We decided not to make it public. Thought it best to keep it our little secret."

"You don't seem very enthused about marrying him."

Sabrina laughed. "I've been married twice before and it's not what it's cracked up to be. But Greg was a celebrity, rich and easy on the eyes. So, I figured '*why not*'? A girl needs more than diamonds to keep her warm on a cold winter night."

Moran studied his hostess while he tried to figure her out. *Is she really Hard-Hearted Hannah or just an act?* Sabrina Van Damme was hard to decipher.

"What kind of motorcycle do you have?"

Sabrina gazed at Moran with dreamy eyes. "A Harley, my '*Hog*' " she said. "Love it."

"Had it long?"

"About a year. Greg bought it for me. A sort of 'his-and-hers' motorcycles. Taught me how to ride and insisted I join that plebian club of his, 'The Harley Rose."

"Did you?"

"Had to. So did my sister. Gave her an excuse to get away from good old straight-laced George."

"They don't get along?"

Sabrina smiled. "Lieutenant, Sam has always been a free-spirit, and being married to George Halpern is stifling her. All he's interested in is getting ahead in politics. She even tried to get him to join us in our biking jaunts," she said and sipped some more gin-and-tonic. "When she got him a Joe Rocket leather two-piece suit for his birthday two years ago, George said he looked like a *putz* in it, so that was the end of that."

The idea of Senator Halpern in leather was too surreal for Moran's mind to hold. The detective shuttered his eyes and quickly shredded the vision. "Samantha owns a motorcycle?"

Sabrina's face split into a grin. "Yes, figured we'd all have the same bike, Harley-Davidson FLTRI, sort of like the Three Musketeers."

"Does that include the riding gear as well?"

Sabrina nodded briskly. "Oh, yes, especially the helmet with that awful tacky decal of a rose on the handlebars."

Moran cleared his throat. "Do you know if your sister was having an affair with Greg?"

Sabrina gazed at the detective. "You certainly are direct."

"I ask because we found a nude photo of her that was taken in Greg Saunders' bedroom."

Sabrina tossed her head back and giggled. "Oh, that? We'd gotten back after shooting skeet at the Pelham Skeet & Trap Club and had a bit too much to drink that night. When Greg suggested a nude picture of Samantha, she said yes. But, as for having an affair, I won't go that far." She stepped in to Moran. "Maybe a brief fling once, but nothing more."

"That didn't bother you?"

"Why? It happened before Greg and I got involved. Besides, it kept everything in the family." Sabrina swallowed some more G&T. "I guess you're going to show George that picture."

"My job is not breaking up marriages. However, I go wherever the evidence takes me."

A stone-faced Sabrina fixed her eyes on Moran while she passed her forefinger over the rim of her glass. "Fair enough."

Moran gestured to the gun cabinet. "I gather you and your sister do a lot of shooting," Moran said. "Does Samantha also own shotguns?"

Sabrina eyed the cabinet and turned back to the detective. "Our grandfather was one of the founders of the Pelham Skeet & Trap Club. And no, Samantha doesn't own any guns. George won't allow them in the house."

"She uses your guns then?"

Sabrina nodded.

"Did you see Greg on the night he was killed?"

Sabrina slammed her G&T down on the coffee table in front of the couch and glared at Moran. "How dare you even consider that I'd be involved in his murder!"

"Easy. I haven't accused you of anything. Just doing my job."

Sabrina exhaled, picked up her glass, and sipped her G&T less politely now. She cocked her head, a quick birdlike movement. "No, I didn't. He had suggested dinner at his place, but I had a splitting migraine and begged off. Took a sleeping pill and went to bed early."

"Can anyone verify this?"

Sabrina gazed up at the ceiling for a moment and finally said. "Uh-uh. Carlos had the night off."

"Do you or your sister do any mountain climbing?"

Another toss of the head and another giggle. "This sounds like an interview for Sports Illustrated; first motorcycling and now mountaineering," Sabrina said.

Moran gave her an apologetic smile. "Part of the job."

"Don't be ridiculous, lieutenant," Sabrina said and motioned to her body. "Do I look like the type? All that ridiculous sweating and grunting just to sit on top of some rock. But Sam did try it some years ago as part of her *no pain, no gain* phase of keeping in shape. Got over that real quick when she broke a nail."

Moran set down his glass on the table as he gathered his thoughts. It was time to ask the question of the hour.

"Does the name Lacy Wooden ring any bells?"

Sabrina's face tightened and darkened. She bolted out of the couch and turned toward Moran. "That slut! Greg introduced me to her at a party once and explained his past relation with her—how he tried to get her on his show and so on. The little tramp thought that because they'd dated a few times, she was going to be the next Mrs. Saunders," Sabrina said, and huffed. "Mrs. Saunders... my ass!"

The sudden change in demeanor brought a thin smile to Moran's face. *The mask had finally fallen off.*

"I recall the press saying they were a serious item," Moran said.

"Bullshit! Pure imaginings. Believe me, I knew my Greg."

"I gather you didn't care for her," the detective said.

Sabrina moved even closer to Moran, stared down at him, glanced briefly to one side, and folded her arms across her chest. She then shifted her gaze back to the cop. "When I heard what'd had happened to her I naturally felt sorry. She may have been an ambitious, no-talent stripper, but actually, I felt sorry for her. I'm really a softy at heart, lieutenant," Sabrina's voice sounded genuine.

Moran gazed at her and smiled wryly. *Mother Teresa with retractable nails.*

"Ever visit the club where she danced?"

"Haven't a clue where it is. Besides I wouldn't be caught dead in that part of town."

"Can you account for your whereabouts on the day she was murdered?"

Sabrina unfolded her arms, let them drop to her sides, turned away and drained her drink. "I was here alone."

"Another migraine?"

Moran's hostess glared at him. "No, I was here getting things ready for my parents' fortieth wedding anniversary party that night."

"That's quite a memory you have for something that happened over a year ago."

"Another one of my many blessings—or curses, depending on the memory."

"Was Carlos here with you?" Moran asked.

"No, he took the Camry to be serviced."

Moran's face blanched.

"Don't look so surprised, lieutenant. To me a car's a car and I save a fortune in insurance and repairs," Sabrina said.

A wry smile crossed Moran's lips—*Not only is she enigmatic but also a penny pincher.* "Were you ever questioned by the police about Lacy Wooden's murder?" Moran asked.

Sabrina froze for an instant, and then turned away from Moran. "No."

"You don't seem overly upset by Greg Saunders' death," Moran said.

Sabrina shrugged as she turned back to face him. "We all deal with grief in our own way."

Moran rose and after thanking Sabrina, walked to the door. When he reached it, he turned. "Something else, how well did you know Paul Myer?"

Sabrina gave Moran a blank stare. "Never heard of the man."

A few moments later Moran sat behind the wheel of his car. He reached inside his coat's breast pocket and turned off the voice-activated recorder. It was the size of a credit card.

Chapter 42

The cafeteria was sparsely dotted with tired looking Sloan-Kettering doctors and nurses. Moran sat alone at a corner table with headphones attached to his ears, listening to the Sabrina's taped interview. The detective slowly turned the cup of coffee that sat in front of him while he pressed the '*Repeat*' button and creased his brow. This was the third time that morning he had heard the tape. Abruptly, Hernandez materialized at the table and cleared his throat. Moran looked up, annoyed.

"How's Sandra?" Hernandez said.

The lieutenant's face relaxed and he removed the headphones. "The same. Sit down, Frank." He motioned to the empty chair across from him. "Dr. Kruger said he'd meet me here."

"What's on the tape? You look upset."

Moran offered the headphones to the sergeant. "I want you to hear this and tell me what you think. I've got a feeling something's amiss but I can't for the life of me pinpoint it."

While Hernandez listened to the tape, Moran took a sip of coffee and tapped his fingers on the table. He watched Hernandez listening to the interview. A few moments later, Hernandez removed the headphones.

"Wow, Samantha and Sabrina are two pieces of work. Think one of them could be Greg's killer?"

Moran thrust his lower lip upwards and shrugged lightly. "We'll see. Any news on Flora King?"

"Went up there yesterday and her neighbor said she left the next day after finding Greg's body. Said she needed to get away for a while. Flew to Nashville to stay with her sister and brother-in-law," Hernandez said. "I got a call from Maureen. The federal IAFIS came up with a blank on the palm print."

"Thought so. You get a name for Flora's sister?"

Hernandez shook his head. "The neighbor didn't know. Flora King wasn't an overly friendly person."

Moran bunched his lips. "I'll call Benedict and ask him to tell his people to keep an eye out for her. By the way, isn't today your day off?"

"Yeah, but as long as I was in this part of town running some errands, I thought I'd—"

Moran bolted up straight. "What did you just say?"

Hernandez repeated it and then said,. "What's the matter?"

Moran snapped his fingers. "That's it!" he exclaimed. "There's a point in the tape where I asked her if she'd ever visited the Chiu's club and she said something like, '*I haven't a clue where it is and besides I wouldn't be caught dead in that part of town.*' If she knew nothing about it, why would she know in what part of town it was located in?"

"I think Sabrina Van Damme just went to the head of the class," Hernandez said. He brought out a booklet from his jacket's inside pocket. "This is the New York Athletic Club's membership list." He slipped it across the table to Moran who opened it and briskly flipped through the glossy pages that contained the names of the NYAC's members—last name first, first name last.

"Most of the city's power brokers are in here. Anyone from our list?"

"Check out the '*M*'s' " Hernandez said.

Moran turned to the last names beginning with 'M.' There were two pages of names. "Can you give me a hint and spare me going through all of this?"

"Try Morrison."

"Of Morrison Savings & Trust?"

Hernandez nodded. "The same. Howard Shillings and Senator

Halpern are also in there. But I thought it interesting that Rosario Mendez would have that particular phone number in her computer filed differently from the others. I crosschecked with the phone company, and there were several calls from Rosario Mendez's office in Mexico to the New York Athletic Club in the last few months. The club operator said it wasn't unusual for members to get calls but she couldn't recall which member got the calls from Mexico."

Moran turned his head toward the cafeteria's entry and caught a glimpse of Dr. Kruger coming toward the table. "Before I forget, Frank," Moran said. He placed Greg Saunders' cell phone on the table. "I'd like you to try and figure out how to access the *Pictures* feature. Greg locked it before he died and we need the password," Moran said.

Hernandez took the phone and gazed at it. "Why me?"

"Because you're part of this '*Gee Whiz Electronic*' generation while I'm an old geezer who still prefers a manual typewriter," Moran said.

"Excuse me," a deep baritone voice said. When Moran and Hernandez looked up, they found Dr. Kruger's somber face staring down at them.

Moran's face was drained to a whiter shade of pale.

"I need to talk to you... in private," the doctor said.

"That's okay," Moran said, and pointed to Hernandez. "He's a friend."

When Dr. Kruger sat down between the two cops, he turned to Moran. "Your wife's improving and I'm going to reduce the sedatives, so she may regain consciousness. However, the chemo is not working as fast as I had hoped," he said and lowered his eyes. "I'm afraid she's going to need a bone marrow transplant. Something I had wanted to avoid with the stem-cell procedure."

"But it could take months or longer to find a donor and Sandra doesn't—" Moran stopped. He felt his throat constrict.

"What about me, doctor. Maybe I'd be a match?" Hernandez

said. He looked at the astonished faces of Moran and the doctor. "Think of it as a Christmas present," Hernandez added with a smile that slowly widened into a grin.

CHAPTER 43

Moran sat with his feet up on the conference table, his brow creased, and his lips pressed together as he paged through *"The Destructive Narcissistic Behavior: Clinical and Diagnostic Implications,"* the book Sandra had been clutching when he'd found her lying unconscious on the floor of their living room. The fact that Lacy Wooden's file lay open on the coffee table and Sandra had this book in her hands meant that she could've been on to something. But it would have to wait until she regained consciousness; it was all gibberish to him. Moran looked at his watch yet again. He'd been at it for a long time, and a headache was beginning to push in behind his eyes like a spiny cactus.

While he concentrated on the book's mystifying contents, the door swung open and Milos Chang stepped into the room. In the AME's right hand were several pages rolled up in a rubber band. Chang's usual rumpled attire had been replaced by a double-breasted Armani over a pinstriped white shirt and a blue polka-dot tie. When Moran saw Chang, he let out a low, slow whistle.

"Got a hot date, Milos?" Moran said. He noticed a mischievous twinkle in the normally inscrutable AME's eyes.

Chang ignored the question and glanced down at the book on Moran's table. "Wait for the movie, the book's a bit dull."

Moran chuckled. "Sandra was holding this when I found her. You've read it?" Moran said. He took his feet off the table.

"A while back," Chang said. "Quite good, but not my thing. Too many patient interviews. I prefer my patients the way they are... dead and silent. How's Sandra doing?"

Moran smiled. "Hernandez was a match and Dr. Kruger has scheduled the bone marrow transplant for the end of the week."

Chang smiled and nodded approvingly.

Moran set the book down and stood up. "So tell me, why so spiffed up?"

Chang tapped the roll in his hand. He removed the rubber band and dropped it on the table. "I'm going to see my agent and figured I'd stop by and give you the DNA test results on Greg Saunders' saliva."

Moran eyed the pages and then looked up at the AME. "You've got an agent?"

"Never mind," Chang said. "Greg's DNA doesn't match that of the semen found in Lacy Wooden nor the bloodstains on Myer's shirt."

Moran frowned and sighed.

"Can't win them all," Chang said.

A wave of annoyance swept through Moran. "Forget about winning or losing. This is more like trying to put pantyhose on a gorilla."

"Cheer up. I sent Myer's skin sample and his shirt fragment to DNA Labs International in Deerfield Beach, Florida. If anyone can perform a test with those samples, it's them."

"They're that good?"

"DNA Labs has been known to get results where the FBI has failed," Chang said. He pressed his lips while he reached into his pocket and brought out a slip of paper. "Here." Chang offered the paper to Moran. "Being of an inquisitive nature, I did some research on the Internet regarding the possibility of a derringer with two different caliber barrels."

"Dexter Industries? Never heard of them," Moran said when he read the note.

"It's a small arms factory in Cicero, Illinois, which four years ago came out with a derringer, the Dexter Special. It had two different caliber barrels, one with a .22 and a .38 and the other with a .38 and a .45 barrel. Sold for under two hundred dollars, but it was discontinued last year."

Moran smiled. "Gee, Milos, there's no end to your talents— medical examiner, poet. And now, detective."

"I was simply trying to satisfy my curiosity. You were right. The angle of the entry wounds ruled out two shooters. It just kept gnawing at me. No big deal, just a couple clicks of the keyboard."

"I'll call them to get a copy of their sales records," Moran said.

"Good luck. From what I saw they're a small, family-run business, which means they probably have a sloppy filing system."

Moran's cell phone rang. When he saw the caller's ID his face hardened. It was Lieutenant Manny Friedman. Moran listened to what the detective started to say and quickly checked his watch. It was nearly five-thirty, which meant that the prisoners' bus for night court arraignments would be leaving soon. "Don't put him on the bus, I'm on my way," Moran said, and snapped the cell phone shut. He knew he had cut Friedman off, but getting to the 19th Precinct as fast as possible was more important than Manny Friedman's feelings.

CHAPTER 44

Moran and a hard-faced Alice Simms entered the Midtown North 19th's glass façade building and strode to the stationhouse's winding staircase. They made their way past several uniformed officers. Other detectives were coming and going on the stairs, and when Moran and Simms reached the second floor, Simms gestured to the sign with an arrow that pointed to the Detective's Squad Room at the end of the congested corridor. While the two detectives edged along the wall to keep out of the way of the human traffic, Simms turned to Moran. "Exactly what's between you and Friedman?"

"Two years ago there was a series of sniper killings in Brooklyn at the *Dream Pizza Parlor*. The M.O. had all the earmarks of another Hubert Singer attack. When Frank and I got there, Manny Friedman—he was a sergeant—was already at the scene. He not only resented us taking over and was abusive both to Frank and to one of his own men. I just pulled him aside and told him off. He was an obnoxious sergeant who's now an obnoxious lieutenant."

A moment later Moran and Simms entered the 19th's half-empty gray-walled squad room. Greenish fluorescent lighting lit the room; a cement floor and avocado-colored plaster walls made the space look more like a warehouse. Rows of disordered desks were occupied by bored looking detectives and plainclothesmen who sat puffing away at stale cigarettes—some typing and others staring at outmoded computer screens. The smoke in the room made it impossible to read the "No Smoking" sign on one of the walls.

"My, my. If it isn't the Caped Crusader and his new Robin," Friedman bellowed from the desk he was sitting on when he saw Moran and Simms.

"Sorry, about hanging up on you." Moran said. He and Simms moved forward. "I wanted to get here as fast as possible."

Simms gave Friedman a cold stare. "Where's the perp?"

Friedman returned the look. "If your boss hadn't hung up on me, I would've told him that the perp, Johnny Drago, aka, John Dragon, Jack Palmer and other assorted names, was shot and killed by one of our uniforms responding to a robbery in progress at a liquor store last night."

"What?" Moran exclaimed. "You brought me down here to tell me the guy's dead?"

"Hold your water, Moran," Friedman said. He gazed across the room and called out to a thin, young looking detective standing by the water cooler. "Hey, Charlie, bring me the Drago evidence bag from my desk." Friedman turned to his two visitors. "I got something you might be interested in."

Moran and Simms exchanged quizzical looks. The young detective trotted over, in his right hand holding an evidence bag with a diamond ring inside.

"We found the ring on Drago's pinky finger. I figure it's about three carats," Friedman said as he brought out a large emerald-cut diamond ring mounted on a platinum setting. He offered it to Moran. "It's a bit too feminine for my taste, but then again, Drago was the kind of guy that liked to show off."

While Moran and Simms examined the gem, Friedman stepped back and lit up a cigarette with a smug smile on his face. Simms furrowed her brow and studied the ring. She drew closer to Moran. "I remember this ring," she whispered. "It was one of the pieces of jewelry on Roth's computer that was sold to Yehoshua."

Friedman gave a slash-like smile. "I hope you don't mind my interrupting, but the reason I called you is because that ring once belonged to Lacy Wooden."

"How do you know that?" Moran said.

Friedman's smile quickly became a Cheshire cat grin. "The late Miss Wooden was not a stupid lady. She'd taken out an insurance policy on her jewelry with The Buckeye Insurance Company two months before her demise. They're located in Columbus, Ohio."

Moran's face flushed. "There's no record of it among her personal effects," he said.

"That's 'cause she bought the policy on the Internet," Friedman said, and eyed Moran with a smirk. He was enjoying his moment of triumph. The Midtown North detective reached over to the desktop behind him. "This came this morning," Friedman said. He handed Moran an envelope addressed to Lacy Wooden from Buckeye Insurance Company. "Lacy's building super brought it over; thought it strange that she'd still get mail. It's a reminder to renew her two-year jewelry insurance policy. There's a list attached of the covered items, in case she needed to make any changes to it."

While Moran and Simms read, Friedman added. "Notice that the last item on the list matches this ring."

Moran recalled that no jewelry had been found in her apartment. He bunched his eyebrows and handed back the fax to a gloating Friedman.

Moran and Simms shared a look—the jewelry Roth sold to his client known as Yehoshua was on Buckeye's list.

"I'd like a copy of this," Moran said.

Friedman lips became a smug smile. "Sure, no problem."

Simms peered at Friedman. "I'm curious. Why are you suddenly being so cooperative?"

Friedman wiggled his fingers and a smile flicked at the corner of his mouth. "It's the Holiday Season and I feel your pain," he said. He looked off for a moment and then returned his gaze to Moran, "I don't want the Commish to accuse me of hindering a murder inquiry. Only promise me that this time when you catch the perp you won't let him go."

Moran's face tightened and he flashed Friedman a hard look. The two lieutenants stared at each other with leaden eyes for a long moment. Moran's mouth felt dry. Any reference to Hubert Singer's escape still stung.

Friedman turned and leaned over the desk. When he straightened, he faced Moran. "Santa has another surprise for you," he said with a twinkle in his eyes. He handed Moran a two-page document. "It's Samantha Halpern's robbery report."

"Come again?" Moran and Simms said in unison.

Friedman grinned. "Thought that might get your attention. Six months ago, Samantha Halpern reported that their apartment had been burglarized. Among the missing objects was that ring. According the B&E squad, Mrs. Halpern said at the time that the ring had been a birthday gift from her husband." Friedman shrugged. "Interesting ain't it? Same ring, two women?" He winked at Moran. "You owe me."

* * *

Pelham, New York— Skeet & Trap Club

Samantha Halpern called out, "Pull!" and aimed her over-and-under Remington shotgun at the clay disc that flew across a gray sky. The two barrels thundered and she watched the untouched disc disappear over the hill and into the trees. Samantha frowned, removed her cushioned shell earmuffs and opened the gun's breach, ejecting two spent shells.

"I just can't stop thinking about who would've murdered Greg," she said. She turned and gazed at her sister who was standing next to a spring-operated disc launcher. "Aren't you upset? After all you were going to marry him."

"Of course, I'm upset, and I miss him terribly," Sabrina said. "But, you know what father always told us: '*Life must go on.*' Now concentrate on your aim... think of Mrs. Hodgkins, our English teacher at Ivey Academy and make believe you're shooting at the old bat."

Samantha emitted a school-girl giggle that was quickly followed by a frown. "You think this Lieutenant Moran's going to show George the photograph?"

Sabrina shrugged and unzipped her khaki shooting vest. "Don't know, but he'll probably will want to talk to you."

Samantha stared at her sister. "He's already called and left a message to get back to him. I just don't need this to get into the tabloids before I talk to George and explain that the damn photo was just a joke."

Sabrina smirked. "I've always found the tabloids to be a source of amusement."

"You would," Samantha shot back. "I for one like my privacy."

"C'mon, try again, and this time remember Mrs. Hodgkins," Sabrina said as she inserted another disc into the launcher.

Samantha reached for the shell bag on a wooden table next to her and hastily pawed through it. She then brought out two shells, reloaded the gun and snapped the breach closed. In one swift move, she placed the gun against her right shoulder and yelled, "Pull!"

The lower barrel thundered and the clay disc exploded in mid-air.

"There you go!" Sabrina called out.

Samantha smiled and ejected the spent shell. She gazed at her sister while her right hand hurriedly reached inside the ammunition bag and brought out two more shells. "That felt good!" she exclaimed and reloaded the gun, raised it to her shoulder, and called out again to Sabrina, "Pull!"

In a robotic move, Sabrina released the target and then shouted, "No... Wait, Sam!"

Too late. Samantha had squeezed the upper barrel's trigger and the breach exploded. She dropped to the ground, her face was mangled and her blonde hair was dyed a crimson red.

CHAPTER 45

Moran stood rooted to the flagstone pavement of George Halpern's penthouse terrace, tracing with his eyes York Avenue's southerly path until it became an invisible point in the horizon. The air was cold but the sun was bright. Puff clouds like suspended balls of cotton dotted the blue sky. The light coat of snow that had fallen during the night was rapidly melting, and he could hear the sound of water dripping from the penthouse's slate roof.

The lieutenant preferred being alone. Inside the senator's spacious condo, he felt superfluous among the guests, like the greenery in a floral arrangement. The small talk consisted mainly of posthumous cookie-cutter compliments about Samantha—*"She was so generous"; "We'll miss her terribly"; "There'll never be another one like her"* etc, etc.

The insincerity of it all was too much for Moran. It also hit too close to home, reminding him of his own possible destiny. *Am I going to end up alone?* The detective's spirit suddenly dimmed and chilled, as the unthinkable entered his mind—the thought of losing Sandra cut through him like a blade of ice.

Samantha's funeral that morning had been at her family's mausoleum at Trinity Church Cemetery on Riverside Drive where generations of Van Dammes had been laid to rest since colonial days. While Moran walked among the mourners along the cobbled walkway, he noted some of the famous names on the gravestones: John James Audubon, which was only fitting since the cemetery was on the site where his home had once stood, John Jacob Astor;

and Clement Clark Moore, author of *'Twas the Night Before Christmas.*

Deathstyles of the rich and famous, Moran reflected when he gazed up at the baroque stone building that overlooked the Hudson River with the name Van Damme chiseled in gothic letters over the bronze door. Despite the fact that the Governor, Mayor Garner, Police Commissioner Newbury and other dignitaries were among the mourners, Halpern had managed to prevent it from becoming the media spectacle that normally would've accompanied the death of a member of one of New York's most venerable families.

From inside the senator's condo, the rustle and rumble of animated conversations went unnoticed by Moran. His thoughts lingered on the bone marrow transplant scheduled for the next morning. He smiled inwardly when he recalled Hernandez kidding Sandra, *"You do realize from now on you and I are blood related—your blood will be my blood."* He was referring to the fact that bone marrow transplant recipients' blood has the same DNA as the donor.

Moran's thoughts turned to Halpern's stone face during the funeral, with its sunken eyes and pasty complexion. The detective hoped with all his heart that he would never have to walk in the senator's shoes. He felt like a cartoon character who's run past the edge of a cliff and keeps on pumping his legs in midair for fear of stopping and plunging into the abyss.

"It was all my fault," a woman whimpered over the staccato clicking of high heels. When Moran turned, he saw Sabrina Van Damme walking slowly toward him. Dressed in a black, knee-length jacket dress and a matching hat on her head she walked with a slight stoop, her face haggard. Sabrina was a shadow of the self-assured, arrogant woman he had met at the Riverdale estate.

"What do you mean?" Moran said.

Sabrina lowered her gaze and fingered the fringe of the jacket. She raised her moist eyes and looked off at the skyline. "I should've checked to make sure Sam hadn't mixed the cartridges," she said. She shifted her gaze to Moran. Her eyes were deadened, like two windows where there had been light, but now there were only shadows. "Sam wasn't the most careful of shooters, always in a hurry. About a year ago, the same thing almost happened. She emptied a box of 12 gauge shells into her ammo bag forgetting that the previous week she had been shooting with a 20-gauge gun. Sam almost inserted a 12-gauge shell behind the 20-gauge one in the barrel. Luckily when I reached inside the bag to reload I spotted the mistake."

Moran nodded and stepped closer to the bereaved sister. "According to the police and coroner's report it was an accident. You can't blame yourself. I really feel bad for Senator Halpern. It's hard enough to lose a wife, but to also lose a child—"

Sabrina's mouth gaped. "Sam was pregnant?"

Moran looked surprised. "You didn't know?"

A stunned Sabrina uttered, "No."

Moran rubbed his brow. "The coroner's report said she was three-and-a-half months along. Didn't she or your brother-in-law tell you?"

Sabrina looked past Moran and smiled tightly. "I guess they wanted to surprise me." Her tone was unconvincing.

Halpern then appeared at the doorway. "There you are, Sabrina." He strode toward his sister-in-law. "I've been looking for you all over the place." When he reached his sister-in-law, he put his hands on her shoulders and gave Moran a sad side-glance.

"Come, let's go back inside," Halpern whispered. Sabrina turned slowly and gazed up at him. "We need to talk, George," she said in a low but stern voice.

Moran watched the two walk back inside the condo, and he turned away with an uneasy feeling. It didn't make sense for Halpern, a man approaching middle-age, not to tell his sister-in-law that after years of marriage he was now going to be a father. And it was even stranger for Samantha not to have told her sister. Moran noted that Sabrina's reaction was one of controlled anger rather than surprise. He also recalled Friedman's words: *"Same ring, two women."*

Moran's mobile phone rang. It was Frank Hernandez.

"Tell me you figured out Greg's cell phone password," Moran said.

There was a moment of silence on the other end and then Hernandez said, "No, but I just got a call back from Verizon. There were no calls to or from Paul Myer's land or cell phone to Mexico or any other country."

"Myer was not a member of the New York Athletic Club, so we know Rosario Mendez wasn't calling him," Moran said. He turned and stared out at the horizon while the wheels of his mind turned. "Myer was used as a patsy to make it look as if he was the one who had transferred the ten mil to Mexico."

"However," Hernandez said, "there is a familiar name in that membership booklet."

"Right," Moran said. He turned around and looked at the guests inside Halpern's penthouse. The cop's gaze zeroed in on a six-foot tall, silver-haired man with strong features in the center of the room. He was surrounded by people eager to speak to him. It was Alan Morrison, and the fact that his host's wife had just been buried didn't stop the mogul banker from holding forth and networking.

"And, I'm looking at him right now," Moran said, and turned away toward the skyline.

CHAPTER 46

When Robert Darcey stepped out of the elevator, he heard the loud ranting of his brother's voice coming from inside his apartment. The cop loped toward his apartment. "Goddammit!! Where the hell is it? I bet you hid it, you... you sonuvabitch!" could be heard through the closed door—Eddie was having another episode.

A moment later, the door swung open and a short, muscular dark-skinned Filipino man with a buzz-cut rushed out of the apartment and bumped into Darcey.

"You handle him, I'm outta here. You couldn't pay me enough to take care of that lunatic! He should be locked up." The man marched past a stunned Darcey toward the emergency stairway.

"Hey, wait!" Darcey called out, but the man jerked open the stairwell door and disappeared. The detective turned and started to enter his apartment. The sound of a door opening from across the hallway made him turn around.

"It's been going on like that for more than an hour," said a woman with an unremarkable saggy face. She wore a windowpane pattern robe, puff slippers on her feet and her gray hair up in curlers. "That man was right, your brother needs to be institutionalized. I think that—"

"I'll handle it, Mrs. Robins, and I'm sorry for the disturbance. It won't happen again."

Mrs. Robins folded her arms under her zaftig breasts and grunted. "Better not, or next time I'll call the cops."

Darcey shot the neighbor a hard look and jammed his index

finger into his chest. "They're already here... remember?" He entered his place and slammed the door shut.

When he stepped into the living room, his eyes widened and he felt beads of sweat begin to form on his brow. He quickly inventoried the space: the sofa's cushions were sprawled slapdash across the room, the small bookshelf near the window radiator was empty, its contents on the carpet in a chaotic pile. From Eddie's bedroom, he could hear the ongoing incoherent ranting. Darcey wrinkled his nose at the stale odor that came from the heap of cigarette butts that lay in an ashtray. He moved to the window and opened it.

Cold fear washed over Darcey as he marched toward his brother's room. Suddenly the door was flung open and Eddie, in a T-shirt and jeans, tramped out, his hair mussed and his face flushed. Darcey grabbed his brother's arm but Eddie jerked free.

"Let go," Eddie barked. "Can't you see what time it is? The program's about to start, and I still can't find the friggin' remote!" Eddie said and continued into the living room.

"What program?" Darcey asked while he followed his brother.

Eddie whirled around, his eyes red and glaring as he headed into the kitchen. "Home Shopping Network, they're havin' a special on men's jewelry—rings, watches, bracelets, you name it. I can't miss this!" Eddie said.

Darcey realized that there were sharp objects in the kitchen. In Eddie's present state of mind, anything could happen. The detective reached for the handcuffs that hung from his belt and ran into the kitchen. When he entered, he saw Eddie opening drawers and starting to empty their contents onto the linoleum floor. The detective leapt forward, grabbed his brother's left arm, and snapped one end of the cuffs on the left wrist and then rapidly did the same to the other wrist. With his arms cuffed behind him, Eddie looked at his brother with a gaze of betrayal.

"You're just like all the rest of them, Bobby. You never liked me because I was always smarter than you!" Eddie bellowed.

Darcey stared at his brother. "Just sit down and shut the hell up. I'll look for the goddamn remote," he said and marched out of the kitchen.

At that moment, like a veil being lifted, Robert Darcey saw that what he had been putting off could longer be denied. He moved to the phone on the end table next to the sofa. Suddenly, from the corner of his eye, he caught a glimpse of a dark plastic object that stuck out from under the sofa—it was the remote. He gave it a quick kick and sent it farther under the sofa, then dialed 9-1-1. From the kitchen, he could hear Eddie sniffling.

"I need an ambulance right away," Darcey told the operator.

CHAPTER 47

The door to Room 1369 slid open and Dr. Kruger, garbed in a protective gown, stepped into the corridor that was lined on both sides with other sterile glass paneled rooms. To safeguard the sterile environment no one was permitted inside the rooms without a protective gown, gloves and mask.

The overhead sign of the archway where Moran paced up and down read: PROTECTIVE ISOLATION UNIT—the area where bone marrow transplant patients, or BMT's, as they were known to the staff, were kept. When Moran saw the doctor, he moistened his upper lip and stepped toward him. "How is she?"

The doctor removed his surgical mask, wiped the plastic shower cap from his head and slipped off his latex gloves.

"Everything went fine," Dr. Kruger said. "She's going to need—" The swish of the room's curtain being opened from the inside startled the doctor and Moran.

"One moment, please," Moran said, and fixed his eyes on his wife. She laid in bed attached to the IV's that had carried Hernandez's harvested bone marrow into her blood system. Several nurses were busy monitoring the IV and the three digital monitors at the side of the bed.

Sandra's tired looking eyes met Moran's and she gave him a brave wink accompanied by a weak smile. The detective wiggled his fingers at her, and he felt an icicle of fear in his gut.

"What happens next?" Moran asked.

"Your wife needs to be totally isolated for the next four to eight weeks until the new bone marrow migrates through her system into the cavities of the large bones—set up housekeeping if you will. We call it *engrafting*. Her body should then start to produce its own normal blood cells. In the meantime, during your limited visits you will need to wear head to toe protective clothing including footwear covers and a full facial plastic guard. There can be absolutely no risk of contamination," the doctor said.

Moran was silent for a moment; then he tilted his head toward Sandra. "She looks awfully weak," the detective said.

Dr. Kruger's gaze caught Moran's face and the dread in his eyes. "And I'm afraid that will continue to be the case for the next several weeks," the doctor said, "She'll experience nausea, vomiting, fever, diarrhea, and extreme weakness for a few days, but at the end of it all she'll be fine."

Moran wiped his mouth with the palm of his hand and turned his gaze to Sandra.

"One more thing," the doctor said. "No flowers, fruit baskets, or plants since they may carry fungi and bacteria that pose a risk of infection."

Moran nodded. "How's my sergeant doing?"

Dr. Kruger grinned. "He can go home tomorrow morning. After extracting marrow from his rear hip bone he's going to feel as if he landed hard on a sheet of ice."

"I gather you took a big amount from him."

"About two quarts worth of marrow and blood."

"Isn't that a lot?" Moran said.

Dr. Kruger briskly shook his head. "It's only two-percent of a person's bone marrow."

A nurse from inside Sandra's room tapped on the room's window and motioned for Dr. Kruger to come inside. After the doctor entered the room, the corridor felt small and stifling to Moran. He stole a glance at his watch—2:45 p.m.

* * *

"It's 2:45," Victor Hernandez said in a low tone to his daughter-in-law as he gazed at his watch. Clad in a navy-blue double-breasted suit over a light blue shirt and a blood-red tie, he blended in with the stodgy staff of the New York Athletic Club. "You set?"

Pilar fidgeted with the wireless microphone that was inserted in the buttonhole of her black velvet pantsuit. A single-strand pearl necklace over a white silk blouse rounded out her ensemble. She ran an anxious hand through her hair and moistened her lips.

"What wives do for their spouses," Pilar said.

"And you're lovin' every minute of it."

"I look like a cow in this outfit," Pilar said.

"Stop it, you're not showing." Victor replied.

Pilar pouted slightly. "You sure?"

"You're not even four months pregnant. Ready?" Victor said patiently.

Pilar tugged at her jacket and adjusted the collar of her blouse. "Whenever you are," she responded, her voice steady.

Victor stood straight and flattened his tie with the palm of his hand. "I think it's time the New York Athletic Club's *new* maitre d' made his entrance," he said.

"Remember, it's not Easter... don't be a ham," Pilar said in a low voice. She spoke into the microphone and informed Darcey and Simms, who were around one of the hallway's corners, that Victor was about to go into the dining room.

At a white-clothed table, Alan Morrison, wearing a brown cashmere sports jacket and an open-collared shirt, sat across from a pudgy middle-aged man with round shoulders who wolfed down large helpings of his turkey sandwich. Morrison picked at his Caesar salad. The two were engrossed in a deep discussion over the effect of the NAFTA trade agreement on the future banking in South America.

"I think the administration has overestimated the potential buying power of the average consumer in the region," said the pudgy man through a mouthful of turkey.

Victor's approaching footsteps were muffled by the cream-colored carpet, and as he neared, he could hear the men.

"I can't agree with that assessment, Tom," Morrison interjected. He pointed his fork at the man. "The international banking community doesn't—"

"I'm sorry, sir," Victor Hernandez said in a stilted tone. "But there's a—"

Morrison looked up and gave the intruder a razor sharp stare. "And you are?"

"Luis, I'm new and I've just come on duty, sir," Victor said. "There's a Miss Rosario Mendez in the hallway asking for you."

The words froze the banker. Morrison flicked his eyes at his luncheon companion and then slowly set his fork down. His normally sallow face was now a white sheet. When Victor and Morrison emerged from the dining room into the hallway, Victor pointed to a young woman who stood near a corner, her back to the banker.

"There she is, sir," Victor said.

On cue, Pilar whirled around and gave Morrison a warm smile. "There you are, sweetie," she cooed.

Alan Morrison stopped and stared at Pilar with a surprised expression. "You're not Rosario Mendez," he blurted out, and then his face reddened. He quickly added, "I mean—"

Darcey and Simms materialized from behind Pilar and flashed their badges at the surprised banker.

"NYPD," Simms announced. The two detectives started toward Morrison, who stood silent. Victor thought he could hear the hoof beats of anxiety and apprehension galloping through Morrison's mind. The banker stiffened and his face blanched. He wiped his forehead with the palm of his hand and started to gasp. For a brief instant, Victor felt sorry for the guy.

The trap that Moran and Hernandez set had worked. If Morrison realized that Pilar was not Rosario Mendez, that confirmed what they had suspected—that Morrison and Rosario Mendez were in cahoots.

Morrison's eyes fluttered, and he bolted to his right. He started to run toward the dining room when Pilar stepped to her side and extended her foot. Alan Morrison flew through the air with outstretched arms like a diver coming off a high board. The sharp crack of bone striking the marble floor echoed through the hallway. Morrison lay face down and emitted a soulful groan, then tried to hoist himself up with his elbows.

"Allow me, sir," Victor Hernandez said, extending a hand to Morrison.

"Get away from me, you cretin!" the banker growled. His eyes were ablaze as he wiped away the thin rivulet of blood that trickled from a cut above his eyebrow.

"Whatever you say, sir," Victor said in his adopted clipped voice. He stepped back and made way for Darcey and Simms, who were rushing toward the disgraced banker.

When Simms finished reading Morrison his Miranda rights, she added, "You're under arrest on suspicion of grand larceny, wire, and banking fraud."

While a chagrined and humbled Morrison was being led away, Victor and Pilar winked at each other and gave themselves a congratulatory high-five.

"That was quick thinking," Victor said, and gave his daughter-in-law an encouraging squeeze on the shoulder.

"I always try to put my best foot forward," Pilar said with a half smile. "You weren't too bad yourself. You should apply for the position."

Victor loosened his tie and unbuttoned his jacket. "No way. *El Cheapo* didn't even give me a tip."

Chapter 48

"Is your bread not done, Moran?" Commissioner Newbury said with a thickened Southern accent. His teeth clenched a half-smoked Dutch Master and slapped his desk—the face flushed.

"No, I'm not nuts," Moran shot back. "I—"

A fuming Newbury would have none of it as he continued his tirade. "How could you and Sergeant Hernandez involve civilians in a sting operation? What if someone had gotten hurt? That was dumber than a bag of hammers," Newbury concluded—another folksy expression. He spun away from his desk and gazed out the window that overlooked Mott Street and the Brooklyn Bridge. "They were right about you. You're an arrogant, *go-it-alone* cop who thinks rules don't matter," he said over his shoulder.

Moran stared at the back of Newbury's head—the neck muscles tight, the ears red. A thick cloud of cigar smoke circled over the commissioner's head.

"I went with my gut and I was right. Besides, there was absolutely no risk to the operation, so what's the big deal?" Moran said.

"I rest my case," Newbury said and turned to the detective. "The NYPD does not outsource. You got that?"

Moran stepped toward the irate Newbury. "Not only is Morrison a longstanding member of the New York Athletic Club, but he's also on their board. Using an undercover cop or even one of the club's people would've meant running the risk that the suspect would've been tipped off and—"

Newbury gave Moran a hard look. "That's the Moran way of doing things, not the NYPD way." He stormed past Moran. "If you and Hernandez had at least let me in on it maybe—"

Moran glanced toward the window. He realized that it all came down to Newbury's pride. The lieutenant gave an apologetic shrug. "I'm sorry… it was my fault, not Sergeant Hernandez's. The fact is we got in and made the arrest without a fuss," Moran said. His lips formed a hint of a smile. "You might say it was '*all of the flavor and none of the calories.*' "

Newbury unplugged the cigar from his mouth and blew out smoke from the corner of his mouth. "I'm not amused," he said as he walked to his desk. Standing over a pile of correspondence, the commissioner leaned in, rested his fingertips on the desktop and took a breath. "I suppose all's well that ends all," Newbury drawled. "Morrison confessed this morning, sweating like a whore in church. He admitted to having used Paul Myer's computer to make the transfers to the Banco de Mexico account. He also explained how he had met Rosario Mendez some years ago when she did a brief stint at the bank after graduating from Columbia. Turns out they were an item for a while."

"Which accounts for his trips to Mexico City," Moran said. "And the fact that Victor Hernandez recognized him as the man Rosario Mendez met with at his restaurant. The story is as old as the hills, older man meets much younger woman and losses all sense of propriety, yada-yada-yada."

Newbury sat down . "What I don't get is why Morrison went to Shilling and insisted on his help?"

"To allay suspicion," Moran said. "He felt that the scheme was so foolproof that no one would ever discover that Rosario Mendez and the elusive Miss Torres were one and the same."

"Any progress in finding her?" Newbury asked.

Moran shook his head. "The Mexican Police can't locate her."

Newbury shrugged gravely. "*Humph.* How ironic. Morrison plans and executes it and will do time, while his cohort disappears with the loot. Like something out of a Hitchcock movie." He narrowed his eyebrows and peered at Moran. "Any progress on my niece's case?" The tone was quiet.

Moran froze, a trickle of apprehension running down his back. It was a question he had been trying to avoid. He started to pace as he weighed whether or not to reveal to the commissioner his new suspicions.

"Is there a problem I should know about?" Newbury asked.

Moran turned, his face screwed on tight. "Sabrina Van Damme."

"What?"

Moran raised a hand, a forefinger extended. "Hear me out. One, Sabrina had motive. She disliked Lacy and was jealous of your niece's relationship with Greg." Moran brought up another finger, "Two, Sabrina owns a motorcycle similar to the one Earl saw outside Chiu's club." Another finger went up. "Three, Sabrina owns a motorcycle suit similar to the one Paul Myer and Earl described. Then there are the letters SA found on Chiu's notepad— the first two letters of Sabrina's name."

"But why kill Myer and Chiu?"

"She could've killed Paul because she feared he might've recognized her coming out of Lacy's apartment. Remember that he said that he thought he recognized something about that person. As far as Chiu's concerned, Sabrina could easily have been the mystery woman who appeared at the club and waited for Lacy."

Newbury grunted. "Not good. Sabrina belongs to one of the city's oldest and richest families," the commissioner said and cast Moran a sharp look. "What about the semen?"

Moran looked down at his shoes and slowly shook his head. "Could've been planted. The DNA didn't match Greg Saunders. As for the gun, I might have a lead."

"Just make sure Sabrina doesn't give us the slip, like what happened with—" Newbury stopped. "Well, you know what I mean."

The lieutenant bristled and felt the muscles in his neck tighten. "She won't," Moran said dryly. The Hubert Singer incident was like a ghost that still haunted everyone.

CHAPTER 49

The rose on the back of the helmet glowed a bright red, as the orange light of the rising winter sun struck it. The rider on the powerful black motorcycle zigzagged and squeezed the bike with calm expertise past the heavy Staten Island truck traffic that plagued the Verrazzano-Narrows Bridge at that early hour.

The sleek motorcycle sped along Staten Island's main thoroughfare, Hylan Boulevard, past rows of strip malls wedged in between new and expensive looking restaurants, supermarkets and shops. The rider's eyes swept the area. New construction had replaced the vacant lots that once dotted the boulevard. In the last ten years, the city's stepchild had become more sophisticated, more urbanized. It was making an effort to lose the stigma of the *boonies* or the *sticks,* the words used by Manhattanites when they referred to Richmond County.

The rider tried several times to pass a van that crept along at the speed of molasses oozing uphill. Every time the bike tried to pass, the van increased its speed and changed lanes to block the motorcycle. Frustrated, the rider fed the bike gas, roared past the van, and looked up at the van's driver—a sour-looking old man who glared at the rider and leaned on the horn.

The cyclist held tight to the handlebars as the tires edged into the left lane while he concentrated on steering the expensive machine. Suddenly, the syncopated wail of a siren approaching from behind made the rider flick his eyes at the side view mirror. A motorcycle cop, with its red, blue, and white lights flashing, was barreling toward him. The rider glanced at his speedometer. It read: 70 mph—*shit!* The speed limit was 35.

Beads of sweat began to slide down the rider's back and the forehead prickled with perspiration. The last thing the stranger needed was to be stopped by a cop. The biker glanced once more into the sideview mirror and slipped into the right lane while abruptly lowering his speed. At that moment, the cop raced past, turned, waved his arm signaling to slow it down, and continued up the boulevard. The motorcyclist let out a breath of relief—the crisis had passed.

Fifteen minutes later, the motorcycle pulled up under the "First Month Free" billboard of the Eltingville Storage Facility. The rider dismounted and took off his helmet. The early morning light cast a shadow on the face that prevented the nearby security cameras from identifying it. From his jacket's side pocket the biker drew out a key and inserted it into the lock at the foot of a large garage-style door. The rider pushed up and lugged the black motorcycle inside the storage area.

A frayed black-and-red rug with an Oriental pattern covered the cement slab floor, and against one of the aluminum walls of the corrugated roofed structure, sat a dust-covered green trunk. The stranger quickly peeled off the black leather suit, rolled it into a bundle, and dropped it inside the trunk. The helmet was tossed in alongside the suit. The stranger then added a small parcel wrapped in oilskin. Next, the figure extracted a duffle bag from inside the trunk and quickly changed into blue jeans and a cable knit sweater.

'*Moran's digging deeper and deeper. Time to ditch everything,*' the stranger mused and closed the lid.

CHAPTER 50

Moran slowly returned the receiver to its cradle. He gave the half-eaten takeout carton of almond spicy tuna a bored look, tossed the wooden chopsticks on the table, and sighed. He had just finished speaking with Sandra. She seemed stronger and cheerier, which in a strange way created mixed feelings in Moran—it lifted his spirits but made him miss her even more.

The sudden jangle of the phone startled Moran out of his reverie. When he answered, the voice on the other end had a Midwest nasal twang and belonged to Clarence Dexter, founder and owner of Dexter Industries. The man apologized for not having returned Moran's call two weeks ago, and went on to explain that they had discontinued the Dexter Special with two different caliber barrels due to poor sales. "Only four firearms dealers—one in Los Angeles, Seattle, Miami and Sandusky, Ohio—had placed orders," he added.

While he listened, Moran could hear the man's fingers tapping a computer keyboard.

"Here they are," Dexter finally said, and rattled off the dealers' names and addresses like a waiter going through the specials of the day.

The derringers were assembled only by special order and only eight had been shipped—three to a Los Angeles firearms store; three more to a dealer in Seattle; one to a Miami store; and the last one to the Lake Erie Firearms Store in Sandusky, Ohio. Clarence Dexter also provided Moran with the serial numbers.

"Mr. Dexter, did you by any chance test fire the derringers after they were made?"

"Eh... yes, as a matter of fact we did. Because they're handmade, we tested each one before shipping. We keep the results on file."

"Could you send me copies?" Moran said.

Dexter enthusiastically agreed, and when Moran hung up, he felt that at last there was a break in the case. At least enough of a crack to allow a small wedge of light into an otherwise dark enigma. The detective quickly came to the conclusion that because federal laws and postal regulations forbade the sale of firearms across state lines, the purchasers of the derringers had to be residents of California, Washington, Florida and Ohio. The thought was rapidly interrupted by the realization that there was also the possibility of sales at gun shows or by private parties.

Moran resuscitated his old IBM Selectric from the maintenance closet and spent the next hour typing out requisition forms for each of the dealers' sales records regarding the Dexter Special. The lieutenant's method of typing was hunt-and-peck—*hunt... hunt... hunt and then peck.* No one used a typewriter these days. Everything was done by computer, but for James Francis Moran that was not an option. His knowledge of computers was limited to browsing through official law enforcement sites that were linked with the stroke of a key.

When Moran faxed the requisition forms, an uneasy thought entered his mind. One of the addresses seemed vaguely familiar. *Why?* He moved to the window and cracked it open. The incoming brisk air bathed his face and he stretched his aching leg—lately the pain was more acute and with increased regularity. *Maybe Chang was right, it was time to see the doctor.* He considered it for an instant, and then quickly pushed the thought aside.

Moran's gaze floated aimlessly over the city, which was covered by a gray sky as his mind delved into its deepest crevices. Why did that address seem so familiar? Then, with the abruptness of a snapped shoelace, it came to him—it was something either Hernandez, Darcey or Simms had mentioned.

What the hell was it?

A frustrated Moran shut the window and returned to his desk. He picked up and reread Samantha Halpern's burglary report while he worked the chopsticks and occasionally dropped a cube of tuna into his mouth, the tuna that by now tasted more vulcanized than cooked. The only item that matched the list on Lacy's insurance list was the diamond ring. *So what the hell happened to the rest of Lacy's jewelry?* The question kept gnawing at the lieutenant while he chewed.

Moran cast a dispirited glance at the invitation to the Annual Christmas Red Cross Gala fundraiser that anyone who was somebody or anyone who wanted to be somebody, attended. Because of his rank and position, Moran was obligated to attend, although he didn't relish going alone.

The office door swung open and when Moran raised his eyes, he saw a cheerless, weary looking Simms shuffle into the office.

"No bad news while I'm eating dead fish," Moran mumbled through a mouthful of tuna. "How was Albany?"

"The same as when you were there, cold and gray," Simms deadpanned. She removed her scarf and stuffed it inside her anorak's pocket. "You were—"

"Before you go on, let me run something by you," Moran said. He handed Simms the list of gun dealers. "Take a look at this, and tell me if any of those places rings a bell."

A bemused Simms narrowed her eyes and scanned the list. When she finished she shook her head and handed the list back to Moran. "No, why?"

Moran told her of his conversation with Clarence Dexter. "I just have the feeling that one of these cities sounds familiar. Anyway, what'd you find out?"

Simms slipped off her anorak and tossed it over one of the chairs. "Your hunch paid off. After traipsing all over Albany and visiting every rent-a-car place in the city, I finally located an out of the way, small independent car rental agency, The Hudson River Car Rental. And guess what? The evening before the Council of Economic Growth dinner at the Clarion Hotel, Halpern rented a car and returned it the next day around three in the afternoon. The dinner wasn't until eight that night and the mileage on the car was equivalent to a round trip to Manhattan. In fact, Senator Halpern is one of their most valued customers. And there's something else I thought was interesting. The agency has a copy of Halpern's driver's license on file. It's a Class DM."

"Which means he can also drive a motorcycle," Moran said.

"And, he had access to his wife's Harley," Simms dropped in.

Moran remained silent for a long moment while he processed the new information. He finally said, "Sabrina said her sister gave Halpern a motorcycle outfit," as Moran massaged his right temple. "He certainly had enough time to drive down here and get back in time for the dinner at the Clarion."

The lieutenant grimaced and plopped himself down into one of the chairs. He let out a breath while he stretched the offending leg. "Of course, we have no proof that Halpern drove into the city that night," he said through gritted teeth.

"You want something for the pain?"

Moran shook his head. "This too shall pass," he said. "If Halpern secretly drove into New York, he could've met with Lacy and taken back the jewelry."

"Why would he?" Simms asked.

Moran spread his hands, turned the palms up. "A lover's quarrel?"

"So where is it?" Simms asked.

"He might still have it stashed somewhere," Moran said.

Simms lowered and shook her head. "I just find it hard to believe that Halpern's a killer. I mean he seems so impeccable and believable."

Moran peered at the cop. "One of the things that differentiates us from animals is our ability to lie. Halpern's a savvy politician. Lying comes with the job. I'm going to have to start charging you tuition, Alice," he said. "Until proved otherwise, everyone's a suspect in a murder investigation. We'll need a DNA sample from Senator Halpern."

Simms placed her hands on her hips. "Don't be lookin' at me, I'm not gonna stick my fingers in that man's mouth," she said with a mock street attitude.

Moran chortled. "I think we can come up with something less invasive."

Simms folded her arms across her chest. "But why would he kill Lacy with that kind of violence?"

Moran gave the detective a patient look. "Tuition's going to go up this semester, Detective Simms," Moran said. "What if Lacy was putting the squeeze on him... threatening to tell Samantha? The commissioner's niece was not exactly Snow White and our *'pillar of the community,'* the senator, has political ambitions that would have been put at risk. But, there's something else I want checked out..." Moran's voice trailed off when he heard the door open.

His eyes darted toward the entrance and brightened when he saw Darcey enter. Moran stepped forward. "Just in time," Moran said, and handed Darcey the dealers' list. "Take a look at this and tell me if any of these places sounds familiar."

When Darcey finished going over the list of gun stores he raised his eyes at Moran and shrugged lightly. "Sorry, no."

Moran pointed his forefinger at the young cop. "You and I are going to the Red Cross fundraiser at the Waldorf this evening."

"What?" Darcey blurted, a wide grin on his face. "I can't believe this—"

"Well, pinch yourself and before you get all mushy-eyed and thank me let me clue you in... you're not going as a guest."

CHAPTER 51

Moran weaved his way through the gathering of New York City's powerbrokers and their female companions in the Waldorf's two-tiered Grand Ballroom. He ignored the side-glances and turned heads that cast disdainful looks at him. The head of the NYPD Cold Case unit was the only man not wearing a tuxedo at the Annual Christmas Red Cross fundraiser.

Moran had never owned a tuxedo. Despite Sandra's pleas, the idea of renting one never appealed to him—'*who would want to wear a suit worn by God knows how many strangers?*' was his philosophy. Moran's faithful standard, a three-year-old black double-breasted Calvin Klein suit he'd purchased at a Men's Wearhouse clearance sale was good enough.

While he snaked through the crowd, he took in the room with its shiny floor and the two tiers of balconies of private booths and a view of the action down on the dance floor. The orchestra at one end of the ballroom played big band music that reminded Moran of an old Hollywood extravaganza film.

Over the giggles of women in silk and satin dresses, who daintily sipped champagne and the occasional laughter of cigar-puffing middle-aged men, Moran picked up inane snippets of conversations while he made his way to his goal.

"*We're going to Switzerland for the New Year to get in some skiing,*" a short, bald man who was as wide as he was tall told his female companion. She was, in Moran's opinion, an example of the Three O's Rule—Overdressed, Overweight, and Over-made-up. Her face looked like an Estee Lauder sample box.

A moment later, Moran reached the finish line--a long table covered with a white linen cloth. On it, an extensive selection of alcoholic beverages and a varied selection of appetizers were being served by a team of tuxedo-clad waiters. Moran ordered a Chivas Regal on ice with a splash of water. While he waited for his drink, his gaze moved over the guests. When his drink arrived, Moran took a sip and from the corner of his eye, he caught a glimpse of Halpern standing in a corner speaking heatedly with Sabrina Van Damme. She was gesticulating wildly, waving her arms like helicopter blades. When the senator put his hand on her shoulder, she slapped him and stormed off.

A more than curious Moran moved quickly along the edge of the crowded room toward Halpern while he craned his head over the throng. The lieutenant's lips formed a thin smile when he spotted an uncomfortable-looking Darcey, in a waiter's uniform, carrying a tray of drinks. The cop/waiter was moving toward Halpern while guests stopped him for drinks.

When Darcey's gaze finally met Moran's, the two cops nodded to each other.

"Your sister-in-law sure packs a wallop," Moran said when he reached the senator. Halpern stood like a sequoia with his fingers wrapped around a half-empty tumbler of scotch-on-the-rocks. He whirled around and stared at the Moran. "Oh, it's you." Halpern smiled weakly. "Sabrina can be difficult at times."

"I got the feeling at your place she wasn't too thrilled to learn that Samantha was pregnant," Moran said in a neutral tone.

The senator blinked and his face tightened. It happened in a wink—Halpern's right cheek had twitched. Moran narrowed his eyebrows as he realized his words had hit a soft spot.

Finally, Halpern swallowed hard. "I find that comment offensive, Lieutenant."

Moran smiled easily. "Oh, I don't know. The fact that you didn't tell Sabrina you and Samantha were finally going to be parents strikes me as a bit odd. Most people would be shouting it from the rooftops," the detective said and drained his glass.

Halpern jerked his thumb at Moran's empty tumbler. "Just how many of those have you had?"

Darcey suddenly backed into Halpern, and the blow caused the senator to spill his drink over his hand. Halpern spun around. "You clumsy fool!"

"I'm sorry," Darcey said, and began to dry the senator's hand with a napkin. "Let me get you another drink, sir," he said. Darcey quickly took Halpern's drink and planted another one in the senator's hand. Before Halpern could react, Darcey had turned and disappeared into the crowd. Halpern shrugged, but when he turned, Moran had also vanished.

CHAPTER 52

The shaft of diffused light that streamed through the window washed over the open pages of the *Civil Procedures* textbook and fell on Hernandez's tight face. He grimaced as he shifted his weight in the hard swivel chair and he tried to ignore the dull pain in his right buttock. Hernandez raised his eyes and glanced at the rapidly darkening clouds as the unseen sun headed for its appointed rendezvous with the western horizon. Hernandez noticed the tiny snowflakes that gently blew past the window—maybe there would be a white Christmas this year. Then the sergeant slowly let out some air and returned to the dull, but necessary reading.

He had chosen to study in the office after everyone had left because concentrating at home was impossible with Frankie, Jr. running around the apartment, playing Cowboys and Indians, and a pregnant Pilar joining in.

The reconciliation with his father and getting to know the man had turned Hernandez's fears of not being able to cope with a second child into eagerness. The idea of realizing the American dream of a home and family in the suburbs didn't seem so distant now.

Hernandez rubbed his eyes with the knuckles of his forefingers and firmly planted his elbows on the desk. The determined sergeant hunched over the pages and murmured the complex wording of the statutes that pertained to the filing of civil actions. The sound of an incoming fax rudely interrupted him. He gave the machine in the corner an impatient look. "Now what?" he said as he got to his feet and strode to the machine. The fax was from the

Lake Erie Firearms Store in Sandusky, Ohio.

He read the fax's contents: one Dexter Special derringer had been sold four years ago and it was to a Douglas Schloessman. The fax gave the customer's age as a sixty-six year old and provided his address and the gun's serial number. When Hernandez returned to his desk, he dropped the fax on the table and moved his gaze to the stack of other faxes that had been received from the Los Angeles, Seattle, and Miami dealers. They indicated that the purchasers were males ranging in age from the early thirties to mid-seventies.

Moran had made a black marker notation on each of the Los Angeles, Seattle, and Miami faxes: *Joseph Carnes, Los Angeles, seventy-four—retired; Robert Osbourne, Seattle, thirty-two—car salesman; Marvin Schuyler, Miami, forty-seven--a real estate developer.*

Hernandez grabbed a stack of Post-Its that lay next to the faxes and scribbled *"Contact the ATF"* and affixed it to the new fax. Then he telephoned Dexter Industries. After the fifth ring, the company's answering machine picked up with the standard '*no-one-is-available*' message. Hernandez left a message for Clarence Dexter, reminding the man that he hadn't sent the ballistics reports on the sold derringers. This was the second time he left the message in the past few days.

Shortly after Hernandez hung up, the phone rang. He decided to let the answering machine take it; he needed to get back to the book. After the fifth ring, he heard the *click* of the answering machine pick up and a familiar voice came through its speaker.

"Milos here, I need someone to—"

Hernandez hurried to the phone. "It's me, Hernandez. What's up, Chang?"

"Surprised anyone's still there," the AME said.

Hernandez twisted his mouth. "I had nothing better to do, so I figured I'd stick around and wait for the phone to ring."

The comment was greeted with a brief silence followed by a

chortle. "Keep the day job. Comedy isn't your strong suit," Chang said. "I put a rush on Halpern's saliva sample like Moran asked, and I just got the results back from the lab."

While Chang read the results, Hernandez's eyes slowly widened. "You've got to be kidding," he blurted out when the medical examiner finished.

"I think you better get a hold of Moran ASAP," Chang said.

* * *

"Not what I wanted to hear, Frank," Moran said into his Bluetooth microphone. "About tomorrow, thank Pilar for the invite, but I want to spend Christmas here with Sandra. Let's say eight o'clock breakfast at Kramer's deli day after tomorrow. It's right around the corner from the office and afterwards I can go get some work done."

Moran disconnected, his demeanor somber. He turned to Sandra who was sitting up in her hospital bed. Her color had come back and she was beginning to look like her old self.

"What's wrong?" she said.

Moran pursed his lips. "Chang called. Halpern's DNA doesn't match Samantha's fetus and his blood type doesn't match the bloodstained piece of latex found in Greg Saunders' kitchen." Moran said and paused for an instant. "But his DNA is a match to the semen found in Lacy," he added.

"So you believe he killed her?"

The lieutenant shrugged. "It does put him at the scene," Moran said. He stepped closer to the foot of the bed. "And we know that the rental car matches a return trip from Albany to New York on the day Lacy was killed. Now, what was it you started to say before Frank called?"

Sandra pushed herself up on her pillows with her elbows and looked at her husband. "I remembered last night what it was I realized before I lost consciousness."

Moran lowered himself onto the bed and through the sterilized suit's plastic protective face mask gazed at his wife. He said, "Good."

"From the excessive violence used to kill Lacy, I think the killer could be a woman—"

"What?" Moran said and shook his head briskly. "No way, Sandy. What about what I just told you?"

Sandra cupped Moran's gloved hands. "Hear me out. As I was reviewing the file I recalled reading sometime back in Horatio Polk's book that malignant narcissism can manifest itself in extremely violent acts against the victim and that in most cases the perpetrators are women," Sandra said and pulled her hands to her chest. "I know what you just told me makes for a strong case against Halpern, but just keep it in the back of your mind."

Moran nodded. "Okay, but I think you're wrong, Remember, I'm the cop," he said and smiled.

"Yeah, but I'm the criminal behavior expert, Kemo Sabe," Sandra replied. "And as long as I'm giving my opinion, I think you should spend Christmas with Frank and Pilar and not here. It'll do you good."

Moran leaned in. "What, and miss out on having rubber turkey in my spacesuit with my favorite girl? Not a chance."

Sandra touched his face mask and emitted a quiet smile. Moran grabbed her hand and squeezed it. She giggled with a glimmer in her eyes. "What a pair we make—Robo-Cop and the damsel skating out onto the uncertain ice."

Moran smiled. "Not so uncertain anymore."

CHAPTER 53

"I left Chang a message this morning," Moran said, "to run a test of Greg Saunders', DNA and see if it matches Samantha's fetus. I also asked him to have DNA Labs International run a test to determine whether the skin under Myer's nails belonged to a man or a woman," Moran said. He ran the palm of one hand along the edge of the plastic menu.

"Why a man or a woman?" Hernandez asked, his focus on the menu's long list of breakfast items.

"Something Sandra suggested," Moran said.

"You think Greg fathered the baby?"

"Samantha's baby wasn't Halpern's, and according to her sister, she and Greg had a fling, so it's possible the baby was Greg's." Moran said.

"Which gives the senator a pretty good motive to kill Greg?"

"It's a good fit," Moran said. "There's also the way Halpern and Sabrina looked at each other the day of the funeral, and her reaction on learning that her sister was pregnant. That and the scene at the Waldorf makes me believe there's more than a brother and sister-in-law relationship between them," he added.

Hernandez massaged his chin and peered at his boss. "This is quite a dysfunctional group of people we're dealing with."

"And don't forget Sabrina," Moran said with an enigmatic smile. "She's certainly fit enough to have carried Greg down to the kitchen. She and Greg were engaged to get married and despite her coolness with her sister being photographed naked by Greg, I'm sure she wasn't happy about it."

Hernandez snorted. "This is turning into a *'cast-of-thousands'* case," the sergeant said.

"I got a call from Simms this morning. When she got in, she found that ATF fax with the info on the derringer buyers. Carnes, the L.A. buyer, is in a wheelchair. The Seattle buyer, Osbourne, is clean as a whistle with no ties to anyone in our case. Regarding Marvin Schuyler in Miami, he's a well-to-do, respected realtor, a member of the Elks, with a wife and two kids and no priors. Darcey's on his way to Ohio to interview the Schloessman guy."

Moran nodded and asked. "Any luck with Greg's cell phone?"

Hernandez shook his head. "Nope. Trying to figure what Saunders could've used as a password is really a tall order. You really expect me to read his mind?"

Moran gave the sergeant a mischievous smile. "Force yourself."

"Okay, fellas, what'll be?" a high-pitched female voice piped in.

Moran and Hernandez looked up but saw no one.

"Down here," the voice squeaked.

When the detectives followed the voice with their eyes, they saw an elderly thin woman with a craggy face and red-framed eyeglasses that sat half-way down the length of her nose staring up at them. Moran eyed her and figured she couldn't have been more than four-feet-seven inches tall. Wisps of strawberry blonde-colored hair that stuck out from beneath an oversized white baseball cap that fell halfway down her brow caught the lieutenant's attention. The name *Nate Kramer's* was sewn in pink letters on the front. She was the only waitress with a white cap; the rest of the help wore black ones.

The woman pointed to the name on the cap with the order pad she held in her left hand. "I'm Ida Kramer," she announced and aimed her pencil at Moran.

An amused smile crept across Hernandez's face. "Related to the owner?"

Ida's quiet brown eyes flashed. "Only by way of alimony checks. Nate's in Miami Beach with Heather, his twenty-two year-old *shiksa* child bride. I got the place, he got the bimbo," Ida spoke without emotion. She turned to Moran. "First time here?"

"Yeah, I usually have breakfast at home," Moran said.

"Me too," Hernandez added.

Ida nodded, "To each his own," she quipped and gazed over her eyeglass frames at Moran. "The usual?"

Moran snorted. "Usual? I just said this was my first time—"

"Lemme see, coffee, black, side order of bacon and an onion bagel lightly toasted," Ida interrupted as she scribbled it on the order pad. She looked up at Moran. "Right?"

A stunned Moran chuckled. "Wow, that's good."

"Not really. After forty years you get a feelin' for what people are into," Ida said in a matter-of-fact tone. She turned to Hernandez. "You're a coffee with milk and pancakes with sausages kinda guy, right?"

Hernandez grinned and nodded. "You betcha."

When Ida finished writing down the order, she looked at the two detectives. "Kinda early for you cops, isn't it?"

Moran and Hernandez exchanged surprised glances. "How did you know we were police officers?" Moran said.

Ida wiggled her fingers and her eyes dropped to the detectives' midsections. "I don't think those small bulges under your jackets mean you're happy to see me," Ida said with a wink. She pushed her eyeglasses up, spun on her heels and walked away.

Hernandez scratched his head as he watched the spunky Ida thread her way through the crowded tables toward the kitchen.

"Sad, still having to schlep tables at her age."

Moran's gaze swept the room. "Before you get too maudlin, look around you. The place is packed, and the menu says it's open from seven a.m. to six p.m. Monday through Friday. Almost office hours, and I'm sure that getting rid of Ida cost Nate big bucks," Moran said.

Hernandez nodded. "Come to think of it, she does seem happy," he said. The sergeant turned to his boss. "So, when do we brace Halpern?"

"Not yet," Moran said and looked into Hernandez's startled face. The lieutenant lifted up his forefinger. "First, it's true we have Halpern at Lacy Wooden's place on the day she was killed, but we don't know the time. Second," Moran said and lifted up his middle finger, "although we know that Halpern owns a motorcycle suit and has a license to drive one, we don't have a motive yet. Nor a gun."

"What about Myer? Think Halpern killed him too?"

"It'd make sense. Maybe our senator was the one paying Myer to keep his mouth shut about Lacy. Maybe he thought Myer might've recognized him in Lacy's hallway that day," Moran said. He scraped his chair closer to the table. "And before you ask, he could've also murdered Rose Chiu. Don't forget that he frequented the place."

"I'd say this investigation is getting to be a pain in the ass, if I didn't already have one," Hernandez said.

CHAPTER 54

The breeze off Lake Erie was crisp. The sun shone brightly against a blue sky as Detective Third-Grade Robert Darcey made his way between the high mounds of fresh snow that flanked the sidewalk. It was a reminder of the snowstorm that had fallen on Sandusky the previous day. Darcey had spent the one-hour train ride from Toledo staring out at the white landscape. It was bare of any foliage, and the wood frame houses along the tracks from which children waved at the passing train made it quintessential middle-America.

When the detective turned the corner onto West Monroe Street, he looked up and saw large waves from the lake striking the breakwater. A few hearty souls who dared the cold were fishing out there. Darcey shuddered, beat his chest with the palms of his hands, and then lifted his coat's fur-lined collar.

A short while later Darcey turned into a flagstone walkway that cut through piles of snow on both sides. He had reached his destination: 608 West Monroe Street, Sandusky, Ohio. The house, a two-story Victorian structure with its snow-covered lawn, white picket fence, front porch complete with Adirondack chairs and a hammock, seemed like the set from the play, *Our Town*. Darcey pressed the rusted doorbell and heard the shuffling of feet approach from within. The door swung open.

"Can I help you?" said an elderly man in a red woolen sweater over baggy pants. His pair of sparkling blue eyes were flanked by two rosy cheeks.

"Douglas Schloessman?" Darcey asked and stamped the snow off his shoes on the welcome mat.

The man grinned. "Yep."

When Darcey identified himself, Schloessman peered at him—the friendly grin was replaced by a wary stare. "A little far from home, aren't you, son?"

"Could we talk inside, sir?"

Schloessman remained silent for a moment and then brought back the grin. "Sure, c'mon on in."

Inside, the air was warm and smelled of freshly baked apple pie. While Darcey followed his host along a musty hallway into the house, he took in the staircase covered by a worn out green rug that led to the second floor. The hallway was covered by a threadbare carpet and its walls by light blue diamond-patterned wallpaper—it was as if time had stood still inside 608 W. Monroe Street.

"Been here long?" Darcey inquired as they entered the living room and his eyes floated around the room. The large wide-screen Sony with an old John Wayne western playing seemed out of place with the 1940s style décor of the room.

"All my life," Schloessman said. "My grandfather built the place and I, like my father before me, was born here."

Darcey nodded and moved to the stuffed couch that had a large quilt rolled up and crammed into one end. A thick corned beef sandwich and a coffee pot with a cup were laid out on a small table.

Schloessman pointed to the couch. "Make yourself comfortable. I was about to have a snack." He gestured to the sandwich. "Not good for my diabetes, but what the hell, once in a while you gotta break the rules."

The old man offered to get something for Darcey, but the detective politely said, "No thanks," as he lowered himself into the couch. Schloessman shrugged and took his place in one of the winged armchairs that framed the brick fireplace that contained a bright fire. The detective cleared his throat and watched his host across from him reach for the sandwich. "I'll get right to the point, sir—" Darcey began.

Schloessman chewed eagerly and gave a warm, friendly inviting smile. "Call me Doug, son; everyone else does."

Darcey nodded. "The Bureau of Alcohol, Tobacco and Firearms' records indicate that four years ago, you purchased a Dexter derringer with a .22 and .38 caliber barrels."

Schloessman swallowed and then took another bite of the sandwich. With his other hand, he pushed back a wisp of thin white hair that fell over his forehead. "Go on," he mumbled through a mouthful of corned beef and bread.

"If you don't mind I like to see it."

"So would I." Schloessman said.

Darcey leaned forward. "Come again?"

"The blasted thing went missing about two years ago," Schloessman said. "And it hasn't turned up yet."

"You report this to the police?"

Schloessman chortled. "If I reported everything I've lost or misplaced, they'd think I was nuts. The truth of the matter is that the damn thing was so small I figured I must've dropped it somewhere in the house. I'm sure it'll turn up when I least expect it."

"After two years?" Darcey said.

"That's the problem with young folks. Always in a hurry, no patience."

Darcey heaved a sigh of exasperation.

"Tell me, son, what's so important about that gun that it'd bring you all the way out of here from New York?"

Darcey watched as his host polished off the rest of the sandwich. "A gun matching that description was used in three murders in New York."

Schloessman wiped his mouth with a paper napkin and pushed his body to the edge of his chair. "Hold on a minute," he said, the palm of one hand held up as if to stop Darcey from getting up. "That's not possible. I just told you I lost in the damn thing here in the house."

"No burglaries or break-ins?" Darcey said.

Schloessman briskly shook his head. "Nope." He leaned forward and poured himself a cup of coffee. "So you see, detective, I'm afraid you've wasted your time."

"Do you entertain a lot?" Darcey pressed.

Schloessman laughed. "Naw, too old for that. My daughter comes to visit every year or so for a couple of weeks but that's about it."

"You think she could've taken it?" Darcey said.

"Jean? I don't recall ever telling her I had it. Besides, she hates guns. Jean's into music, a real talent."

"Oh, what exactly does she do?"

Schloessman's eyes glimmered and he rose to his feet. "Here, let me get you a picture of her," the old man said with obvious pride. He walked out of the room.

While Darcey waited for his host to return, he pushed himself off the couch and stepped to the nearby fireplace. The warmth felt good. He leaned in, held his palms over the flames and rubbed them together. When he straightened up, he focused on the photographs on the mantle: a black-and-white picture of a much younger Schloessman, with a petite brunette and a dark-haired, light-colored eyes child in a plain sleeveless dress standing between them. The girl appeared to be around five years old. Next to this picture was a large color photograph of an older Schloessman and the petite woman, who now looked emaciated and frail. Both were dressed in formalwear and seated at a table holding glasses of champagne.

"That's me and Helen on New Years Eve in Toledo, six years ago. She passed away six months later—colon cancer," Schloessman said when he entered the room.

Darcey turned around and faced his host. The cop's gaze fell on the large silver frame that Schloessman clutched in his left hand.

"Here she is... almost lost her when she was eighteen," Schloessman said, and then handed the picture to the detective.

Darcey gave a polite smile as he grasped the photograph.

"What happened?" the detective murmured while his eyes focused intently at the black-and-white glossy portrait of the young woman in the picture.

"She was coming home for Christmas after her first semester at the University of Toledo. It was snowing heavily and visibility was almost zero when she hit a patch of black ice on the road. The car plummeted down a steep embankment," Schloessman said and heaved a breath. "Another motorist saw what happened and contacted the state troopers, but the storm worsened into a blizzard. It took two days before a search-and-rescue operation could be mounted. When they found her, she was barely clinging on to life. It was so terrifying, that for years Jean had nightmares about it and—" Schloessman stopped suddenly and peered at his guest. "Something wrong? You don't look so hot," the old man said to an ashen Darcey.

The detective raised his eyes and gazed at Schloessman with a befuddled expression. "Is... is your daughter, Jessie Rand?" Darcey stammered and returned his look to the glossy portrait. Saul Goodwin's words came back to him: '*Some German-sounding name, Schleper or Schhoo something or other, can't remember exactly;*' '*When Jessie arrived fresh off a small town, San... something or other in Ohio.*' The names *Schloessman and Sandusky* came to mind.

Schloessman's face beamed. "She was a star on Broadway, you know. I see you've heard of her."

A numbed Darcey handed the picture back to his host. "Who hasn't?" was all the detective could manage.

Later that evening, on the return flight to LaGuardia Airport, a still flabbergasted Darcey sat in economy class staring out the window at the dark clouds that raced past. The detective's mind was full of questions. Douglas Schloessman on the surface seemed like a nice enough sort of man but something was out of sync. When the flight attendant swept past, Darcey stopped her and asked for a double Jim Beam, neat. The pert middle-aged dyed blonde with *FRAN* embossed on her nametag gave Darcey an odd look that was quickly met by Darcey's *'you gotta problem with that?'* stare.

What the hell, he was thirty-five thousand feet up, off-duty, and the day hadn't exactly been without its surprises. He needed that drink.

CHAPTER 55

When Kevin Palmer stepped off Amtrak's Lake Shore Limited, the hands of Pennsylvania Station's art deco brass clock pointed at seven p.m. A medium-size brown valise bounced against his left thigh as he made his way through the throng of commuters to the Eighth Avenue exit. He passed the newspaper stand and felt the icy stare of the two uniformed cops who loitered nearby. Palmer didn't like being watched—he'd had enough of that in prison.

"Screw you," Palmer muttered and quickened his pace. After zigzagging across the wide avenue while dodging honking taxis and cars, Palmer ambled into the Hotel Pennsylvania's cavernous marble lobby and walked to the check-in counter. The attractive, young East Indian clerk flashed her dark eyes at the roll of bills that Palmer pulled out of his blue jeans. Her eyes widened as she watched him slowly count off six fifty dollar bills for that night and place them in a neat stack on the counter.

Palmer raised his aqua blue eyes at her, and with a razor thin smile, wrote his name on the registration form—Jason Bourne, the name of the hero from *The Bourne Identity,* his favorite book. He even wrote down a made up address in Nixa, Missouri, as his residence—the fictional Bourne's birthplace. Palmer enjoyed pushing things to the limit.

When the ex-con entered the room, he placed the '*Do Not Disturb'* placard on the door knob and clicked the lock shut. He then moved toward the bed, tossed the valise on it, and stepped toward the window. Palmer gazed out at Penn Station across the street and watched the heavy traffic of buses, cabs and private cars as they maneuvered around jay-walking New Yorkers. It felt good to be back in the Big Apple after so many years.

He drew the curtains closed, quickly peeled off his black leather car coat, draped it across one of the chairs and opened the suitcase. He brought out the bottle of Johnnie Walker Black that rested under his shirts and cracked it open. He took a long pull of the dark amber liquid, straightened to his full six feet, and wiped his mouth with the back of his hand.

He glanced at the radio clock's digital display: 8:00 p.m.

"Time for a nap," he muttered. "This is goin' to be one New Year's Eve to remember."

* * *

Inside Apartment 10B in the Upper Westside, Pilar Hernandez was hard at work in the kitchen preparing three dishes, each containing twelve seedless grapes. With them were three champagne flutes on a plastic tray. "Hey, you guys!" she called out. "Time to stop working. It's ten to midnight!"

A few feet away in the living room, Alice Simms and Frank Hernandez sat at the dining table feverishly working on Greg Saunders' cell phone.

Simms pushed herself away from the table. "I give up," she said and stared at the phone as if were about to come alive or mutate into some alien creature. "How the hell does Moran expect us—"

"Me. He expects *me* to crack the code," Hernandez interjected.

"Whatever. It's like trying to win the lottery," Simms said.

Hernandez passed his fingers through his hair and leaned back. "Well, you know what they say, '*you can't win if you don't play,*' " the sergeant said. He rested his elbows on the table. "I think it has to be a name, a number, something that was important to him," he said. He shrugged. "At least that's how I would pick a password."

Simms rolled her eyes. "We've tried combinations of his date of birth, address, and his social security number in a thousand different ways. What else can it be?"

Pilar glided into the room and placed a tray of dishes, a bottle of Korbel, and three flutes on the table. She grabbed the remote and turned on the *Dick Clark New Year's Eve Special.*

Simms cast an odd look at the twelve grapes in each of the three dishes. "What is this for?"

"It's an old custom from Spain that my grandmother brought over," Pilar said. "You eat one grape for each second just before the stroke of midnight. It brings good luck during the coming year."

Simms gestured to the cell phone on the table. "Something we could all use."

An hour later, a cheery Simms left the Hernandez apartment. She felt unusually optimistic about the New Year, and thought perhaps Pilar's grape ritual wasn't such a nutty idea after all.

When she exited the building, the icy air made her fold her arms against her parka. She braced herself against the cold and with a hurried pace, started for her car, which was parked under a street lamp in the building's front parking area.

As Simms marched toward her Volvo, the sound of rustling caused her to stop and turn around. The detective instinctively reached inside her purse and then realized that the Glock was still in her car's glove compartment. A calico cat jumped off the hood of a parked SUV and scampered away into the darkness, Simms' heart also jumped. Annoyed at herself for overreacting, she shrugged and continued walking.

Soon she heard the sound again. She stopped and spun on her heels. This time there was nothing. An edgy Simms dropped her hands to her sides. "Whoever's there, I'm a police officer!" she bellowed. The words were answered by the meowing of the cat from another part of the parking area. Detective Simms squinted. She sensed her throat tighten and mouth go dry while she peered into the shadows. Nothing.

When Simms reached the car and inserted her key into the

driver's door lock a sudden, powerful force slammed her body against the car's side and her face struck the car's roof. Stunned, she felt a warm trickle of blood slide down her forehead as she struggled to straighten up and turn around. But the assailant had the advantage.

"You've made a big mistake, moron. I'm... I'm a cop," Simms stammered.

There was no reply, just more pressure on the back of her head. Her attacker placed the palm of one hand over her mouth, and Simms grunted as she tried to scream. She kicked her assailant with the back of her foot and her mind raced to guess where the attacker's feet were in order to grind one of her stiletto heels into them.

Simms felt two powerful fingertips press against her neck just below the ear, and she lost consciousness as a tsunami of darkness engulfed her.

CHAPTER 56

When Moran walked into Nate Kramer's with Hernandez and Darcey, he found that the lunch crowd had already taken most of the booths against the right wall. The lieutenant frowned while his gaze arced through the eatery searching for a secluded table where they could talk. Ida intercepted the trio and stepped in front of them. She glanced up at Darcey. "I see you've brought backup," she said. "Follow me."

The trio filed behind Ida past the noisy tables of other diners. "You're a dangerous woman," Moran said. "You've stolen our hearts."

"I'm been known to have that effect on men," Ida said over the clamor of voices and the clanging of plates. She wiggled her four-foot-seven-inch frame and sprightly weaved her small frame past customer-filled tables to a corner at the back of the deli.

"Maybe we should've taken a cab," Moran said.

"Stop whining," Ida snapped over her shoulder. "We're almost there."

When the group reached a solitary table in a corner, Ida stopped. "There you go," she said. "Only one I got left."

Hernandez gazed at the kitchen doors only a few feet away and saw the line of waiters and bus boys rushing through it. "Kinda close and noisy isn't it?" He jerked his thumb at the kitchen.

Ida craned her neck and gazed up at the cop. "Look on the bright side. You'll get the food sooner and warmer," She set three menus on the table. "I'll be back," Ida said.

The three detectives settled into their seats as Ida breezed away.

"Somehow, I empathize with Nate," Moran murmured. "Anybody heard from Alice?" He slid one of the menus toward Hernandez while a bus boy set down three glasses of water.

"No, and I'm getting concerned. Since she left our place day before yesterday, no one's seen hide nor hair of her. Pilar called her place and got the answering machine. I called her cell and got her voicemail," Hernandez said.

"Same here," Darcey chimed in.

"Let's put an alert out on her car," Moran said. "I don't like this," the lieutenant added. He gazed at Darcey who was concentrating on the menu. "Now that we know Jesse Rand's real name, find out everything you can about her."

From across the table, a dour Darcey lifted his eyes and faced his boss. "Will do… but…" he started and paused. He moistened his lips and continued. "I mean—"

Moran set his menu down and focused hard on the young cop. "We all know you've got a soft spot for her, but you admitted that it was odd that Mr. Schloessman's derringer mysteriously disappeared. Humor me, check her out."

"But we don't even know if that gun is the murder weapon," Darcey said.

Hernandez turned to Darcey. "That's why we need to check her out."

A crestfallen Darcey quietly nodded and returned to the menu.

Ida appeared at the table. "Okay, fellas, time's money. What'll be?" she said.

After everyone placed their order and Ida left, Moran edged his chair closer to the table.

"I got a call from Chang this morning. Samantha's baby was definitely Greg's, and the skin under Myer's fingernails isn't Halpern's or Greg's. We're now waiting on the chromosome part of the test."

"Sure takes long enough," Hernandez said.

"Not enough skin tissue," Moran responded. "Any progress with Greg's cell phone?"

Hernandez reached into the pocket of his three-piece blue suit and drew out the phone.

"Nothing, nada, nil, squat, zil—"

Moran waved his hand. "Okay, okay, got the picture."

Darcey took a sip of water and turned to Hernandez. "Try *JFOX*," Darcey said.

Moran and Hernandez looked at each other and then stared at Darcey with widened eyes.

"Why?" Hernandez said.

Darcey shrugged. "Simple. You said that Saunders was very proud and thankful to his character, *James Fox*, for winning him two Emmys. So, why not use it as password?"

"Why not indeed," Hernandez said. He activated Greg Saunders' cell. At the *Pictures* prompt, he punched in *JFOX*.

Hernandez's face brightened. "I'll be damned, it worked!" he exclaimed and placed the phone in the middle of the table.

The folder contained three items:

1. *Cast and Crew*
2. *Sabrina*
3. *The Four Musketeers*

The sergeant selected the first one: a photo of the cast and crew on the set of *Bachelor Dad*. The second picture was of Sabrina and Greg seated at a restaurant with their arms intertwined. When Hernandez selected *The Four Musketeers* picture, he stopped. He peered at it and pointed to someone in the frame. "Who's that?"

An inquisitive Moran and Darcey leaned in to peek over the sergeant's shoulder at the picture.

"Oh, boy!" Moran said. "See if the password works for the voicemail."

Hernandez pressed the cell's *Speaker* key and set it down on the table.

George Halpern's voice blared. "*I know you're there so pick up the—!*" and then stopped.

"What happened?" Moran asked.

Hernandez said. "Sounds like Greg answered."

"What's the date and time?" Moran said.

"Ten o'clock, the same night that Saunders was murdered," Hernandez said.

The lieutenant picked up the phone and gazed at it. "No end to the surprises."

CHAPTER 57

The Lakeside Hotel and Spa Resort in New York's Putnam County, which first opened its doors in the early 1960s to city dwellers seeking the mountain coolness during summer was closed for the winter. That didn't stop Kevin Palmer from driving his ex-wife's Volvo up the winding gravel driveway. The car's headlights reflected off the retinas of some of the fauna that inhabited the surrounding woods and eerily illuminated the deserted buildings while the chirr of crickets serenaded the night.

Palmer cranked down the window and let in the crisp night air. He breathed deeply and tossed out a cigarette butt. "You okay?" Palmer asked as he turned around to a handcuffed, gagged and blindfolded Alice Simms. She lay across the back seat. "Sorry we had to spend the night in the car, but I couldn't risk being spotted with you in the back seat like that. But I'll make up for it."

Simms emitted a mournful moan through the duct tape that covered her mouth. A moment later, the Volvo drove past a row of log cabins and stopped in front of the door of the last one.

"We're here, honey," Palmer called over his shoulder. Moments later the ex-con was dragging Simms out of the car. "You'll remember the place," he said. "We always loved it, so I figured it'd be the ideal spot for us to get back together."

Simms violently shook her head and moaned loudly. With his valise clutched in one hand, Palmer pushed his ex-wife in front of him toward the cabin's front door. Simms grunted when she tripped and fell on the flagstone walkway. Palmer grabbed her by an arm and yanked her to her feet. "Let's try to be more careful," he said. "We have a long night ahead of us."

When they entered the cabin, Alice Simms, whose body shivered from the cold and dampness, was propelled onto one of the twin beds. Palmer moved to a rustic wooden table that had a hurricane lamp its center. He set the valise down and lit the lamp, then opened the suitcase and brought out his bottle of Johnnie Walker.

"I'll light the stove," Palmer said and nodded to the potbelly stove in a corner. There was a stack of wood piled next to it. "I know you don't drink, so I'll do it for both of us."

He took a pull of the scotch, and a moment later when Simms' blindfold and duct tape had been removed, the detective gasped. Her eyes beamed recognition as they swept the room—the red checkered cloth curtains, the stove, the small kitchen near a window, and the dark rustic walls with lithographs of colonial scenes, all brought back memories of happier times. This was where they had spent their honeymoon in what felt like an eternity ago.

"You've gotta be out of your mind," Simms said, her voice filled with contempt. "When the hell did they let you out?"

Palmer curled his lips into a sneer. "About a month ago, but I've been dreamin' of this moment for a long, long time." He drew out Simms' Glock service pistol from his waistband then laid the gun down on one of the night tables next to the bed, took off his coat and tossed it on the small couch near the bed.

Simms gazed at him while he moved toward the woodpile—the lumberjack woolen shirt and tight blue jeans over the Wellington boots accentuated Kevin Palmer's physique as he carried himself with the agility of a mountain lion.

"How about taking the 'cuffs off?" Simms said in a softened tone.

Palmer finished lighting the stove and stepped toward the bed. He loomed over her, his legs apart and his fingers starting to unbutton his shirt. "All in good time, Alice, all in good time," he hissed. "First the parka comes off. Let's find out how the years have treated you."

"You do realize my partners are probably looking for me?"

Palmer shrugged. "So what!" he said. He unlocked one end of the handcuffs and snapped it around one of the posts of the headboard. When he took off Simms' parka, he surveyed her fit, svelte body. It was covered by a yellow v-neck sweater and a pair of designer jeans. "Lookin' good, baby," he said

"Wish I could say the same about you. By the way, my cell phone has a GPS locator that's automatically activated when the phone is turned off for more than twelve hours."

Palmer snorted. "You really expect me to fall for that?"

"Everyone in the squad has one. But fine, Kevin, don't believe me. But come morning you're gonna be sitting in jail facing, among other things, kidnapping charges," she said. "If you take me back now, I'll just say I ran into you and you wanted to talk. No charges will be pressed."

Palmer crinkled his forehead. "Nice try, but no dice."

"C'mon, Kevin. You were with Special Forces; you know about GPS locators," Simms pressed and riveted her eyes on Palmer's questioning look.

Palmer studied his ex-wife's face for a moment. "Okay, okay, where's the friggin' thing?" he finally said.

"In my purse… in the car."

A smile crossed Palmer's face and broadened into a grin. "You must think I'm stupid," he said. The ex-con took off his belt and stepped toward Simms. "Let's make sure you don't decide to be a hero and try to escape while I'm out there." He bound her ankles with the belt and walked out. A few minutes later Palmer re-entered the cabin with the mobile in his hands. When he tried to activate it the mobile's screen read: *Enter Passcode*

"What's the passcode?" Palmer said.

"One-one-eight," Simms said, and watched as her ex-husband activated the phone.

"You got two voicemails," Palmer said, and retrieved them. When he finished listening to them, he removed the cell from his ear and faced Simms.

"Some guy named Darcey and another one from a Hernandez. They want you to call them. What are they, boyfriends?"

"You might say that," Simms said. "A girl does get lonely."

Palmer smirked and tossed the mobile on top of his coat. When he removed his shirt, his lean muscular torso was exposed. He strode toward his ex-wife and slowly pressed his body against hers. Beads of sweat prickled Simms' mocha-colored forehead while she clenched her jaw and turned her face away from Palmer. When his hands reached under her shirt and touched her breasts Simms bristled and tensed. She spat in his face.

Palmer laughed and wiped the spittle away. "That's what I've always liked about you... spunk," he said. He lifted up her skirt and stripped off his pants.

As he lay on top of her, the pungent, stale smell of Palmer's whiskey breath made the detective twist her mouth and turn away to avoid his open mouth. But handcuffed Alice Simms was no match for Kevin Palmer.

At the same time eighty miles to the south, in a darkened kitchen, a Blackberry vibrated and beeped.

CHAPTER 58

"I located Alice!" Hernandez exclaimed as he burst into the Cold Cases & Apprehension Squad's office. Moran and Darcey were seated in their shirtsleeves at the conference table hunched over a photograph.

Moran looked up. "Where the hell is she?"

Hernandez moved to the table and from his jacket pocket brought out his Blackberry and pressed a couple of keys. "When I went to the kitchen this morning I found it beeping," Hernandez said while he set the handheld on the table. "According to the navigation map, her cell phone sent the signal from a place called The Lakeside Hotel and Spa Resort in Putnam County about eighty miles away. It's on Peach Lake."

"It's open this time of year?" Darcey said as he gazed at the map on the screen.

Moran picked up the Blackberry. "Which means Simms didn't activate her phone until now, and that's not like her. Any messages?"

"That's what's strange. Nothing. And when I called no one answered."

Moran tapped his lower lip a few times with his index finger and then pushed himself to his feet. "Send her a text message and if she's doesn't respond, we'll know something's definitely wrong."

While Hernandez typed out, *'Are you okay?'* on the handheld's screen keyboard, he glanced at the photograph on the table. "I see you enlarged Greg's mobile picture."

"Which adds another dimension to the case," Moran said.

When Hernandez sent the message, a disheartened Darcey slid the picture across the table toward the sergeant. "Never would've thought it," Darcey murmured. Hernandez studied the photograph of Greg Saunders, the Van Damme sisters and another woman, all of them astride separate black Harleys and garbed in black riding outfits.

"Sabrina did say they were like the Three Musketeers," Moran said. "So what's Jessie Rand doing in the picture?" He grabbed his jacket from the back of his chair and slipped it on, then pointed at Darcey. "Let's you and me pay Miss Rand, slash, Schloessman a visit," Moran said. He turned to Hernandez, "Call the Putnam County State Police Barracks and have them pay the resort a visit. I think Simms is in trouble."

* * *

Inside the cabin, the mid-morning light filtered through the thin damask curtain that covered the front window. The sound of Simms' cell phone's ring broke the silence of sleep and Kevin Palmer stirred. He rubbed his eyes and turned to a still asleep Simms, whose right wrist was still handcuffed to the bed's headboard. Palmer checked his watch and nudged his ex-wife. "Wake up, it's almost eleven," he said.

He threw off the covers and exposed Simms' curled up nude body, then sat up and gazed at the cell phone that continued to ring from across the room. "I'll get it," he murmured.

A moment later Palmer stared at the screen's text message. "What the hell is this?" he barked. He marched to the bed with the phone in his hand. "You told me the phone emitted a GPS signal *only* when it was turned off. You goddamn lied to me!"

"So did you last night," she said with a mocking tone. Barely covered by the bed sheet, Simms sat up and leaned against the headboard. "So much for Mr. Macho," she added. Simms covered her mouth with the free hand and giggled. "I guess Mr. Happy wasn't up to the job last night… too much booze or too little man."

Palmer glared at Simms, his eyes ablaze. He threw the cell phone at his ex-wife and Simms ducked. The missile narrowly missed her head and crashed against the wall above her.

Simms looked at the broken phone that lay next to her. "Nice."

Suddenly, Palmer's fist struck the detective's mouth. "You think you're funny, don't you, bitch!"

The force of the blow dazed Simms for a moment. When she shook off the dizziness, she touched the corner of her mouth with her fingertips and felt the lower lip start to swell.

"You haven't changed. Always free with the fists," Simms barked. "You're not so much angry at me as you are with yourself, especially after last night." She made quotations marks with her fingers, "The rape that couldn't happen." She smirked. "Since you couldn't screw me, go screw yourself."

Palmer gritted his teeth while he clenched both fists and started toward the bed.

"That message was from Detective Sergeant Frank Hernandez, and if he doesn't hear from me, State Troopers are going to be knocking the door down to this place. And there's no phone in the cabin. Way to go, Kevin!" Simms shouted.

Palmer flattened out his hands. He moved toward Simms, his gait slow and deliberate.

CHAPTER 59

Moran and Darcey sat waiting in silence on a cream-colored divan, aimlessly looking around at the living room's décor: expensive porcelain vases on faux marble columns and framed lithographs by Erte, Dali and Arp on the white walls. A large gold-trimmed mirror that hung over a red sofa. A marble-top table with a Lalique clock embraced by a sculpted nude woman. Music softly flowed from a replica 1930s radio/CD player that sat in a corner on top of a wide-screen television set.

"You'd think Norma Desmond lived here," Moran said from the corner of his mouth.

"I sorta like it," Darcey replied. "I think—"

The sound of soft footsteps made the two cops turn. Jessie Rand glided into the room carrying a tray with a porcelain teapot, three cups and a small silver dish filled with sugar cubes.

"Sorry, but the cleaning woman misplaced the sugar," Rand said as she walked toward the two detectives. She set the tray down on a table that was between two nearby satin covered chairs in front of the divan. With gazelle-like grace folded her lithe frame into one of the chairs. The light from the panoramic window that faced Central Park bathed the dancer's complexion. It also highlighted the thin crow's feet at the corners of her eyes, which sparkled with sexuality.

When Rand crossed her ankles—right over left—the slit of her dress' skirt revealed a pair of long, shapely legs. Darcey smiled and focused on the sapphire blue eyes that mesmerized him from the chair.

Moran sniffed the air and turned to his hostess. "What's that you're wearing?"

"Hmm?" Rand said.

"The perfume," Moran said. "It's smells familiar."

"Chanel No. 5. Sorry, if it bothers you, but—"

"Not at all, it just reminds me of someone I knew a long time ago," Moran said.

Rand shifted her gaze to Darcey. "Dad said you visited him," Rand said. Her fingertips played with the ends of her hair. "He liked you and was sorry you wasted your trip."

Darcey remained silent, his gaze fixed on Rand. He finally cleared his throat and moved to the edge of the divan. "I found out your name isn't Jessie Rand and that you're not English," Darcey said.

Rand smiled pleasantly. "Guilty as charged. It's Jean Schloessman, born and bred in Sandusky, Ohio. The center of the universe to my father," she said. "But I'm sure Saul Goodwin told you all that." The English accent had evaporated.

Darcey remained silent with a nonplussed look on his face. "Word travels fast," he said.

Rand smiled. "The theater world is a small place."

Moran made no sound while he concentrated on his hostess— attractive, elegant, in good physical shape and yet possessed of a femininity that belied her true sexual preference.

When the dancer shifted her weight in the chair, Moran's eyes went to Rand's left lower leg. He quickly motioned to the long scar that ran up from the ankle to the calf.

"Accident?" he said

"What?" Rand said. A surprised look appeared on her face. She flicked her eyes at the scar. "Oh, that. Yes." She then picked up a small remote from the coffee table and turned off the music.

"I gather it's from the car accident you had when you were a freshman in college?" Moran asked.

Rand looked at Darcey. "I see dad left no stone unturned," the dancer said. "He's very protective of me and to this day the accident still haunts him." She shifted her gaze back to Moran. "The answer is no."

"So where did you get that scar?"

"I fail to see what relevance that has," Rand snapped back. She gathered herself and smiled tightly. "Sorry, it's just something I'd rather forget. It happened five years ago, and I really don't want to go into it."

Moran gestured again to the scar. "Is that why you don't dance anymore?" he pressed.

Their hostess poured tea into the cups. "That and age," Rand said, as she poured.

Moran nodded. "Miss Schloessman—"

"Miss Rand, please. I legally changed the name some years ago."

"No problem," Moran said. "We need your help in clearing up certain things in our inquiries into the murders of Lacy Wooden, Greg Saunders, Rose Chiu, and Paul Myer."

Rand finished filling the cups and leaned back in her chair. Her eyes met Moran's with unflinching steadfastness.

"I don't mean to sound callous," Rand said, "but that seems a lot of dead people."

"We think so," Darcey piped in.

"For starters what do you know about the relationship between George Halpern and his wife, Samantha?" Moran asked.

Rand flipped her right hand in a dismissive wave. "We all knew they didn't get along. Sam wanted more excitement in her life and George... well, George is George. Always worried about his public image."

"Anything between him and Sabrina?" Darcey asked.

Rand turned to him, her eyes flashing surprise. "I... well... eh...," she stammered. "Oh, I suppose with Sam gone it'll do no harm to say it."

Moran and Darcey exchanged glances.

"About six months ago, one night Sabrina and I were here alone. You know... girl's night. After two bottles of Chardonnay, she opened up." Rand rose and walked to the window and looked out at the park. "She said that George suspected Sam of having an affair with Greg Saunders, but since he was out of love with his wife, he didn't seem to be very upset about it," Rand said as she looked out the window and her voice trailed off.

Moran asked. "Do you know if Sabrina and Halpern were carrying on a relationship?"

Rand spun on her heels and faced the lieutenant. "She never came out and said as much, but I had the feeling they were."

"Anything you'd care to share with us regarding Lacy and Halpern?" Darcey said. "We know they had something going on and that he lavished her with expensive gifts." Darcey said

Rand made her way back to her chair. She sat and then crossed and uncrossed her ankles. "One afternoon during dance class I noticed that Lacy wasn't herself. Her timing was off, and she was making mistakes she wouldn't normally make. So after class, I pulled her aside and asked her what was wrong," she said.

"And?" Darcey said.

Rand took a sip of tea. "She confessed that she and Halpern had been seeing each other. You know, the usual May/December affair, and that he showered her with jewelry. She complained that he was too possessive, an older version of Paul Myer," Rand said, and moistened her lips. "To make a long story short—"

"I love long stories," Moran interrupted.

Rand shot the lieutenant an annoyed glance. "She told me that the last time they met he was totally out of control. Said if he ever found out she'd been double timing him he'd kill her."

"You sure?" Darcey asked.

Rand raised her look at the young detective. "Those may not have been her exact words but that was the gist of it."

"Miss Rand," Moran said carefully, "if it became necessary, would you be willing to testify or sign a deposition to that effect?"

"Of course. If he's Lacy's killer, I'm not going to stand idly by and watch him get away with it. She was a good girl who got caught up in her own ambitious dreams."

"Like yourself?" Moran said briskly.

Rand's face muscles relaxed and she smiled—a pencil thin smile. "In a way," she said. The dancer looked away for an instant and then returned her gaze to Moran. "And as long as we're on the subject of George Halpern, I should mention that at this year's Fourth of July party at Greg's, I overheard him tell Greg to leave Lacy alone or pay the consequences."

"That's not in the police report. Why didn't you come forward with this information after Greg was killed?" Moran said.

Rand shrugged. "Because George had a little too much to drink and was angry. People in that state often say things they don't really mean. Besides, the cops never bothered to interview me. I've told you what I heard, but it's not an accusation."

"Thank you, Miss Rand. You've been very helpful," Moran said. He reached into his pocket and brought a small folded copy of the *Four Musketeers* picture and laid it on the table.

"Can you tell us something about this?"

Rand glanced at it and her eyes saddened. "Of course. Hard to believe Sam and Greg are gone."

"Who took the picture?" Moran asked.

"Greg's housekeeper."

"Do you own a Harley?" Darcey asked.

"No," Rand said crisply.

"Any motorcycle?" Moran said.

Another crisp "No."

Darcey lifted one of the cups of tea and took a sip. "Whose Harley is next to you in the picture?"

"Greg's. He had two," Rand said.

Moran asked Jessie Rand about her relationship with Lacy Wooden, and the dance teacher told how Lacy was a promising student who stood a good chance of making it in show business. Rand went on and explained that she had recommended Lacy to Saul and Greg in an effort to jumpstart the young woman's career.

When Rand finished, Darcey pointed at her. "You also played a role in getting her a job at 'The Little Foxes' club."

Rand blinked twice and fingered her right earring. "Lacy needed money and the club was a popular hangout frequented by important people. I figured somebody might spot her."

"Did you go there a lot?" Moran asked.

"No, I do my entertaining more privately," Rand deadpanned.

Darcey cleared his throat. "When we first met, you mentioned you were gay. Did you and Lacy have more than a teacher-student relationship?"

"Normally, I'd find that question offensive. However, given the circumstances, I can honestly say that the answer is an unequivocal no," Rand said. She maintained her eyes on the young detective. "As I said, Lacy had a lot of promise, and I just wanted to help her, but we were not personal friends."

"One more question and then we'll be on our way," Moran said. "How well did you know Paul Myer?"

Rand pursed her lips and her face darkened. "Only that he was a real hard-ass who came around the studio to pick up Lacy," she said. "Never liked him. A pushy, jealous jerk. Nothing else."

A short time later when Moran and Darcey reached the door of the apartment, Moran turned and faced Rand—another one of Moran's Lieutenant Columbo moments.

"You wouldn't know what happened to your father's derringer?" Moran said.

Rand shook her head and shrugged. "Other than a pair of old shotguns, I never knew my father owned any weapons," Rand said. "My mother and I hated firearms, and dad always kept them safely stored away."

Moran nodded and started to turn away and then stopped. He turned and once more faced Rand.

"By the way, do you have any property on the Jersey Shore?"

Rand chuckled. "Not till I save up my first couple of millions."

When the two detectives climbed into their Crown Victoria, Darcey started the engine and turned to Moran. "She sure was sensitive about the accident she had," Darcy said.

"Yeah, but I can understand her not wanting to relive it. After all, it ruined her career," Moran wrinkled his face. "However, I admit she's a strange woman. But then almost everyone in show business is."

"She seemed nice enough under the circumstances. God knows the only thing we didn't ask was if she knew what happened to Amelia Earhart."

Moran gazed at Darcey and nodded. "Remind me to do that next time," he said, and then snapped on his seatbelt.

Darcey turned to the lieutenant. "By the way, who did that perfume remind you of?"

"My ex-wife."

CHAPTER 60

Alice Simms sat in her Toyota's passenger seat and staring out at the landscape of pine trees that blurred past her window. She shifted her weight and felt the tug of the handcuff on her right wrist. It was attached to the door's handle.

"We've been on the Thruway for three hours. Where the hell are we going?" Simms asked as she massaged her bruised jaw.

"Canada, where we can start a new life together," Palmer said.

"Snap out of it, Kevin. It's over between us."

Palmer reached out and cupped Simms' free hand. When she didn't withdraw it, he smiled. "No use denying it, Alice, you still have feelings for me."

Simms contemplated the ribbon of road that was being swallowed up by the car and pulled herself away. "Don't get your hopes up. Got anything to keep warm? It's freezing."

"Then just shut up for the rest of the trip," Palmer barked.

"I promised not to scream if you took the gag off but nothing was said about not talking."

Irked, Palmer turned on the radio and loud punk rock music filled the car.

Simms kept her eyes focused on the road ahead. "I'm hungry and I have to pee," she said.

Palmer turned to his ex-wife. "What?"

Simms turned to her ex-husband. "Pee, as in using the Ladies' Room... Rest Room... Toilet... Latrine."

"Why the hell didn't you go before we left?"

"Because one of us was in a hurry to leave before the cops came, remember?" Simms said.

Palmer squinted while he peered through the bug-splattered windshield. He pointed to a sign announcing that Millie's Mini-Mart & Gas Station was a quarter of mile away at the next exit.

"Fine, but I'm going inside with you."

Simms snorted and chuckled. "Right, like the attendant's going to allow that."

Palmer pursed his lips. "I'll be waiting right outside. Better not try any funny stuff," he said. He gestured to the Glock that was inside his waistband. A moment later, the car rolled into Millie's gas station area and came to a stop in front of the mini-mart.

Palmer and Simms entered the empty store with Simms' parka folded over her right hand which clutched a small purse. The parka hid the fact that the other end of the handcuff was gripped tightly by her ex-husband. Palmer slipped his other hand under the coat and unlocked Simms' handcuff.

"Remember the Glock," Palmer whispered. He glanced at the only other person in the mart--a lanky, blonde pimpled-face teenager behind the counter. In a raised voice he added, "I'll wait for you right here, honey." While Palmer waited, the attendant kept his eyes on the scurvy- looking customer from behind the counter.

"Whaddya lookin' at?" Palmer snarled. "Gimme four of those." He pointed to a stack of Mounds chocolate bars that lay in a box behind the attendant. "And two Cokes." He gestured to the soft drinks refrigerator behind the clerk.

When the clerk set down the chocolate bars and the sodas, he glanced at the Toyota that was parked facing the store. "So where are you folks heading?" the teenager asked.

Palmer laid down a five-dollar bill on the counter. "What's this, The Larry King Show?" He brought out a pack of cigarettes from his woolen shirt's pocket, and placed a cigarette between his lips.

"Sorry, sir, but no smoking's allowed," the clerk said.

As Palmer, looking annoyed, opened his mouth to speak, Simms hurried out of the ladies' room toward the counter.

"About time," Palmer said.

Simms turned to the young clerk. "You gotta serious leaking toilet in there," she said, and jerked her left thumb over her shoulder toward the restroom.

When the attendant saw Simms and Palmer drive off, he walked into the ladies' room and stared with his mouth agape at the lipsticked message on the mirror.

"I am police officer Alice Simms and I'm being kidnapped. This is no joke!!"

CHAPTER 61

In a booth at Rafferty's Chinese Kosher Restaurant & Bar, Assistant Medical Examiner Milos Chang sat clad in an Armani double-breasted suit next to an attractive, much younger-looking Asian woman in a tailor-fitted black dress. The small diamond earrings and the jade necklace that graced her slim long neck made her the poster-woman for New York City sophistication.

In front of them were two filled champagne flutes alongside an ice bucket with a bottle of Dom Perignon immersed in it.

The woman picked up one of the two books that lay next to her glass and gazed at the dustcover: *'Passion and Other Vices: The Poetry of Sex by Milos Chang.'*

"It was very sweet of you to dedicate it to me," she said in a soft, mellow voice.

Chang took a sip of his champagne and looked at his companion. "Why not, Joyce? You were the one that inspired me and made it all possible." He took her hand.

Joyce smiled and gently kissed Chang on the cheek. "You realize I can't be your agent anymore?"

Chang shrugged. "Who cares, lose an agent, gain a—"

A loud "Ahem," interrupted the AME. When Chang and Joyce looked up, they saw Moran towering over them. "Sorry, I'm late," he said and gave Joyce a curious look.

Chang smiled. "This is Joyce Tan, my former agent," the AME said and squeezed Joyce's hand..

Moran nodded at the woman and when he sat down across from the couple, he noticed the champagne bottle. "Nice to meet

254

you," he told Joyce. His gaze darted from her to Chang and back. "Is this some kind of celebration?"

The couple squeezed each other's hands and Chang cast Joyce a tender glance. "Joyce and I were married a couple of hours ago by Judge Berti over at the Municipal Building."

The couple riveted their glimmering eyes on Moran as the words slammed into him. He finally reached over and grasped Chang's glass. "Sorry, but I need this more than you." he said. Moran raised the champagne glass to the couple. "Congratulations," he said and drained it.

"Every poet needs a muse, and I found mine," Chang said. He slid the other book toward the still shocked Moran. "I autographed it for you."

Chang brought out an envelope from inside his jacket pocket and handed it to Moran who bunched his eyebrows and peered at Chang. "Why the secrecy about you two?" Moran asked as he tapped the envelope against his fingertips.

Chang and Joyce looked at each other. "We didn't want any fuss or wisecracks from a certain party whose last name begins with an *H.*"

Moran laughed. "Okay, so what's in here?" He nodded toward the envelope.

"The reason I asked you to meet me before departing for the Caribbean. It's the results from the lab in Florida."

When Moran reached the last paragraph of the two-page report, he raised his gaze at Chang.

"Will this hold up in court?" Moran asked.

Chang nodded. "I think so, but it won't be easy. DNA Labs International is the best, but as you read, the sample is so minute and deteriorated that their result is more of an opinion than a conclusion. And the same holds for the bloodstain on the shirt."

CHAPTER 62

Sandra lowered Chang's report away from her face and gazed at her husband with broadened eyes. "This certainly adds a new dimension to the case," she said. "The chromosome count of 46 mentioned here holds true for either a normal male or female. I agree that the small amount and poor state of the skin and bloodstains makes it a matter of guesswork to determine whether the chromosome constitution is XY or XX, male or female."

"Which means we still don't know the sex of Myer's killer, or for that matter, of Lacy's and Rose Chiu's killer," Moran said.

Sandra heaved a small sigh and set the report down next to the table by her hospital bed. "I still feel that Lacy's killer could be a woman. However, regarding Paul Myer and Rose Chiu, I don't know."

"One gun for all three killings, the killer is one and same," Moran said. He scratched the nape of his neck and continued. "Sabrina's a strong, fit woman, and so was Samantha. Any woman who can handle a Harley has to be in shape. And they both had skin almost alabaster white, just like the skin under Myer's nails."

"But, Halpern also matches that description," Sandra put in.

Moran fixed his eyes on his wife. "I know," he said, and frowned.

"What's wrong?" Sandra asked.

Moran smacked his lips. "Here's my problem with Halpern. We've got him at Lacy's place on the day of the murder, but we don't know the exact time and we can't tie him to the gun because we can't locate it," Moran said. He then sucked in air. "And we know he spoke with Greg Saunders on the night he was killed.

256

Halpern found out that his wife was pregnant with Greg's baby and confronted him that night. But again we can't place him there... yet."

Sandra nodded. "And you still can't explain why Sabrina would kill Myer."

The lieutenant pushed himself up from the edge of the bed, folded the report, and jammed it into his pocket. "I keep going back to what Myer said. Something struck him familiar about the individual in Lacy's hallway. Since the stranger's face was covered by the helmet's tinted visor, I'm thinking smell."

"Perfume?"

Moran nodded. "Could be, and if that's the case it had to be a very unique kind of perfume," Moran said. "And Myer decided to blackmail that individual. I'll bet—"

Moran's cell rang. It was Hernandez. When the lieutenant finished listening he flipped the cell closed. His worried expression said it all.

"Simms' car was spotted at a Thruway toll booth north of Albany with a man driving. I've got to get back to the office," Moran said. "The NYSP has a fix on car."

* * *

It was nearly dusk, and creeping Utica commute traffic on the New York State Thruway made Kevin Palmer jittery as he sat behind the wheel of the Toyota. The semi in front of him was doing five-miles-an-hour and the fast lane was moving even slower.

"What's the hell's goin' on?" Palmer said and hit the steering with the palm of his hand.

"I gotta pee again," Simms said.

Palmer shot her a hard look. "Suck it in, Alice. We got bigger problems. I didn't like the way the last toll booth attendant looked at you."

Simms stared out at the semi. "Whatever, but I gotta pee."

Palmer glowered at his ex-wife. "You went at the gas station."

"That was a can of Coke and over two hours ago. Plus, it's cold."

Palmer gave the side view mirror a quick glance and then jerked the car into the fast lane. The honk of the horn from the car behind him went unchallenged. He fixed his attention on the flashing lights twenty-five yards ahead.

"Hell!" Palmer shouted. "The cops are runnin' a roadblock up ahead."

"Oh, good, that means I can use the bathroom," Simms said.

Palmer shot her a sideways glance. "Keep it up and you're gonna need a dentist," he said. He turned the car hard to the left onto the grassy snow-patched narrow divider. "Gotta get outta—" Palmer started to say when sound of rapidly approaching sirens interrupted him.

"Give it up Kevin," Simms pleaded. "All you're going to do is get yourself killed."

"I'm not going back inside," Palmer said. He turned to Simms, his eyes moistened. "All I ever wanted was to give us another chance. What's so wrong about that?"

The sound of nearing sirens from the other direction startled Palmer. His face was ashen and perspiration began to form on his face. Kevin Palmer was trapped.

"Please, Kevin, let's just—" Simms said and stopped when she saw the barrel of the Glock pointed at her head.

CHAPTER 63

When novice Trooper Gavin Dawes, a recent transfer to Troop G from Buffalo, left his wife and five-month-old son that morning to go to work, he had no idea that his day was going to develop into a possible standoff with a crazed kidnapper.

As Trooper Dawes drove the lead car toward the stopped Toyota, his stomach tightened. He turned and looked at his superior, a burly fifteen-year veteran sergeant in the passenger seat and swallowed hard.

"Don't worry Dawes, you'll do just fine," the sergeant said. "He'd be a fool not to give himself up."

The younger trooper nodded and accelerated the cruiser. "I just hope he doesn't hurt the hostage," Dawes said. His jaw was set hard when the car screeched to a stop twenty feet away from the Toyota. After Dawes and the sergeant climbed out of their car with guns drawn, a loud gunshot came from inside the Toyota.

"Oh, shit!" the sergeant shouted and both men raced toward the stopped car. When they neared, a badly shaken Simms opened her door and stumbled out. She was clutching her stomach.

"Are you okay, ma'am?" Dawes asked.

The NYPD detective grimaced, shook her head and looked at the troopers with tear-filled eyes. With a shaky finger she pointed to the inside of the car, but when she opened her mouth to speak no sound came forth.

A moment later, when the sergeant yanked the Toyota's driver's door open, his face paled.

Kevin Palmer fell face up, halfway out of the car. The flow of blood running down the right side of the head and the Glock in his right hand told the story.

With his arms around a distraught Simms, Trooper Dawes reached the driver's side and the NYPD detective gazed down at her ex-husband's body.

"He's finally free of his demons," Simms said in a low voice and turned away.

CHAPTER 64

"Thanks, Captain," Moran said and hung up the phone. He turned to Darcey who was seated across from him. "That was Benedict. Flora King got back yesterday from Nashville," Moran said. He tapped the Traffic Control Division's five-year-old report with the tip of his index finger. "The proverbial '*other shoe*' has just fallen," Moran said. He pushed the report toward Darcey. "Take a look at this."

Darcey studied the one-page report and set it down on the table. "So, Jessie Rand's ankle scar was due to a motorcycle accident on the FDR Drive."

Moran nodded. "She was driving and was sideswiped by a delivery van that almost ripped her foot off. I think we've been had by Miss Rand. Run a DMV check on her in New York, Ohio, and New Jersey under both names, Rand and Schloessman. Also, check those names for any properties or leased homes in the Jersey Shores." He rose from the chair, stepped to the blackboard and picked up a piece of chalk. "S... A", Moran murmured as he wrote the letters on the board.

He stepped back and looked at the letters. "What if—" the lieutenant began and strode back to the blackboard. "If instead an '*A*' Rose Chiu was really writing the start of a '*C*'?"

"Schloessman," Darcey said with a blank expression.

Moran turned around and walked to the table. He faced the seated detective. "Exactly."

"But that means that—" Darcey started to say.

"That Jessie Rand could be Lacy's and Myer's killer," Moran interjected. "God knows she's fit enough to have taken on Myer."

"That still leaves the question of motive."

Moran sat down. "Try this on for size. Lacy and Rand have more than a teacher-student relationship. They go on holidays together to the Jersey Shore and Atlantic City. I'm sure the '*R*' in Lacy's diary stands for Rand and the picture on the veranda on a beach could be Rand's place. One day Rand finds out Lacy is having a fling with both Halpern and Greg Saunders. Jealousy rears its ugly head. She shows up at Lacy's apartment and overhears Lacy and Halpern. Rand waits and when the senator leaves she enters and in a rage kills Lacy. She exits the place and runs into Myer, who recognizes something about her, which could be the Chanel No. 5 she was doused in when we interviewed her. When sleaze-ball Paul Myer starts to blackmail her, she kills him."

Darcey slowly nodded. "Okay, a possible scenario. But it doesn't explain Rose Chiu."

An enthusiastic Moran slammed the palm of his hand on the table and leaned forward. "That's easy," he said while Darcey with a mesmerized look on his face stared at his boss. Moran went on. "I asked Chiu if Lacy was a switch-hitter, she responded, '*Who knows, god knows she was pretty enough to attract both sexes.*' Then Chiu described an unknown woman who visited Lacy at the club. That woman could easily be Jessie Rand. Our dancer realizing that Chiu could possibly link her to Lacy decides to silence her."

Just then the door to the office opened. "And how do we go about proving all this?" Hernandez said from the doorway.

Moran and Darcey turned to the sergeant. "Chang said that the bloodstains on the back of Myer's shirt was the rare AB type. We need to ascertain Rand's blood type."

Hernandez walked farther into the room. "That's not going to be easy."

"Not really," Moran said and picked up the accident report. "It says here that at the time of the accident Jessie Rand was transported by ambulance to Bellevue's emergency room. They must have her blood type."

Darcey said. "Rand's skin complexion does match the skin under Myer's fingernails."

Moran peered at Hernandez. "How's Alice doing?"

"Coping," Hernandez answered.

"Get her on this ASAP. It'll do her good." Moran said. "Let's talk with Flora King about the last time she cleaned Greg Saunders' place."

* * *

Flora King, a medium built African-American with gray-streaked hair neatly gathered in a snoop, sat in a large La-Z-Boy chair as she took a deep breath from the oxygen mask she pressed against her nose. The fingers of her other hand held a lit Virginia Slims. She gazed up at Moran and Hernandez who were standing over her, removed the mask and took a couple of frantic drags from the cigarette.

The sergeant looked at the green oxygen tank next to her. "Don't you think that's dangerous?"

Flora's face blossomed into a grin and looked at the cigarette. "I've tried giving 'em up but found it useless. My motto is, '*If you can't beat 'em, join 'em.*' "

"Do you still do housecleaning?" Moran asked

Flora shook her head. "Can't," she said and gestured to the oxygen tank. "The good Lord didn't give me a husband, so instead he threw this in," she said and gestured to the tank. "I'm sixty-three and too dependent on it. That's what I was going to tell Mr. Saunders on the day—" Flora stopped and bit her lower lip.

"How long did you work for Saunders?" Moran said.

"A little over five years."

"When was the last time that you cleaned his house, specifically the bedroom?"

Flora passed the palm of one hand over her floral-patterned housecoat and gazed at the ceiling for a moment. "Eh, late in the afternoon of the day before... before I... found him," she finally stammered. "By the time I left it was nearly seven."

"You cleaned every day?" Hernandez said.

"No, but Mr. Saunders was having guests over that week and wanted everything to be particularly spotless."

"By spotless I assume that the bed was perfectly made up and clean," Moran said.

Flora narrowed her eyebrows, and then straightened herself. "Of course. Only thing on that bed was the cover and four oriental cushions."

"No chance of any loose strands of hair being on it," Hernandez asked.

Flora's face tightened. "Not when I clean!"

Moran dug into his pocket, drew out three photographs and handed them to the cleaning lady. "Have you ever seen any of these people at the house?" Moran said.

Flora studied each of the photographs. While she peered at the pictures she alternated breaths of oxygen with drags from the cigarette. Finally, she pointed at one of the pictures.

"This one, a couple of times. Miss Sabrina."

Hernandez pointed to Samantha's picture. "What about her?"

Flora looked at the photograph. "Oh, yes, she was there quite a bit," she said. The cleaning lady pursed her lips. "Never thought it right, her being married and all."

"What about her husband, Senator Halpern, the man in the other photograph?" Moran said.

Flora studied the photo and gazed up at the lieutenant. "Only once, at a Fourth of July party last year. Mr. Saunders asked me to stay and help out. At one point I heard them arguing out on the patio."

"Over what?" Hernandez said.

Flora shrugged. "Couldn't it make out, but it was heated."

"What about this?" Hernandez handed Flora the enlarged picture from Greg's cell phone.

Flora gazed at the *Four Musketeers* cell picture and laughed. "They were a crazy bunch. Loved their motorcycles. I remember taking this."

"The other woman in the picture, Jessie Rand. What can you tell us about her?" Hernandez said.

Flora King handed the pictures back to Moran and took a deep drag from the cigarette. "Nothing. She came around once in a while with Miss Sabrina. Some kinda dancer, I think," Flora said and shrugged. "That's all I know."

Moran and Hernandez exchanged glances and then watched Flora King help herself to another breath of oxygen and one long final drag.

* * *

As the Mercury Marquis that carried Moran and Hernandez from Flora King's home crossed the Henry Hudson Bridge into the northern tip of Manhattan, Hernandez's Blackberry buzzed. "It's a text message from Alice," Hernandez said and answered. A moment later he turned to Moran in the passenger seat.

"Hospital records show that Jessie Rand's blood type is 'O'," Hernandez said. "The same as Myer's, so that isn't Rand's blood on the back of Myer's shirt. And, Ohio and New York DMV don't have a motorcycle registered to Jessie Rand or Jessie Schloessman, but—"

A somber Moran stared out his window. "It just keeps getting better, doesn't it?"

Hernandez kept his eyes on the road ahead while he accelerated the car into the fast lane. "However, Ohio has a black Harley registered to a Douglas Schloessman in Sandusky and—"

Moran's face brightened and looked at his sergeant. "Which means that Jessie could've been using her father's motorcycle," Moran said with eagerness.

"He sold it three years ago to a neighbor's son who still owns it." Hernandez said.

CHAPTER 65

After Carlos Ivanovich led Moran and Simms into Sabrina's living room, the valet turned to the two detectives and gave them a cold disdainful look. "Miss Van Damme will be down shortly," the valet said. He turned and left the room.

Simms waved her hand in front of her face. "Phew! Breath like a flamethrower. Not exactly 'Mr. Personality' is he?" she said.

"I'm sure that down deep he's all cuddly and warm," Moran said.

The door opened and Sabrina came into the room—a black silk blouse with an open neck tucked into a pair of long wide-bottom matching pants covered her supple frame. "Whatever it is, I hope it won't take long," she said with all the warmth of an arctic snowstorm. She sailed past the two detectives and slid into a chair. "I have another engagement."

Moran stepped toward Sabrina. "We've ascertained that at Greg's last July 4th party your brother-in-law and he got into a rather nasty argument."

"Ahem. Excuse me," Simms coughed out and tugged at her anorak. "Could I use the bathroom?"

Moran turned to the detective and glared at her. "Now?"

"Sorry, but coffee goes through me like... well you know," Simms said meekly.

"How vivid," Sabrina said. "There's one outside in the hall, first door on the left."

As soon as Simms left, Moran turned to his hostess. "Can you tell me anything about their argument?"

Sabrina leaned back, her hands clasped and resting on her lap.

"There's nothing to tell. George had had a little too much to drink and he accused Greg of having an affair with my sister."

"We've ascertained that Greg was the father of Samantha's child. Do you think Halpern knew your sister was pregnant?"

"I hate to disappoint you, but mind-reading is not one my attributes," Sabrina said. With gazelle-like grace, she levitated off the chair and walked toward the brass bar cart a few feet away.

Moran, zeroing in on the glittering diamond tennis bracelet that dangled from Sabrina's right wrist, made a mental note. "It doesn't bother you that your sister was sleeping with the man you were supposed to marry?"

"I knew they had a brief fling way before Greg and I got hooked up," Sabrina said. "But Sam swore to me that it was over and I believed her. Obviously that wasn't quite true," Sabrina added. Her composure remained cool and collected.

"Why did you slap your brother-in-law at the Red Cross affair?"

Sabrina eyes flashed surprise and her face tensed. She turned toward Moran and shot the detective a cold stare. "You don't miss a thing, do you?"

"Observation is my job."

Sabrina emitted a thin smile. "George had the audacity to say that Sam's death was my fault."

Moran inched closer. "Oh?"

"Like I said, Sam was a bit careless, and it wasn't the first time she had mixed up the cartridges. The last time it happened, I noticed it and was able to warn her in time. George feels I should've checked her cartridge bag before we left the house," Sabrina said and brushed away a strand of blonde hair from her forehead. "And in retrospect..." Her voice faltered. She inhaled deeply and continued, "I feel partly at fault and I'm learning to deal with it."

"There have been rumors that you and your brother-in-law were lovers. Is that true?"

Sabrina snorted. "I see you've spoken to Jessie Rand."

"Were you?"

Sabrina was nearly at the bar cart. "No. His marriage was not a happy one and sometimes when he needed a friendly ear, we'd have lunch somewhere or he'd come over."

Moran's kept his eyes on Sabrina searching for some sign of discomfort—a twitch, an unnatural fluttering of the eyelids, tiny beads of perspiration on the forehead or a twisting of the mouth. But there was nothing. *Either Sabrina Van Damme was the greatest actress in the world or Rand was mistaken*, the lieutenant mused.

"What's your poison?" Sabrina asked from the cart. "I'm having a high-ball."

"None," Moran said. "Isn't a little early in the day?"

Sabrina cackled. "It's never too early," she said. "By the way, what's taking your friend so long? I hope she's all right."

"I'm sure she is. Is there anything you can tell me about Halpern's relationship with Lacy Wooden?"

Sabrina continued mixing her drink. "Only that she was a piece of trash that preyed on men like George."

"What does that mean?"

Sabrina flicked her wrist in the air. "Men approaching their twilight years with unhappy marriages. The never-ending story of man having to have his mate," she said. "Why?"

Moran moved toward the bar cart. "I'm just trying to get a handle on George Halpern."

"Good luck," Sabrina said. "I've been trying for years without any—"

The door slowly opened, and Simms entered the room.

Moran and Sabrina turned to the detective. "What took you so long?" Moran asked.

Simms gazed at Sabrina and gave her an apologetic smile. "Way too much coffee," the detective said and eyed the bracelet on Sabrina's right wrist. Simms gestured to the ornament. "That's absolutely stunning."

Sabrina cast an abandoned glance at the bracelet. "Thank you."

"May I ask how many carats is it?" Simms urged on with an admiring gaze.

Sabrina looked at the diamond bracelet with an indifferent glance. "I really don't know."

Moran looked at his watch and turned to Simms. "We've got to leave or we're going to be late for our meeting with the Commish."

When the two detectives drove out from the Van Damme grounds onto the blacktop road, Simms reached into her anorak's pocket and drew out a small sealed evidence bag.

"Here you go," Simms said as she steered the car and handed Moran the bag.

The lieutenant peered at the bag's contents—a single strand of blonde hair.

"Didn't think you'd pull it off."

A smiled peeked across Simms' face and her eyes glimmered. "Easy, went upstairs, found her bedroom, went inside the bathroom and got it off a brush on the counter," Simms said. She tapped the purse that was strapped across her shoulders. "I also got her prints off the brush."

"You are truly a woman of many talents," Moran said.

Simms skillfully threaded the sedan through the narrow road that led past other mansions. She turned to the lieutenant. "The bracelet she was wearing is an exact match to the one Lacy exchanged the Movado watch for," Simms said. "And it's on Buckeye's insurance policy list."

CHAPTER 66

When Halpern's secretary, the statuesque Cynthia, heard heavy footfalls enter the office, she whirled around and her silky blonde hair fanned out around her shoulders. Her blue eyes widened, and she glared at Moran and Simms as they strode toward her desk. Moran flipped his badge at her. "Don't bother to announce us."

When Moran threw open the door he was greeted by a scowling Halpern who was in his shirtsleeves behind the large mahogany desk with the phone receiver in his hand.

"Never mind, they're here," Halpern said into the receiver and placed it on its cradle.

The senator jumped to his feet, his face reddened and his body tense. "Have you lost your mind, Moran?"

Simms stepped out from behind her boss. She reached into her purse and drew out a folded document. "This is a warrant for your arrest for the murder of Lacy—" the detective began.

Halpern's jaw fell open. "Murder!" the senator exclaimed. "You've really screwed up this time Moran. I'll have your badge for this."

"By the time all this is over you'll be welcome to it," Moran said. He turned to Simms. "Read him the Miranda rights." Moran stepped forward with a pair of handcuffs in his hands.

Halpern stared at the steel bracelets and then at Moran. "Just a sec—"

"I suggest you keep quiet," Simms said.

An ashen Halpern gazed at her and then shifted his attention to Moran. "Please... hear me out. I didn't kill her. I swear," he said.

He flopped into his chair and wiped beads of sweat from his brow with a handkerchief. "I admit I was infatuated with Lacy for the usual reasons a man like me falls in love with a woman half his age," Halpern said. "But I didn't kill her... I couldn't have... loved her too much," he said. The words came out quickly as the two cops neared the desk.

"It's been established that the semen found is yours," Moran said. "We know you bought several pieces of jewelry from Max Roth that are part of Lacy's missing jewelry. You gave the diamond ring to your wife and a diamond tennis bracelet to your sister-in-law. Right?"

Halpern nodded. "Lacy exchanged the Movado for the bracelet. She didn't have much class."

"We know you rented a car here in Albany, drove to New York, and returned it the next day—the same day that Lacy was murdered," Simms said.

Halpern raised his opened hands as if trying to ward off the verbal attack. "Okay, okay, I was there that day," he said. The senator slowly hoisted himself off the chair and massaged his temples. He turned to the detectives. "I drove down to see if I could persuade Lacy to change her mind about ending our relationship. She had this impression that Greg Saunders was going to marry her," Halpern said and turned his eyes away. "Stupid girl," he muttered. He turned back to the cops. "We talked, one thing led to another and we had sex. When we finished I thought I had won her back, but then she said *'That's the last time, George. Consider it a going away present.'* I lost it, called her a whore, punched her, and she fell to the floor unconscious. I then went to where I knew she kept her jewelry, took back my presents, and walked out. When I left her she was unconscious but still alive."

"What time was that?" Moran said.

Halpern pursed his lips and gazed up at the ceiling for a moment. "About eleven or eleven-thirty that morning."

"Except for Lacy's and Myer's prints the police didn't find any other prints in the place," Moran said. "Care to explain?"

"I wiped off every place I'd touched."

"Why? What were you afraid of?" Simms pressed.

Halpern snorted. "When I hit her and saw her lying there without moving, at first I thought I killed her or done serious damage. I panicked and…" Halpern's voice trembled and faded. "I took my handkerchief and—"

Moran nodded. "Got it. So where's the jewelry?"

"In my safe, over there" an agitated Halpern said. He gestured to the sofa that lay against the opposite wall. "It's behind the couch. I knew this day would be coming."

"How's that?" Simms said.

"When Max called me and told me that an NYPD detective had interviewed him regarding the jewelry," he fixed his eyes on Simms, "his description of that detective matched you. I knew it wouldn't be long before someone would put two and two together."

Minutes later, Moran spread the contents of a black silk bag onto the desktop. When the two detectives finished sorting the jewelry, Simms turned to her boss "Except for the ring and bracelet, it's all here."

A disheartened Halpern ran his fingers through his hair. "Am I going to be arrested?"

Moran and Simms looked at each other, and then the lieutenant shifted his gaze to Halpern. "There's no one around to file an assault complaint and a good lawyer could make the case that Lacy voluntarily returned the jewelry to you when she broke up with you. Besides, you have enough on your plate explaining all this to your constituents."

Moran started to turn away and stopped. "You didn't kill Greg Saunders' did you?"

Simms stared at Moran as if he'd lost his mind while Halpern's eyes widened and his hands fell limp to his side.

"Wha… I…. No, of course not," the senator said.

"I didn't think so. It would've meant getting your hands dirty,"

Moran said. He shifted his gaze to a Simms. "Let's go Alice. We've got work to do."

CHAPTER 67

The circular marble lobby of the Federal Courthouse hummed and vibrated with the sound of shuffling of feet and murmurings from the throng. Two revolving doors spilled people in and let them hurry off into the six-pillared corridors that spiraled like arms in different directions.

Clayton Bigelow, a rugged individual with a steady look and his hair buzzed military-style, stood against a corner wall. He glanced at his watch for the third time in the last ten minutes. It was 10:45 a.m. He let out an impatient stream of air, adjusted his corduroy tan jacket and stretched his tall frame, while he watched the crowd at the revolving door. Finally, his eyes squinted when he saw Moran enter.

Bigelow raised his arm. "Over here!"

"Good to see you, Clayton," Moran said when he reached the man. "How're you liking it at the new U.S. Immigration and Citizenship Services?"

Bigelow shrugged. "Same food, different bowl," he said. "Only the name has changed." He reached inside his jacket and brought out an envelope. "Here." Bigelow handed it to Moran. "I've got a meeting with the Assistant U.S. Attorney in ten minutes. This is all we've got at USCIS on Carlos Ivanovich. You were right there's more to Carlos Ivanovich than meets the eye."

Moran studied the sealed envelope in his hand and then switched his gaze to the Homeland Security immigration agent. "Give me the Reader's Digest version."

Bigelow pursed his lips. "You'll have to settle for the peanut shell version. His real name is Jaime Serra and he was a member of

Colombia's Special Forces unit. His job was to *neutralize* dangerous government dissidents. When the new left-wing regime came into power, it became unhealthy for him to remain in the country. That's when the State Department, which had backed the old government, came to the rescue. He was vetted, then given a new name, and a new life."

"If the father was Russian, why the name Serra?" Moran said.

"Mother's maiden name. His father didn't marry his mother," Bigelow said.

Moran nodded. "I thought there was something fishy about him," he said. "So he's a trained killer."

"Few better," Bigelow said. "You'll find all you need in there." The agent motioned to the envelope. "Including his blood type. Now I gotta split." Bigelow said. He turned and vanished into the crowd.

Moran slid the envelope into his jacket and snaked his way through the crowd toward the street. When he reached the building's portico, he saw Hernandez racing up the stone steps.

"What are you doing here?" the lieutenant asked.

Hernandez, panting, clutched at his chest. "Hold... hold on..." he stammered. Finally, he caught his breath. "Simms told me you were here. I ran all the way over to—"

"I was on my way back. What's happened?"

"You're not going to believe this. Earl Schuyler was arrested yesterday afternoon at the Little Foxes Club for running a prostitution ring."

"Huh?"

"Heard it over the radio. I immediately called a friend of mine at Vice and he said the place had been under surveillance until a year ago. Rose Chiu was suspected of running a call-girl service with some of the dancers, but Vice had never been able to get the DA's office to move on it and was ordered to scrub the operation."

Moran wrinkled his face. "That was before Shilling's time. You don't think the fact that some of New York's powerbrokers frequented the place might've had something to do with it, hmm? So what happened to change things?"

"Earl beat up one of the girls pretty badly, she went to the cops," Hernandez said. "The judge slapped him with a million dollar bail. Vice figures that Earl was the enforcer who kept the girls in line for Rose. The complainant said it wasn't the first time he had worked over a dancer."

Moran, perplexed, stared at his sergeant, "Interesting. Maybe we should have a talk with Earl."

An impish smile slowly appeared on the sergeant's face. "He made bail."

Moran's eyes narrowed "On a million dollars?"

"Earl's brother put up the bond overnight and he got released early this morning," Hernandez said.

Moran looked away for an instant while he rubbed the bridge of his nose with the tip of a forefinger. He then returned his gaze to Hernandez. "Who's the rich brother?"

Hernandez shrugged. "Don't know, but I can find out."

CHAPTER 68

"**I** appreciate you letting me come along," Captain Darryl Benedict said to Moran as they stood in front of Sabrina Van Damme's door.

"Thought it only fair since the murder took place in your town," Moran said. He turned to the four NYPD uniforms behind them. "When the door opens, two of you grab the valet and hold him. The rest of you follow us inside." Moran pushed the doorbell button with his thumb.

Carlos, impeccably dressed in his valet uniform, opened the door. His pale face was expressionless while his gaze took in Moran and Benedict. "I assume you wish to speak with madam. She's in the living room," he said. At that moment, two uniforms sprang up from behind Moran and flanked Carlos.

"Don't even think about moving," one of the uniforms told him.

The valet smiled complacently. "Wouldn't dream of spoiling the party."

Moran glared at Carlos—something wasn't right. Followed by Benedict and two uniform cops, Moran strode through the open doors of the living room. When Moran and the Pelham police captain strode farther into the dim room, they were silhouetted by the shaft of light that came through the opening of the partially drawn curtains from behind.

A cold voice from the center of the room spoke. "I'd appreciate it if you two moved out of the light so I can see you," Sabrina said. Moran peered and saw the glow of a cigarette from where the voice came.

When the two cops side-stepped into the darkness, the light revealed Sabrina seated in an armchair gracefully dressed in a black-and-white bellbottomed pants suit and her blonde hair in a neatly coifed French twist. The glint of the diamond earrings caught Moran's attention.

"Well dressed as always," Moran said.

Sabrina emitted a pencil thin smile. "I try my best."

Moran and Benedict began to move toward Sabrina. The sound of a hammer being cocked froze them.

"Stop right there," Sabrina said, her voice calm and determined.

Moran peered through the dimness at a tiny glint of light that reflected off the steel-blue barrel of the over-and-under shotgun set in the crook of Sabrina's left arm—it was pointed directly at him and Benedict.

"When I saw that your Detective Simms had been in my bathroom," Sabrina said, "I knew this day would arrive. Carlos saw you drive up." Sabrina said in a monotone tone. "Sorry if I'm not a very good hostess today and remain seated."

Moran flicked his gaze to the two uniforms at his left and extended his arm. "Stay put!" he ordered. "Leave the guns holstered."

Captain Benedict stepped out from behind Moran and started to move toward Sabrina.

"Just put the weapon down before someone gets hurt," the Pelham Chief of Police said in a calm voice.

Moran stepped forward and pointed at Sabrina. "You killed Greg Saunders, and Carlos was your accomplice."

Sabrina gazed at the lieutenant with leaden eyes. "How did you ever come to that conclusion?"

"We matched the hair found on Greg's bed to you. Saunders's cleaning lady's schedule for that day puts you in the house on the night of the murder. A latent palm print was found on the wall over Saunders's bed and it matches the one lifted from your hairbrush. The fingerprints match the ones on file with the ATF when you applied for a gun license. Also, Greg was tied up by a left handed person and I noticed when we met that you're left-handed."

Sabrina kept her eyes riveted on the lieutenant while she took a slow drag from the cigarette and let out a thin stream of smoke. "This is fascinating, please go on."

Moran said. "Carlos's blood, type B, matches the blood found on a torn piece of latex in Greg's kitchen. Saunders's blood type was A. The chromosome makeup of the bloodstained latex was male, and Carlos is the only one you would've trusted to help you. My first choice was Halpern, but after digging deeper I decided that he was too soft for a job like that."

The lieutenant took two steps forward. "Don't," Sabrina said and nudged the shotgun at him.

Moran stopped. "I submit that being aware of the continuing relationship between Samantha and Greg on the day of her death you saw Samantha throw in the wrong shotgun shells into her cartridge bag. You even might have put them in yourself. At any rate you decided to let fate handle things and not interrupt your enemy while she was making a mistake. Everything else after that was an act on your part."

Sabrina's mouth tightened for an instant and then she smiled thinly. "Actually, Samantha mixed up the shells all by her klutzy self. But you're certainly a clever little man."

"I like to think so," Moran answered. "By the way, did you kill Lacy Wooden?"

Sabrina took another puff. "No, someone else had that pleasure."

"Would you care to tell us why you killed Saunders?"

Sabrina cackled and the sound echoed throughout the room. "The bastard wanted to marry me for my money while he was diddling Lacy and my sister. The little twit thought I wouldn't find out."

Moran nodded. "I'm curious. How did you know Detective Simms had been in your bathroom?"

"She made the mistake of laying the brush face down. I never do that. You really should tell her to be more careful, women notice these things."

"I will."

"So what's next, we stand here all day?" Benedict said.

Sabrina crushed out the cigarette in a nearby ashtray and placed her hand on her lap. "No, I have other plans," Sabrina said. The shotgun started to come up.

From behind Moran and Benedict, two gunshot bursts thundered in rapid succession through the room. Sabrina's body twitched violently and then slumped backwards in the chair revealing a massive circular crimson red stain that had rapidly started to spread over the front of her black-and-white pants suit.

Moran whirled around and glared at one of the uniforms, a young blond cop with boyish looks and a dumbfounded expression on his face. The young cop lowered his eyes and stared at the service revolver in his right hand as if the gun had gone off by itself. Moran turned and ran toward Sabrina.

Captain Benedict turned to the stunned cop. "You were told to keep your guns holstered," he exclaimed.

"She... she brought the gun up. I thought—" the cop stammered.

"The damn thing's empty," Moran called out.

Benedict turned and saw Moran standing next to Sabrina's body with the shotgun in his hands and the breach open.

The Pelham police captain's jaw dropped open and he marched toward the Lieutenant. When Benedict reached the dead woman and Moran, he gazed down at Sabrina and then his eyes drifted to the shotgun. "I'll be a monkey's uncle, she planned it so we'd be the ones to take her out."

"Suicide-by-cop," Moran said and snapped the breach closed.

The sound of heavy footfalls entering the room made Moran and Benedict turn around.

Clayton Bigelow and a man in a charcoal gray single-breasted suit marched in. Between them walked Carlos Ivanovich.

"What the hell's this?" Moran blurted.

"Easy," Bigelow said. "We need to talk, now!"

Moran pointed to the stranger with Bigelow. "Who's he?"

"You can call me Mr. Smith," the stranger said, his face impassive and tight. "And I represent a higher authority."

"You work for Hebrew National?" Moran said with a look of pretended astonishment on his face.

"There's nothing funny about this," Bigelow said.

The man called Smith said, "Carlos Ivanovich is a very important asset to this country's fight against organized terrorism in Latin-America. That's all I can tell you."

Moran's face tightened and he gritted his teeth. "We have proof that Carlos Ivanovich is involved in the murder of Greg Saunders and—"

Mr. Smith stepped forward. "I understand how you feel, but you got your murderess. Case solved," he said, He pointed to the dead Sabrina. "Carlos explained his part. He was merely an accessory. The lady asked him for help, and being a loyal servant, he came to her aid. According to him, she was the one who set up the contraption that killed Mr. Saunders. All our man did was bring an unconscious Saunders to the kitchen and at her request left. End of story."

Moran snorted. "You actually believe that?"

Mr. Smith shrugged lightly. "You have to admit that Miss Van Damme was an expert with shotguns and had the physique to do the job. It sounds plausible to me," the man said. "But let's cut to the chase. Carlos Ivanovich is officially United States Government property and therefore New York State putting him in jail is not an option."

"So he gets a free pass?" Moran said.

"He'll be relocated somewhere else and as far as New York is concerned, he never existed. Are we clear on that?"

Moran swallowed hard. "You're from Langley, right?"

Mr. Smith gave an enigmatic smile. "That information is on a need-to-know basis only, and that's not the case here."

Moran turned to Bigelow. "If you knew about this why the

hell did you help me?"

"I'm not privy to everything that goes on at Homeland. I'm Immigration. I didn't know how deep this all went until yesterday."

Moran nodded. "Sure, like JFK didn't know Marilyn Monroe." He then shifted his attention to Carlos, who stood impassively next to Bigelow.

"You knew she was going to do this, didn't you?" Moran said.

The valet shrugged. "The way I see it everyone has a right to choose how they die."

CHAPTER 69

"You're telling us that the man who put up the bond for Earl Schuyler is the same person in Miami who purchased a Dexter derringer?" Schilling said from his seat behind the desk.

"When Hernandez told me that Earl's brother had posted bail," Moran said, "we contacted the bail bondsman. One hundred thousand dollars was wired from a Miami bank. The account was in the name of a Marvin Schuyler."

Shilling shrugged with a baffled expression on his face.

"It all fits," Moran went on. "I remembered that Earl's last name is Schuyler, and the guy that bought a Dexter derringer in Miami was a successful developer named Marvin Schuyler. Earl said he came from Central Florida and just to make sure that he was indeed Earl's brother, we checked into ATF's records of the purchase of the derringer. Marvin Schuyler was born in Kissimmee five years before Earl. And Earl's Social Security file has Kissimmee as his place of birth."

Schilling looked at Commissioner Newbury, who was seated on the sofa across the room next to Moran. "What do you think of all this, Horace?"

The commissioner coughed and crossed his legs. "It's very possible that Earl Schuyler, whom we now know to have been Rose Chiu's enforcer, killed my niece," Newbury said.

Shilling narrowed his eyebrows and cast the commissioner a doubtful look. "With a gun belonging to a brother who lives in Florida," the DA put in.

"I'll let Moran paint the rest of the picture," Newbury said.

Moran lifted himself off the sofa and lumbered to the center of the room. "Lacy figures she's got Greg Saunders all wrapped up around her little finger. Even sees herself as the next Mrs. Saunders. After all, she's younger and maybe prettier than Sabrina. Which is why she dumped Halpern. Lacy then decides to quit dancing or whatever else she did at Chiu's club and Rose won't have any of it. In steps Earl."

"Does he own a motorcycle?" Schilling asked.

"Not here, but we're checking with Florida," Moran said. "But it does bring up the point that except for Earl no one has ever said they actually saw the killer ride a motorcycle, only that he wore a riding outfit."

Schilling shifted his weight in his chair and steepled his fingers. "What about the possibility of Rose Chiu owning one and Earl having access to it?"

Newbury scoffed. "For crying out loud, the woman was paralyzed."

Moran's lips formed a razor-thin smile. "Not all her life. And Howard is right. I thought the same and asked Simms to check with DMV for any records on Chiu."

Shilling gestured to the lieutenant. "Go on."

Moran started to pace in front of the DA's desk. "After Earl killed Lacy he ran into Paul Myer in the hallway and figured the cops would play the hot-headed boyfriend card," Moran said. "And he was right." Moran stopped and looked at Schilling, who was slowly rolling a silver ballpoint pen between his fingers. "Earl's no fool," he went on. He's got the survival instincts of an alley cat. Something not to be underestimated."

Schilling dropped the pen on the desk and looked up at the lieutenant. "Motive?"

"Unexpectedly, Myer got released and this worried Earl. We know that Paul was seen hanging around the club and he most likely knew Earl. Remember, Paul said that when he was on his way to Lacy's apartment, he passed someone in a motorcycle rider's outfit and that he recognized something," Moran said and paused for a moment. He then added, "Could that something have been Earl Schuyler's cologne?"

"Cologne?" Schilling said.

Moran moved toward the desk. "When we interviewed Earl at the club after Rose was murdered, Hernandez and I were almost knocked over by Earl's cologne. Hernandez recognized it as *Paco Rabanne*. And knowing Paul Myer, he probably tried to hustle Rose and Earl."

"Okay, I can buy into that," Schilling said.

"This all works for Myer but what about Rose Chiu?" Newbury said.

Moran peered at the Commissioner. "I don't know the answer to that yet, but I've ordered Hernandez and Simms to pick up Earl for questioning."

Schilling turned to Moran. "I'll tell the assistant district attorney handling the Vice case against Schuyler to make a motion to vacate bail. If Earl Schuyler is a murder suspect I don't want him on the streets."

"The Dade County Sheriff's Office is leaning on Marvin Schuyler as we speak," Moran said. "In my opinion he was either duped into giving or selling the derringer to his brother, or Earl stole it. We know he's a respected member of the business community, and I'm sure he'll cooperate."

CHAPTER 70

With Rose Chiu's lizard-skin phonebook in his hand, Moran angrily shoved his chair away from his desk and faced Hernandez. "Whaddya mean, Earl Schuyler's disappeared?" Moran shouted. "And where the hell's Simms?"

"She's still over at DMV," a red-faced Hernandez muttered. "Like I said, when Simms and I got to Earl's place and started up the stairs to his apartment on the second floor, the building's manager stopped us. When we told him where we were going he said he'd seen Earl with a suitcase leave the building earlier this morning."

Moran rose, the phonebook clutched in his right hand. "Did he know where Earl was going?"

Hernandez shook his head. "Nope, just that he got into a waiting cab."

"Did he give you the name of the cab company?" Moran pressed.

"Yep. Crestwood Taxi Company. I've got Darcey out there now."

The phone on top of the conference table rang. "That must be the Dade County Sheriff's Office calling back," Moran said and moved to the telephone. "Called them earlier and left a message." When Moran answered, his face broke into a wide smile. "Thank you, Sheriff Martinez," he said and hung up. Moran turned and pointed at Hernandez. "Earl visited his brother about a month before Lacy's death for a couple of weeks; a couple of days later, his brother, Marvin, discovered the derringer missing and immediately thought of Earl. Seems his brother kept talking about how nice it'd be to have a small gun like that."

"Did Marvin report the incident?" the sergeant said.

"No, and he's facing possible charges of failing to report a lost or stolen weapon," Moran said. "A misdemeanor at most—a fine and slap on the wrist. Put out an APB on Earl, and get his DMV picture in every newspaper and newscast," Moran said and returned to his desk. "Let's give him the full celebrity treatment."

Hernandez said. "It'd be great help if Dexter Industries got their ballistic reports to us."

The door swung open and Alice Simms walked into the office. Moran turned to face her. "I hope you're the bearer of good news."

"Rose Chiu owned a black Yamaha Stratoliner motorcycle," Simms said.

Moran creased his brow. "But that's not the bike everyone's described."

Simms nodded. "I thought the same and checked out the Stratoliner on Yamaha's website. It's very similar to a Harley and easy to get them confused at a distance. For whatever reason, Chiu kept the registration up to date," she said. Simms then opened her notepad. "The woman's so-called '*traffic accident*' consisted of her missing a curve on the Long Island Expressway near Montauk Point while driving her Yamaha Stratoliner. Rose Chiu had more alcohol in her bloodstream than a brewery when her bike slammed into a tree and threw her," the detective said. "DMV has a record of it because her license was subsequently suspended."

Moran strode to the conference table and set down Chiu's phonebook. He opened it and pointed to an entry written in black ink—*Skillman, James*—followed by a local telephone number. "Take a good look at this."

While Hernandez and Simms gazed at the name, Moran edged in close and stuck his forefinger on top of the name, and then set down Chiu's Post-It with the SA scribbling next to the name. "Notice anything?"

Hernandez and Simms shifted their eyes to the Post-It. "What about it?" Simms said.

"All this time we thought that Rose's killer's name began with the letters *SA*, a least from what we could make out from her handwriting. However, take a close look at the way she connects the 'S' and the 'K' when she wrote *Skillman*."

The two detectives leaned in and peered closely at the entry.

"I don't get it," Hernandez whispered.

"Hold on," Simms suddenly blurted. She jammed her index finger over *Skillman*. The way she connects the S and the K...it—" Simms stopped and looked up at Moran, her face a question mark.

Moran straightened up and loosened his tie. "You're on the right track. If we examine her Post-It closely, at the top of her 'A' there's appears to be a tiny continuing line that could be the start of a 'K,' " Moran said. "We're going to need the opinion of a handwriting expert, but I'm sure we're right."

"Fine, but what does that have to do with Earl Schuyler?" Hernandez said.

Moran emitted a 'cat-that-ate-the-canary' smile. "Rose Chiu called Earl, '*Sky*,' short for Schuyler."

Simms face brightened. "Chiu was beginning to write out the name *Sky*," she said.

"Exactly. So, boys and girls, we've got a pretty good idea that Earl is our man, motive and opportunity, but it's all circumstantial. We need that derringer to tie him to the killings."

"Plus a motive," Hernandez said.

Moran glanced at his watch. It was three o'clock. "It's two o'clock in Illinois," he said and started to walk to the telephone. "Time to give Clarence Dexter another reminder. How busy can they be in beautiful downtown Cicero?"

CHAPTER 71

The Crown Vic cruised off the Staten Island Expressway's Richmond Hill/Hylan Boulevard exit. When it came to a stop at the red light, Hernandez turned in his driver's seat to Moran. "I'm still surprised at how fast Clarence Dexter e-mailed the ballistics report. Less than a half an hour after you spoke with him," he said.

Moran smiled. "Phrases like, '*obstruction-of-justice,*' '*accessory-to-murder*' and '*aiding-and-abetting,*' suddenly make people eager to cooperate." He focused on the two side-by-side color photographs of Earl Schuyler on the front page of the *New York Post*. "Wanted for Murder—Armed and Dangerous"—was printed underneath them. One of the pictures was of the suspect with his red handlebar moustache, and other was the same picture without the bushy appendage.

Moran pointed to the picture of Earl without the moustache. "This computer-enhanced version should cover all possible changes our man might've attempted."

"Except for adding a wig," Hernandez said.

"We still have his face," Moran said as the engine revved and the sedan sped down the four-lane boulevard.

Fifteen minutes later, the two detectives climbed out of the car and ignored the "No Entry-Eltingville Storage Facility" sign posted on a side door. They pushed it open. The swarthy man wearing a red turban neatly wrapped around his head and a zipped up long-sleeved sweater looked up. "Lieutenant Moran, I presume," the man said with a sub-continent accent.

Moran nodded and gestured to his sergeant. "You must be the

owner, Mr. Singh. This is Sergeant Hernandez."

Singh nodded. He grabbed a thin file on the Formica counter that lay alongside pens and pencils neatly arranged like flatware on a tablecloth. He walked out from behind it. "As I said over the phone, I recognized Mr. Schuyler from his picture on the news," Singh said. "This is his paperwork." The owner handed Moran the file.

When Moran opened the file he briskly flipped through its contents: a rental agreement and copies of Earl Schuyler's driver's license and a deposit check. He looked up at the owner. "That's it?"

Singh smiled and shrugged. "I am afraid there is nothing else. Mr. Schuyler is a good customer, pays on time and there is never any complaint."

"What about a key?" Hernandez said.

The owner frowned. "I am afraid that without a warrant I cannot comply. I consulted my attorney."

Moran looked around the small office. He pointed to a small section of exposed wiring in a corner. "That's a fire hazard," Moran said and turned to Hernandez. "We should let the Fire Department know about it."

Hernandez gazed at a surprised looking Singh and smiled wryly. "Sorry, but we have to call *'em as we see 'em.*"

A broad smile materialized on Singh's face. "There is no need to complicate matters, Lieutenant. In fact, I told my attorney that it would be wise to cooperate since this was a murder investigation."

Shortly afterwards, Moran and Hernandez were inside storage area number four, taking in the place. In a corner, a black tarp lay against a wall. A few feet away sat a beat-up green trunk.

Moran looked down at the frayed black-and-red rug with an Oriental pattern. "Look familiar?"

Hernandez's gaze went to the rug. "Same color as the threads on Myer's shoes." The sergeant focused on a large dark stain on the rug. He crouched down and with the tips of his fingers touched the stain. "Motor oil."

"Has to be a motorcycle," Moran said, "The place is too small for anything else."

Hernandez's eyes went to a slight indentation in the rug. "Looks like something a motorcycle kickstand would make."

"With the license number out there he won't get far," Moran said. "Make a note to have Forensics check the rug for bloodstains."

The two cops moved toward the trunk. It was closed and locked. Moran and Hernandez shared a look and a moment later the tip of the blade from the sergeant's penknife started to pry open the flimsy lock.

"You're pretty good at that," Moran observed.

Hernandez chortled. "Picked it up in Boy Scouts," the sergeant said over his shoulder.

"Never doubted it for a moment," Moran said.

Moran opened the trunk lid and grasped the bundled black leather motorcycle suit. His gaze fell on the decal on the back of a black helmet: a red rose superimposed over motorcycle handlebars.

"Can't imagine Earl being a member of the club," Moran murmured.

Hernandez turned and looked at the decal. "It's not the same decal." He pointed to the rose, "This one's only got four petals, and the real one has six. Also the handlebars are not like the others."

"You know about motorcycles too?" Moran asked.

Hernandez shrugged. "Not really, but these handlebars are low while the others rode high."

"Looks like Earl was trying to frame someone from the Harley Rose Club. Always said he was cunning," Moran said. He set the helmet down next to the suit, reached inside the trunk and pulled out a small empty oilskin wrapping. He handed it to his sergeant. Moran then extracted an empty duffle bag.

"There's nothing in the oilskin," Hernandez said from behind Moran. "But I'd say these stains are gun oil residue."

The lieutenant turned around and looked at the unfolded

oilskin in Hernandez's hands and the oil stains. "Probably belong to the derringer," Moran said. "Okay, get some uniforms out here and let's go catch ourselves a killer."

CHAPTER 72

During the forty-mile drive north on the Taconic State Parkway, Moran and Hernandez sat quietly. Moran stared out at the passing towns where mothers where stirring to get their children ready for school buses and fathers were leaving for the long commute to work. Occasionally Moran would clear his throat or grunt. He glanced a couple of times at the silent sergeant, who seemed lost in thought. While Hernandez steered the sedan over the cement ribbon of road, he yawned a couple of times, which made Moran do the same and both men shared an uneasy laugh. They looked at each other as if each knew what the other was thinking. Manhunts were always risky affairs.

Three hours earlier, the sound of Moran's phone had filled his dark bedroom and caused the lieutenant to pop open his eyes and bolt up in bed. When he glanced at the radio/clock's green LCD it read 4:45 a.m. It had been the Police Headquarters' operator telling Moran that a Major Edward Thorsen from the New York State Police had just called regarding Earl Schuyler.

When Moran called Thorsen, the major spoke with clipped military exactness—a no-nonsense kind of officer.

At 7:35 a.m., Moran and Hernandez pulled into the parking area of the Mohansic State Park. As they climbed out of the car they spotted in the shadows of the gray dawn several NYSP cruisers and clusters of men in gray woolen winter uniforms and broad straight-brimmed hats on their heads. From one of the clusters an officer turned, broke away and started walking toward the two New York City detectives.

The approaching tall, straight as a ramrod, NYSP trooper

carried his chin out, and his chest puffed out while he strode with West Point precision toward Moran and Hernandez. A polished black leather belt and holster girded his narrow tight waist.

"Here comes 'Smokey the Bear,' " Hernandez said beneath his breath.

When the trooper reached the two detectives, he gave a sharp salute. "Major Edward Thorsen," he announced.

"I'm Lieutenant James Francis Moran and this is Detective Sergeant Frank Hernandez," Moran said tersely.

"How do I know that?" Thorsen snapped.

Moran and Hernandez shared a glance. They opened their topcoats, and flipped out their identifications and showed them to an unsmiling Thorsen. "Come with me. We found the motorcycle you were looking for. It's over there." He gestured to a small circle of troopers.

When the trio arrived, the circle opened, and Moran and Hernandez stared at Rose Chiu's black Yamaha Stratoliner. Thorsen stuck his right thumb between his belt and uniform. "Before we go any further, let me get one thing clear. There's a jurisdictional problem."

Moran eyebrows narrowed. "Oh?"

"This is New York State Police turf, so any inquiries or investigations are to be handled by us," Thorsen said. "You two can come along only as observers but stay in the rear."

"You seem to forget that the suspect is wanted for three murders in my city," Moran said.

Thorsen nodded firmly. "You want to take him back to New York City, you go through channels."

Moran and Hernandez shared another look. "Fine, Major. So, what else do you have?" the lieutenant said.

The major peered suspiciously at Moran. "I've heard of you from colleagues, Lieutenant, and I know you like to do things your way, so I'm keeping an eye out. Don't even think of breaking my rules."

Moran gave an impish smile. "Would it help to tell you that

I've reformed?"

Thorsen stared hard at Moran. "No." He then led the two detectives to the edge of the parking lot's blacktop and pointed to a series of footprints on the dewy grass. "A trooper spotted the Yamaha and the lettering Stratoliner on the gas tank, exiting the Taconic State Parkway and followed it at a distance to this spot. He checked the license number that you'd put out and called it in."

"Why didn't he arrest him right then and there?" Hernandez asked.

"Your bulletin said the suspect was armed and dangerous," Thorsen said. "Our policy is not to approach unless we have backup. The trooper said he saw the man dismount from the bike and when he took off the helmet, except for the absence of a moustache, he matched the APB. The trooper watched while the guy headed into the woods with a long object in his hands."

"A rifle?" Moran said.

"We don't know, but I'd have to assume so," Thorsen said. "This is not a large park, not like the ones in the Catskills, but that's Storm Mountain." He pointed to a tall rise that loomed over the crest of pine trees. "If he makes it up there we're looking at a long search."

Moran followed the series of footsteps in the grass into the dense forest of pines with his eyes and then looked up at the mountain.

"Tough terrain," Moran said.

"That's why I've called in helicopters and our snipers—"

Moran bristled and stepped toward Thorsen. "Snipers?"

Thorsen stood at attention to his full six-foot-four-inch height. "We have to go in there and find your man. If he has a rifle he could pick us off one-by-one. I'm not taking that risk," Thorsen said. Then he relaxed and gazed at Moran with a tinge of compassion in his eyes. "This fugitive of yours, any chance he might give himself up?"

Moran slowly shook his head. "Uh-uh. Earl Schuyler isn't the type to rot in jail for the rest of his life. From what I make of him, he's an old country boy from Florida who probably knows how to survive in the woods, which is why he came here."

Thorsen adjusted his hat and pursed his lips. "I was afraid of that."

The flashing tri-color roof lights of a dark gray SUV as it entered the parking lot made the three men turn their heads. Thorsen's face tightened once more and he looked at Moran and Hernandez with steely eyes. "They're here. Let's go. You two at the rear."

CHAPTER 73

"*E*arl Schuyler... Earl Schuyler... This is the New York State Police, come out with your hands in the air.*" The voice boomed through a megaphone and echoed repeatedly through the woods as twenty troopers spread out in line formation with Major Thorsen in the center trampled through plants and bushes. At each end of the line was a sniper with a scoped M-22 rifle cradled in his arms.

A New York State Police helicopter circled above as *"Earl Schuyler... Earl Schuyler... Show yourself"* blared from its loudspeaker.

Moran and Hernandez walked a few paces behind the line, each with the Glocks in his hands.

"Dudley Do-Right up ahead better not see these," Hernandez said and nodded to his gun.

"Screw 'im," Moran grumbled. He grimaced. The right knee was throbbing like there was no tomorrow. He looked up at Storm Mountain—it now seemed nearer. Moran checked his watch and saw they had been walking for an hour.

The megaphone and the chopper's loudspeaker continued to repeat their ominous message. No trooper in the line spoke while the morning light that filtered through the pine trees filled the range with an eerie aspect. Only the booming megaphone and the helicopter's loudspeaker gave it any sense of reality.

"Watch out for the bogs," Thorsen called out.

"Too late," Hernandez murmured and pulled his left leg out from a black-water leaf- covered mud-hole.

Suddenly a rifle shot pierced the air and whistled through the trees. It came from somewhere in the lower base of the mountain. Then another shot cracked through the air like a whip as everyone hit the dirt. Moran and Hernandez peered out into the thick forest from their prone positions. "I think it came from over there," Moran whispered and jerked his thumb to the right.

"From the sound I'd say a little over a hundred yards away and up," Hernandez said.

Suddenly Thorsen called out. "Everyone stay down!" It was answered with several *Rogers* and *Ten-fours*. Thorsen craned his head backwards. "You people okay back there, Moran?"

"Fine!" Hernandez shouted back.

Moran gazed at his sergeant. "You game?" he asked with a mischievous glint in his eye.

Hernandez grinned and nodded. "But I go first."

"Wait a—"

Hernandez nodded down to Moran's knee. "Let's not go through this again," the sergeant said. He pulled off his topcoat, rolled it up and placed it against the base of a pine tree. When his boss did the same, the sergeant began crawling toward his right with Moran close behind.

The first twenty-five yards were tough going as Hernandez led the way through thick underbrush while trying to avoid the bogs, which were visible only because the sunlight reflected off their surface.

Hernandez stopped. His boss's breathing was becoming heavy. The sergeant turned his head and gazed at Moran. "You okay?"

Moran looked exhausted, his face smudged with black tar and mud. Dry leaves stuck out of his hair. "Besides freezing my butt off," the lieutenant said. "Like my grandmother Fiona would say, *'Never better, laddie.'*"

Hernandez smiled and continued crawling uphill in the direction of the shot. Twenty yards later the sergeant stopped behind a moss-covered boulder and held his hand up. "Wait, I hear something up ahead," he whispered.

With the use of his elbows, Moran inched his way up and

reached Hernandez. The lieutenant squinted and peered over the stone. He made out the partial dark profile of a figure on a small bluff hunched behind a tree. A rifle with a scope was aimed toward the area where Thorsen and his men were. Moran slid his body away from the boulder and felt pebbles underneath his stomach. Too late. When he finished sliding over to his right, the pebbles rolled down the small incline. In the stillness, they sounded like an avalanche.

"Who's there?" Earl Schuyler called out and aimed his rifle toward the two detectives. With an unsteady voice he shouted, "Don't... don't come any closer. Go back!"

Then the rifle barked, and a bullet ricocheted off the boulder sending shards of granite over Hernandez's head.

"This is Lieutenant Moran, NYPD, Earl. Remember me?" Moran said. He started to slowly crouch toward the suspect.

"Stay here, Frank, in case he tries to make a break for it," Moran whispered. The sound of the circling helicopter made Moran look up—it was lower and circling right above them. The cop waved his arms at the chopper signaling it to move away. "Friggin' Smokies," he murmured. "They'll get us killed yet."

A spooky silence had fallen over the forest. The only sound was the breathing of the two detectives and the chopper's rotating blades. Then soft snowflakes began to fall and quickly dissolve when they hit the ground. The temperature was dropping and dark clouds had moved in.

"Shit," Moran hissed. He clenched his teeth and stood behind a large pine tree. "Earl, it's cold out here, I'm tired and hungry, and the weather's getting ugly. I think it's time to stop this bullshit and give yourself up."

The nearby lonesome howl of a wolf reverberated through the forest. "You hear that, Earl? He's hungry too. It's time to come in," Moran shouted.

Silence.

Moran stepped out from behind the tree as Hernandez arrived. "Are you crazy?" the sergeant said.

The Lieutenant spoke in a raised voice. "Earl's not stupid," Moran said. He craned his head toward where the fugitive was. "Right, Earl?"

Again, silence.

Moran turned to his partner. "He's tired and hungry like us, and knows it's the end of the fourth quarter," he said. Moran stepped out from behind the tree and started to slowly walk up the embankment toward Earl. "Don't prove me wrong, Earl. Throw the rifle down, step out into the clearing, kneel, and put your hands behind your head."

The deafening whirr of the chopper's blade caused Moran to look up—the helicopter was hovering two hundred feet above.

"Christ!" Moran said when he spotted the barrel of a rifle projecting from the chopper.

"Frank, you see him?" Moran said.

Hernandez squinted and looked through the branches to a grassy knoll that was surrounded by thick vegetation and trees. "Barely, he's crouched on the other side of the knoll behind one of the trees. His back's to the chopper."

"Cover me before they get into position," Moran said. He pointed to the chopper. "The bastards are gonna kill him in a few seconds."

Moran ignored the pain in his right knee as he dashed over the dense underbrush and winter foliage up the slope before Hernandez could react. A moment later, when Moran neared the knoll, he turned and looked up the chopper. He stretched out his arm and flashed his badge at the aircraft. "NYPD... Get outta here... NYPD!" Moran yelled as he crawled up the incline. He realized he must've seemed like a madman, but he had to stop them from killing Earl Schuyler.

James Francis Moran wanted—needed--to bring Earl in alive. First, it was Hubert Singer's escape and then Sabrina's *suicide-by-cop*. This was now a matter of pride.

When he reached the knoll, Moran shifted his eyes back to the chopper and heaved a sigh when he saw the rifle recede. The gamble had worked—the NYSP sharpshooter wasn't going to run the risk of firing at an unclear target and hitting the NYPD lieutenant. A much relieved Moran watched the chopper bank and vanish over the treetops.

Suddenly, two bursts came from Earl's rifle and fragments of dirt and gravel flew around Moran's feet. The cop zig-zagged toward the safety of a large round granite boulder a few feet away. Out of breath, Moran knelt on his right knee behind the large rock. "For chrissake's," he moaned and switched knees. "I'm getting to old for this crap," he muttered. He cupped his mouth with the palm of one hand. "Earl, I know you don't want to do this!" Moran yelled. He was certain Earl had missed him on purpose. There was no way that Earl could've missed at that distance.

Then he heard movement from the slope on the other side of the knoll and a moment later he watched Hernandez crouching up the incline with the Glock in his hand—the sergeant was only a few feet from the clearing. The fugitive, caught between the two cops, had only one way to run and that was directly toward Major Thorsen and his men. That was not option for Moran.

"Earl... Earl!" Moran called out. "Better us than them!"

More silence.

"Screw this," Moran said, and then jumped to his feet. He lumbered out into the clearing. When he saw Hernandez reach the knoll, he called out to his partner. "Where is he?"

Hernandez lowered his Glock. "You gotta see this," the sergeant said. When a perplexed Moran entered the clearing, he turned to where Hernandez was looking. Sitting on the ground in with his legs crossed sat a weeping Earl Schuyler. The rifle lay a foot away.

Moran and Hernandez carefully approached Earl from opposite sides and when they reached him, Hernandez kicked the rifle out of Earl's reach.

"Cuff him," Moran said.

"I... I... didn't want to kill Rose," Earl sobbed while he rocked back and forth. "She was always good to me, but after all I did for her she was going to kick me out like a dog."

The lieutenant knelt in front of Earl. "Go on, tell us all about it. We'll find out anyway."

Earl slowly raised his head, the eyes red and moist. He winced when he felt the handcuffs tighten around his wrists behind him.

"She was gonna sell the club to some jerk…" Earl said and his voiced trailed off. He sniffled. "Never once thought about me. Told me that I'd be taken care of by the new owner," Earl said. "Horseshit."

"Where's the derringer?" Hernandez said.

"In my back pocket."

Hernandez patted Earl down and drew out the Dexter derringer.

"What happened with Lacy and Myer?" Moran said.

Earl looked up, with a glazed stare boring into Moran's face. "Rose only wanted me to rough up Lacy a little bit. When I got to her apartment, I heard arguing inside. Her and another guy were shouting at each other; I figured it was another John and decided to wait in the stairwell," Earl said and lowered his eyes to the ground. "When the guy left I walked in. She was in a bathrobe and… well… things got out of hand. She became uncontrollable and… I…. I lost my temper. Before I knew it, there was a knife in my hands. It's all hazy. Lacy wanted to stop working for us."

"What about Myer?" Hernandez said.

Earl shifted his eyes up to the sergeant. "Piece of shit, tried to blackmail Rose and me. Said he recognized my cologne when I passed him in the hallway… frigging bullshit, just a lucky guess. Rose went along for a while, and I was the go-between."

"So you were the one who visited Myer at his apartment," Moran said.

Earl nodded. "Yeah, but only for a few times."

"Then Rose told you to take care of him," Moran said.

Earl shook his head briskly. "Uh-uh. That was my idea. The little twerp needed killing. I'll never forget the look of surprise on his face when he met me at my storage place," Earl said and snorted. "Thought he was going to collect a payoff." He gazed at Moran and sneered. "Yeah, he got paid off all right, a one way ticket to hell."

Moran nodded and bunched his lips. "Where you'll probably run into him."

"I'd like to know why you shot him twice after he was dead," Moran said.

Earl bunched his eyebrows and shrugged. "I wanted to make sure the bastard was really dead."

Hernandez held up the derringer with the tips of his thumb and forefinger and examined it. "Not much to it."

"Just like Earl," Moran said.

Thorsen led a group of troopers into the clearing. "We'll take it from here, Lieutenant. That man is our prisoner!"

Moran turned on his heels. "Those are our cuffs on him. We made the pinch, and therefore, it's finders-keepers."

Thorsen edged forward. "Consider yourself and your partner under arrest. I'm charging you with interfering with a State Police operation, obstructing an arrest, disobeying direct orders," the irate major said. "And, about a half-dozen other charges that I'm sure we'll come up with."

"Then you better be ready to explain authorizing cold-blooded murder," Moran barked.

Thorsen froze. His mouth opened and his eyes broadened. "What the hell are you pulling here?"

Moran shrugged and glared at the infuriated major. "You ordered your men in the chopper to shoot without a clear target. We could see the fugitive wasn't making any threatening moves," the lieutenant said. He stepped closer to Thorsen. "Your men were about to kill him without cause."

"What?"

"When Sergeant Hernandez and I arrived, we found the suspect sitting where he's now in a highly emotional state and the rifle on the ground a foot away from him," Moran said.

Thorsen shifted his gaze toward Hernandez. "He's right, sir," the sergeant affirmed.

Thorsen moistened his lips and turned to a sturdy trooper with sergeant stripes who stood to his left. "You know anything about this?" The trooper shrugged. "We'd need to talk with the pilot, but they've flown back to the base in Poughkeepsie."

Major Thorsen switched his gaze back to Moran. He jerked his thumb back toward the parking lot. "Take your prisoner and get the hell out of here," Thorsen said. "And, don't let the door hit you in the ass."

Moran turned to Hernandez. "You heard what the man said. Let's get the hell out of here."

CHAPTER 74

The sun, against a cloudless blue sky, shone brightly over the city, and the glistening mounds of fresh snow piled against the sidewalks sparkled as if covered with diamond dust. The snowstorm that had besieged the city for the last two days had moved out to sea, and things were getting back to normal—chaos, noise and controlled mayhem would once again reign. All of which provided the ideal backdrop for finally bringing Sandra Moran home.

The late model metallic silver Cadillac XLR Roadster pulled up to the Patient Discharge door of Sloan-Kettering Memorial Hospital and stopped behind a white Mercedes-Benz sedan with Connecticut plates. The driver's window on the sedan cracked open and a plume of smoke floated from inside.

James Francis Moran placed his *'Police Official Business'* placard against the Cadillac's windshield and extracted himself from behind the wheel, making sure that his head cleared the convertible's metal roof. He strode to the Mercedes and rapped the window with his knuckles. "Move the car, this is a no-parking zone," the lieutenant said.

The uniformed chauffer cast Moran a dismissive glance and continued to smoke. Moran straightened and gazed at two approaching uniformed police officers who had exited through the hospital doors. The older cop had sergeant stripes on his sleeve. Moran strode toward them.

"Sergeant," the lieutenant said. "If that Mercedes doesn't move in thirty seconds issue it a summons and have it towed. Is that clear?"

The two uniforms looked at each and then at Moran. "And you are?"

Moran showed them his badge and ID. "Official business."

The sergeant looked over Moran's shoulder at the parked roadster and the card against the windshield. "I gather that's your car, sir."

"Yes it is," Moran said and returned to the vehicle.

Two minutes later when the Mercedes pulled away from the curb, Moran inched the Caddie up to the spot formerly occupied by the chauffeured car. He climbed out and saw Sandra being wheeled out by two female Filipino nurses.

When his wife and the nurses reached the car, Sandra eyes broadened. "Don't tell me you leased a car just to pick me up?"

Moran gave Sandra an enigmatic smile and opened the passenger door. After the nurses placed Sandra inside, they closed the door and Moran went to the driver's side.

Sandra looked at her husband with curious eyes. "I know that look, James. What's going on?"

Moran turned from his seat and faced his wife. "It's not leased. It's ours, bought it yesterday and just picked it up."

"What! This has got to be an expensive—"

Moran turned the key and the V-8 Northstar engine purred. "It is, but you and I are starting a new life as of right now," Moran said. The car pulled away from the curb and entered the stream of traffic. "Now that Dr. Kruger has finally let you come home and the prognosis is positive, you're going to see a lot of me."

Sandra turned in her seat and looked at Moran. "Exactly what does that mean?"

"For starters, I packed for the both of us, everything's in the trunk and if I missed something, you can buy it when we get there."

"Get where?"

"The Hamptons."

Sandra arched her eyebrows. "It's winter. There's no one there at this time of year."

Moran smiled. "Exactly why we're going. There are two bottles of Dom Perignon in the back seat, and we're going to finish every single drop." He pointed to the roof. "By the way, this folds into the trunk."

"James," Sandra murmured in a suspicious tone. "Are you thinking of retiring?"

Moran kept his eyes on the road as the car turned onto 58th Street and followed the sign that indicated the entrance to the Queens-Midtown Tunnel. "No. Did it, I presented my resignation to Newbury day before yesterday effective immediately. After what you've been through, I realized that it's time we spent more time together. Also, my knee could use the rest and I've got a whole collection of recipes I want to cook for you."

Sandra remained silent for a long moment. She reached over and with the palm of her hand, cupped Moran's fingers that rested on the beige leather gear shift, then leaned in and bussed Moran on the cheek.

"Now, God help us all," Sandra cooed and smiled—a warm smile that said it all. She returned her gaze to the road ahead. "Sorry I got it wrong. Always thought Lacy's killer was a woman."

"You didn't get it wrong. You said it *could've* been a woman," Moran said while the coupe idled in traffic at the tunnel's entrance. "If it hadn't been for the raid on Rose Chiu's club, Earl Schuyler stood a good chance of passing under the radar."

Sandra gazed out her window at the rows of cement and concrete buildings that surrounded them. "I wonder how many other Lacy's are out there, lured by Manhattan's serenade, beckoning to them like a siren's song?"

EPILOGUE

After seven hours of narrow, rough roads through a landscape that varied from low desert to rain forests, a svelte, attractive woman in her mid-thirties with a small but aristocratic straight nose and high cheekbones and a deep tan stepped off a 1960's Opel bus in Lima, Peru. She straightened the jacket of her black leather pants suit and checked the handcuff that linked her graceful wrist to a leather attaché case. It was common practice for thieves to rob sleeping passengers on the local buses.

During the trip, although the bus smelled of sweat and stale herbs, the woman did the proper thing and discreetly covered her nose with a silk handkerchief during the entire trip while occasionally smiling politely at her inquisitive fellow passengers.

On the gray concrete of the rundown bus station, the woman moved aside while the other travelers passed by her. Most were small, bronze-colored Peruvian men and women of different ages wrapped in colorful outfits with brown bowler hats that rested on their jet-black hair. Some gave toothless smiles to this oddly dressed traveling companion while others simply nodded their heads. A tiny old woman with a craggy, deeply tanned face stopped and whispered something in her native Indian tongue and offered the traveler a wooden cage that contained a speckled feathered chicken, which she politely declined.

Moments later, she walked out of the station's restroom, jutted out her strong chin and shook loose her chestnut hair. She fixed her steady dark brown eyes on the billboard across from the street that read: *BIENVENIDOS A LIMA*. She strengthened her grip on the handle of the attaché case and headed for the nearby queue of colorfully painted old taxis.

A few minutes later, the attractive woman climbed out of a dilapidated cab and entered the marble vestibule of the Banco del Peru where she was escorted by a young boy dressed in a bellboy uniform to the bank's second floor.

"Señor Del Valle, will be with you in a moment," the bellboy said when he let her into a spacious carpeted, well appointed room where an elaborate handcrafted massive wooden desk sat against the backdrop of a fabric covered wall. When the bellboy left, the woman reached into her purse, drew out a small key, and unlocked the handcuffs.

"Buenos dias, Miss Mendez. I am Francisco Del Valle," a deep, cultured voice said from the doorway. "I am glad that you are all right. We were beginning to be concerned since we expected you yesterday," he continued while he walked toward his guest.

She spun around and faced a tall, swarthy man with touches of gray in his dark hair. Mendez quickly took in the banker's pin-striped blue serge three-piece suit—*handsome in a provincial sort of way*, she thought.

"The bus from La Paz had problems and I had to wait for another one, but it was the safest way of getting here."

The banker nodded and smiled knowingly. "Unfortunately, Bolivia is not quite up to our standards," Del Valle said and gave his guest a broad smile as a row of perfect white teeth came into view. His eyes darted to the attaché case. "I trust there was no problem?"

Mendez stepped to the case and snapped open the two locks. "None. And I hope none has arisen since we spoke."

Again the broad smile. "Not at all," Del Valle said and drummed his fingers on the case's lid.

Mendez smiled tightly and opened the case while she kept her eyes on the banker enjoying his obvious anticipation. Del Valle's face beamed when he saw the Rio Tinto bearer bonds that filled the case.

"I assume that it is all here," he said softly.

"All ten million dollars," Rosario Mendez purred. "And I assume that the bank has prepared the funds."

"Eight million U.S. Dollars will be wired to your account in Rio de Janeiro. I trust you are satisfied with that amount," Del Valle said.

Mendez smiled. "Two million for the bank and eight for us isn't a bad day's work. The cost of doing business!"

Del Valle gazed at his visitor appraisingly. "I do not suppose you would care to share with me how you came into this fortune."

Mendez looked at the Peruvian banker with leaden eyes. "A very generous friend."

Del Valle nodded. He raised an eyebrow, gave her a warm smile and placed his hand on the former Banco de Mexico executive's forearm. "If you are not too tired," he said. "I would consider it an honor if you would have dinner with me tonight."

Mendez's eyes twinkled. "Why not?" She knew one could never have too many friends.

The phone on the Del Valle's desk rang, and a moment later, the banker answered. He turned to his guest. "It's for you."

"Everything is fine, you were right, Mr. Del Valle has been very helpful," she said and winked at the banker. "I'll be arriving on tomorrow's afternoon flight, see you at the airport."

* * *

On the other end of the line on the top-floor apartment of a one of Rio de Janeiro's tallest buildings, a trim chiseled featured man in a double-breasted tuxedo responded. "Can't wait to see you." When the man replaced the receiver on the cradle, he turned away, and from the corner of his eye caught his reflection in the gilded frame mirror on the wall. He stopped and smiled—the image pleased him. He ran his fingers through his wavy light-brown hair.

The man stepped to a nearby lace-covered table and set down the crystal tumbler of whiskey in his hand next to a silver framed

New Yorker magazine color photograph. He turned his head briefly toward the closed door and the muffled sounds of animated voices and music that came from behind it and then turned back toward the table.

The man slid open a drawer, and with his long slender fingers, moved aside a Beretta automatic pistol with a silencer attached to it's business end. He picked up a gold lighter and an unopened pack of Gitanes cigarettes and laid them on the table. He closed the drawer and lit a cigarette. The man lifted his gaze and looked out his window to Sugar Loaf and the statue of Christ that overlooked Rio de Janeiro. He then lowered his gaze to the picture frame and the four-year old date on the upper right-hand corner of the print. It was a picture of a luminous, trim woman in a strapless red dress seated next to a pasty face uninteresting looking man. They were both smiling at camera. His hair was long, dark wavy with wisps of gray. His eyes were light-hazel. The caption read:

"The New York City Spiritus Award winner, Criminal Psychology professor Sandra Mazzetti and Dr. Hubert Singer, professor of Comparative Philosophy."

The stranger smiled—the only remnants of his past were his light-hazel eyes. His face hardened. Rosario Mendez, the ambitious young banker who managed his account at Morrison Savings & Trust years ago whom he befriended, was a loose end that had to be dealt with.

THE END